THE BLUE DOOR

Es muss sein!… Es könnte auch anders sein
—Milan Kundera

1

THERE WAS, FIRST, THE DREAM. WHICH SHOULD have alerted me, except that I'm not normally into dreams. But this one I found strangely disquieting, and carried it with me, like a persistent tune in my head, throughout that long day. Until the shocking moment in the early dusk. The kind of moment that once turned the life of Kafka's Gregor Samsa upside down. But this was not fiction. It happened. And to me.

Not that the dream had any direct bearing on what happened in the evening. But in some subliminal way, and with hindsight, there did seem to be a connection which I have not been able to figure out. Nor, I must confess, have I tried. I believe that dreams belong to the night in which they're dreamt and should preferably not be allowed to spill into the day. This time it was different.

In the dream I am embarking on a long journey with my family, moving house. My wife Lydia is there, but also three children, three little girls, very blonde, with very blue eyes. This is perturbing. We do not have children, and after nine years of marriage it still hurts, although both of us have become skilled at pretending

other lives

a novel in three parts

André Brink

 SOURCEBOOKS LANDMARK™
AN IMPRINT OF SOURCEBOOKS, INC.®
NAPERVILLE, ILLINOIS

Published by Sourcebooks Landmark, an imprint of Sourcebooks, Inc.
P.O. Box 4410, Naperville, Illinois 60567-4410
(630) 961-3900
Fax: (630) 961-2168
www.sourcebooks.com

Brink, André Philippus
  Other lives : a novel in three parts / André Brink.
    p. cm.
  I. Title.
  PR9369.3.B7O78 2008
  823'.914--dc22
                            2008015045

Printed and bound in the United States of America.
BG 10 9 8 7 6 5 4 3 2

For Geoff, Stephen, Kerneels
publishers, friends

it doesn't matter; not anymore. Lydia gets into the front of the truck with the driver. The girls are already in the back, perched high up on the mountain of furniture like little monkeys. I join them and we drive off very slowly, the load swaying precariously. It is a sweltering day and the children are perspiring profusely, strands of their blonde hair clinging to their cheeks and fore-heads. They seem to have difficulty breathing.

Before we have reached the first corner, I realize that we will never make it like this. We need water for the journey for the children to survive. I start hammering with my hands on the cabin of the truck. The driver stops and peers up at me, a surly expression on his thick face which is turning an ominous purple.

"I've got to get water for the kids," I explain. "I left three bottles on the kitchen sink."

"We don't have time," growls the driver.

"I won't be long," I insist. "And they won't survive without water in this heat."

He mutters a reply, mercifully inaudible, and I jump off.

"Just drive on slowly," I try to placate him. "I'll soon catch up with you."

The girls begin to cry, but I give them a reas-suring wave as I trot off into the simmering and searing white day.

Only when I arrive at the kitchen door do I realize

that I have no keys with me. Glancing round to give another wave to the children, I hurriedly begin to jog around the house to find a means of entry. Only after three exhausting rounds do I spot a half-open window. In the distance, the truck is beginning to disappear in a cloud of dust.

I manage to climb into the house and collect the bottles of water. They are ice cold against my chest. But now the window through which I have entered is barred, and I lose precious time rushing this way and that through the house. Everything seems locked and bolted. I become aware of rising panic inside me.

Then at last, somehow, in the inexplicable manner of dreams, I am outside again, still clutching the water bottles to my chest. By now the truck is nowhere to be seen. Only a small cloud of dust, the size of a man's hand, hangs in the distance.

I start running. In the heat my legs turn to lead. But I persevere. I have to, otherwise my family will be lost: they do not know where we are heading for, I am the only one who knows the address. On and on I run.

From time to time I catch a glimpse of the diminishing truck. On, on, on. I have to. I just have to.

In the distance I can hear the thin voices of the children wailing, more and more faintly. Once I believe I can hear Lydia calling:

"David! David, hurry!"

Then that, too, dies away.

In the ferocious glare of the day I redouble my efforts. But in the end I am forced to admit that it is useless. I shall never catch up with the truck. I shall never see Lydia and the children again.

That was where the dream ended.

2

THROUGHOUT THE DAY IT ACCOMPANIED ME— the vivid remains of the dream, the sense of loss. A sad intimation of mortality. Which was uncalled for, really: I am only forty-four. I am supposed to be in the prime of my life. *Nel mezzo del cammin di nostra vita.* In the generally accepted view I have had a successful career, a happy marriage, good and sustaining relationships with friends. I have taught a generation or two of schoolchildren a basic under-standing of language and of history; over weekends and holidays I have been able to indulge my private passion for painting, to the extent of taking part in a few group exhibitions and of renting my own studio, a garden cottage belonging to a ramshackle old house in Green Point, far enough from our large, comfortable flat in Claremont to offer a feeling of escape and privacy.

Over the years, ever since I first ventured to take part in an exhibition, I had been toying with the idea of one day giving up teaching to paint full time; but some kind of innate caution—reinforced, no doubt, by my family's convictions about the need for a married man to have a "respectable job"—had always held me back. After another surprisingly successful exhibition in Observatory at the end of last year, several friends suggested that the time for the break had, surely, come. This time they were much more insistent than before. "There are no kids involved, David," said my friend Rudy, whom I have known since our university years at UCT. "You have a wife who is an architect and surely earns enough to keep you afloat. You have, as far as I know, no huge debts to settle, no financial obligations to family or friends, no plans to get involved in risky investments, you and Lydia are both disgustingly healthy, you're in the gym three times a week, there are no threatening illnesses in the family: so why the hell don't you take the plunge?"

Why the hell indeed not?

Still the memory of my father? Could be. A prudent man, a toes-together kind of man, a man of considered and considerable judgment, who'd spent all his life escaping from the memory of the Great Depression that had ruined his family and landed them in the unaccommodating streets of Johannesburg. A man conditioned by counting his pennies never to take unnecessary risks, never to stand surety for man or beast, never to borrow from anyone, never to purchase anything that could not be paid for in cash. He gave me the biggest hiding of my life when as a boy of nine I slipped out of the house one Wednesday afternoon when I was supposed to study for a math test, to go to a fun fair, where I spent twenty cents of my own pocket money for a ride on the Big Wheel. He never discouraged me in my attempts at drawing and painting—in fact, he occasionally put a couple of my pictures up in his functional gray office—as long as I did not lose my perspective and indulge in such amusing but ultimately frivolous pursuits at the expense of earning a proper living through a decent job. And a decent job was not only one that brought in a steady income, but preferably one that was also of some value to fellow Afrikaners.

He would certainly have frowned at the idea of my renting a studio. That would have been regarded as lowering a harmless dabbling in art to indulging a private vice. But of course he did not know about the place. Very few people did. In the beginning I kept it as a secret even from Lydia, and it was only when—as was her custom—she was dealing with the household accounts at the end of one particular month that she came upon the bill for the rental of the studio and confronted me with it. One of the worst fights of our entire married life. I felt singularly outraged by her accusations of trying to set up some lewd love nest, as if I had suddenly been stripped naked in public. It was like the day—I was thirteen or fourteen—when my mother found under my bed a tin of condensed milk I had taken from the pantry and she took the strap to me. (It was only years later that it dawned on me that her addiction to corporal punishment was the only way she could ever stand up to my father's unquestionable authority.) As if the beating in itself was not enough, she insisted that for such a serious offense the punishment had to be inflicted on my bare backside in the presence of my three younger brothers and two older sisters. I shall never forget that day. And now Lydia was reviving it in all its unbearable humiliation.

It was not the stealing of the condensed milk as such, I felt, which was at stake. That in itself might well have been a punishable offense (though not in such an extreme manner). But it was the invasion of my privacy, its public exposure, which I found unforgivable. Throughout my life I have felt this urge to have a space that was entirely my own, that could not be violated or invaded by anyone. Even, I'm afraid, in my married life with Lydia I have constantly lived with the deep need to keep something to myself which I would never, ever share with her. Not that I ever tried or even wished to cheat on her, to be involved in anything clandestine, be it some secret passion or a dubious financial transaction. But I needed a space, whether physical or emotional, that would be mine only, inaccessible to the rest of the world. Perhaps it was simply the consequence of growing up in such a big family, which made privacy something of a luxury. I remember how often I would fall asleep at night clutching my blankets very tightly to my neck, convinced that as soon as I had dropped off someone—a brother, a sister, a parent, a stranger—would steal into the room and strip away the blankets to expose me to their rapacious eyes.

So it took a long time before Lydia's discovery of the studio could be resolved. In fact, for several months I stopped going there altogether. It was no longer mine. But in due course the need to draw and paint—or simply the need to smell linseed oil and treated canvases and brushes again—became so overwhelming that I had to go back. After that, the pleasure was always somewhat attenuated, as Lydia developed a habit of dropping in on me unannounced whenever she "happened to be in the vicinity" to share a cup of coffee, fruit juice, a biscuit, or a piece of chocolate, even a glass of red wine. But the relationship between us was steady and sure enough to bear the strain. And often her visits would expand into long rambling discussions—holidays imminent or recent, friends and acquaintances, other people's children, the rapes and murders and political scandals of the day—and even, occasionally, into unexpected but quite satisfying little bouts of lovemaking on the floor, the unwieldy couch covered in paint-stained, faded green cloth, once even on the long table in front of the window where I usually stacked my painting paraphernalia. After such a visit a fair deal of tidying up was invariably required—Lydia has always been a great one for setting things right, and would insist on helping, even if I might have secretly preferred to see to it myself, in my own good time; if ever—leading to spring cleanings that left me feeling abandoned in a place that had suddenly become alien; a castaway on a desert island. And when, eventually, I would scrape together the courage to take up my brushes and start on a clean canvas, each venture would be, as Eliot would have said, a wholly new start and a different kind of failure. It reached the point where I seriously considered finding a new studio altogether, in a different and distant part of the Cape, Noordhoek or Durbanville or wherever, where nobody, and certainly not Lydia, would track me down again. But I could not bear the thought of risking another discovery, another fight with Lydia.

For the moment I still held on, even though I had been using the place less and less during that particular autumn. Perhaps it was simply the cold that began to affect me. There was no central heating in the cottage, only a fireplace in the living room where I mostly painted; but I did not like the fuss of cleaning the grate afterward.

So there was, I think now, a general sense of something running out, running down. Within a foreseeable future I might have to move out. I might as well return to the small storeroom at my school I'd used as a studio before moving to the cottage. Which would be a way of giving up. A way, I thought melodramatically, of dying before my death. That, certainly, was how it felt after waking up from the dream.

I had spent most of the day trying to work, and not succeeding. Starting on two or three canvases, then scraping off the paint or simply abandoning them on the floor against the wall. Partly my desultory mood came from knowing that in the late afternoon I would have to pack up anyway. We were having guests for dinner—the architect Steve and his lovely wife Carla—and Lydia was expecting me to come home well in time with the shopping she had meticulously listed in the morning. Knowing in advance that the working day would have to be cut short before things had run their natural course was enough to unsettle me and break my concentration, inhibit my imagination. And there was still the aftermath of the dream.

3

B Y MID-AFTERNOON I COLLECTED THE THINGS I meant to take home with me—my leather jacket, some mail, a small pile of essays I had hoped to mark during the day, a sketchbook, three old drawings I wanted to look at overnight in the hope of finding ideas for the next painting, a gilt frame—and placed them on the small rosewood table just inside the front door. From that moment on I remember in acute detail every single thing that happened, every step I took, as if it all had been registered by a surveillance camera.

My car was parked higher up, just off High Level Road, but I wanted to walk. It was only a short distance: down the steep side street to Main Road and left to Giovanni's delicatessen. I had come this way innumerable times over the past few years since I started using the cottage, yet somehow they all seemed strange today. Not like real buildings, but like cutouts of a stage set, two-dimensional, flimsy, hardboard. As if there was nothing at all behind the façades. The old Edwardian house with the green gate hanging from one hinge. The pseudo-Jugendstil block of flats with multicolored washing suspended on the balconies like a scene from Seurat or Monet. The three "modernized" houses on the right crouching behind high railings topped with electrified wire. The small box-shaped building with windows boarded up and billboards announcing its imminent demolition. A row of garages with uniform drab brown doors. More evidence of renewal in dolled-up façades, imitation Cape-Dutch gables, and inane Tuscan chimneys as one approached the Main Road. The streets and people appeared more real than the buildings. Two obese black nannies pushing white babies in prams, one navy blue, one maroon. A small gathering of bergies rolling joints and drinking blue-train from bottles inadequately stashed in newsprint. Two youngsters in T-shirts and jeans laboring uphill and stopping every few meters to kiss and caress, the man barefoot (long, broken, black toenails) and with tousled Rastafarian hair, the girl with bare midriff and the imprint of a chocolate hand on her left breast. An old couple waddling downhill, the woman carrying a worse-for-wear bouquet of daisies and rather faded blue delphiniums. Two small girls bobbing uphill, their faces smudged by large cones of pink ice cream. The streets were rather dirty, littered with beer cans, empty takeaway cartons, crumpled balls of wax paper, several lumps of dog shit, a gaggle of gulls gathered around a dead fish.

Then left along the Main Road, and into Giovanni's.

A woman with lank, oily hair served me with hands on which the fingernail, like bunches of blotched peas, had been bitten to the quick.

"Thanks, lovey," she said without looking up.

I took the two plastic bags and left, feeling even gloomier than before.

Uphill, then left at the black garden gate which needed a coat of paint, and round the back of the house to my garden cottage.

Just as I am about to unlock the blue door it swings open and a slim young woman comes out on the narrow stoop. She is dark of complexion, with long curly hair and the blackest eyes I have ever seen. She is wearing a white T-shirt and jeans, and her feet are bare.

"David!" she exclaims as she puts her arms around my neck and kisses me with her full, moist lips.

I cannot move. I want to say something but cannot find my voice. All I know is that I have never seen her in my life before.

Behind her two small children, a girl who seems to be about five, a boy surely no older than three, both as dark and black-eyed as their mother, come running to me with shouts of glee.

"Daddy! Daddy!" they squeal, their voices shrill with excitement.

4

THE INTERIOR BEARS NO RESEMBLANCE TO THAT of the cottage I left less than an hour earlier. The rosewood table inside the front door is still there, but the things I left on it—the leather jacket, the mail, the unmarked essays, the sketchbook, the drawings, the broken gilt frame—are missing; and everything else is unfamiliar. The furniture, the carpets, the curtains, the pictures on the walls, everything. Even the layout of the place, as far as I can make out, has changed. For one thing, it looks much bigger. From the entrance there is a wide passage with doors on either side, leading to rooms I do not recognize. The ceiling looks higher. From the hall I can see through a door into what appears to be a spacious and somewhat untidy lounge. It has a large fireplace with an ornate Victorian mantelpiece which I have never seen before.

Involuntarily I take a step back to look, once again, at the front door from the outside. This is indeed the blue door I painted six years ago when I first moved in. I recognize the small tortoise-shaped scar left by a flake of paint that has come off, and two parallel scratches just below the keyhole.

"What's up?" asks the young woman. She seems both amused and bemused as she scrutinizes me. "You look as if you've lost your way or something."

I want to say, "Who are you? What are you doing here?" But I cannot find my voice. And by now the two children have caught up with me, each grabbing me by a leg, clamoring to be picked up.

Apologetic and embarrassed, I dump the plastic bags on the floor and bend over to pick them up, one by one, first the girl, then the little boy. They cover my face with wet kisses. Somewhat hurriedly I put them down again.

"Excuse me," I stammer. "I—honestly, I—"

"Ah," says the woman. "I'm glad you remembered to bring the stuff." She takes over the bags and turns round to go deeper into the house, moving smoothly on her bare feet (there is only the sensual, almost inaudible, sucking sound of the soft soles on the tiles) while the children keep tugging at my legs.

Then I hear her call from inside: "David! Where are you?"

I try to move past the children, but with each of them clinging to a leg it isn't easy to move.

On the way to the passage opposite the front door I pass an oval hall table littered with mail. Noticing, in passing, my name, I stop involuntarily to flip through the envelopes. There are three accounts addressed to me. A card with an invitation to an art exhibition, bearing the name of a gallery on the back. A letter with a typed address: Mr. and Mrs. D. le Roux. Then a large envelope, A4 size; looks like a catalog. As I pick it up, yet another letter falls on the floor. I stoop to retrieve it, and immediately recognize the handwriting. It is my youngest brother's; he has the commendable if irritating habit of sending a photocopied letter every week in order to "keep the family together." This one is addressed to David & Sarah le Roux.

I am still staring at the address when the woman calls again from the back of the house: "David? Where are you?"

I clear my throat. Still staring at the envelope, yielding to a sudden feeling of recklessness, I call, "Sarah—?"

"I'm in the kitchen."

"But where—?" I begin, then give it up and try to find my way to where the voice has come from.

The kitchen is large and flooded with light. It looks recently renovated, although it already bears signs of the kind of destruction and dilapidation only small children can wreak: some broken tiles, muddy footprints on the floor, a broken red plastic bowl, tatters of newsprint everywhere, finger-painted artwork clinging desperately to the fridge, cat litter and a food bowl scattered near the back door.

Sarah, if that is who the stranger is, is unpacking the plastic bags on a homely old kitchen table in the middle of the floor. The children are clamoring to "see, see," so I deposit them on the table just to make the noise subside. Which is effective inasmuch as it curbs the decibels, but brings what politicians term "unintended consequences" in its wake when the boy manages to tear open the pack of sugar and spill the contents across table and floor.

"Tommie!" yelps the young woman, lunging forward and managing to save the eggs as the carton slides perilously close to the edge. "David!" she cries again, "For God's sake, don't just stand there. Help me!"

It takes a while to unpack everything on the table and deposit the protesting children on a cabinet out of reach of the stove.

"Well!" she says at last. A few strands of her dark hair cling alluringly to her forehead, one of them in a delicate S over her small nose. Her black eyes smile. "At least you remembered everything, which must be something of a first. Except that you added chocolates." She accusingly holds up the slab. "They were not on my list."

"Guilty as charged," I admit.

"Chocky, chocky!" screeches the boy.

"Yes, please," adds the girl, an angelic expression on her face. "We were very good, Daddy. And you promised—"

"After supper," says their mother gently but firmly. I am struck by the easy way in which she handles both them and the household. I am conscious of her very dark eyes and unruly hair, the slimness of her figure— she appears to be in her late thirties, but with a litheness that would be captivating in someone ten years younger. And—emphatically—her pretty slender feet. The kind of woman, it occurs to me, with whom I might fall in love. If I were free. But there is, of course, the rub. I am not free. Only, that in this totally weird, bewildering situation everything suddenly seems to be up for redefinition.

There must be some mistake. And I must get out of here before it becomes an impossible tangle.

"You have to excuse me," I say precipitately. "I'm not sure about what is going on here, but I really have to go."

"Where?" asks Sarah in obvious surprise. "You've just come home."

"I—I forgot to lock my car."

"Can we go with you, Daddeeee?" pleads the girl.

"No, Emily, you stay," says the mother. "You can help me make the sauce for the chicken. And when Daddy comes back he can bathe you."

Squeals of delight.

Flustered, I back out of the kitchen and return to the entrance. I take my time to look around. My throat feels constricted. There is something very wrong here.

Perhaps there is an easy explanation for the whole mystery, but right now it escapes me.

As I open the front door a blast of cold wind forces me back. Instinctively I reach for the small table where I left my jacket but of course it is no longer there. Annoyed, and leaving the door open, I return to the passage. From close to the kitchen I call out, "Sarah, where's my leather jacket?"

She appears in the kitchen door. "What are you looking for?"

"My leather jacket."

There is a frown between her dark eyes. "Leather jacket?"

"Yes. I left it at the front door when I went out earlier."

"But you don't have a leather jacket, David," she says.

"But I—" I shake my head.

She comes to me. "Are you sure you're all right, darling?"

"Of course I'm all right! It's just that—" I sigh. "Never mind. I'll try to sort it out." Although I do not have an idea of how to go about it.

When I look back from the hall, she is still standing at the kitchen door, staring at me with a puzzled, concerned look on her face, the fingers of one hand pushed into tousled black hair. I feel an urge to go to her, to reassure her, perhaps—preposterous thought!—to take her in my arms and comfort her. But how can I do that? I have never seen this person in my life.

Behind her I see the children, their eager little faces. Tommie is leaning forward as if preparing to stand on his head. Emily holds one small hand with perfect starfish fingers outstretched toward me. They seem frozen in their positions.

I go out into the wind, pulling the blue door shut behind me.

My car is still where I parked it in the early afternoon, in the side street just down from High Level Road. Without thinking, I slide into the driver's seat, close the door, and start driving home.

5

THE ENORMOUS APARTMENT BUILDING IN Claremont looms ahead in the early dusk. I have never noticed it before, but today I am struck by how much it resembles Brueghel's Tower of Babel—although there is nothing dilapidated about this one. It is vast and solid, arrogantly modern, rising in layer upon layer, with yawning glass-and-chrome entrances on all four corners. As there are rows of cars queuing up to enter, I find a parking spot outside in a small side street, about a block away.

I hurry to my entrance at the northwest corner and go to the lift. The inside of the building appears gloomier than usual, which may account for the fact that I find myself in a lift I do not know, on the indicator panel of which only even-numbered floors are listed. Curious that I should not have noticed this before. But I shrug it off. Instead of going straight up to 13, I take the lift to 12, from where I can easily mount the single flight of stairs. Except that, for some reason, the staircase is not where it used to be in the past: there are stairs going down from here, but none leading up to the higher floors.

After a while I decide, rather peeved, to return to the lift and go up to 14, from where I may find a way down. But this lift does not go any higher than 12.

There seems to be no alternative but to go down to the ground floor again and find another lift. However, as it turns out, the one with the even numbers does not stop at the ground floor but continues all the way to the basement. Swallowing my mounting irritation, I get out to take another lift. But in the basement all the lights appear to have burned out and I simply cannot locate anything. I start feeling my way back to the first lift, but in the dark

I cannot find my way at all and have to start crawling along the wall hoping to find an opening of some kind.

After what seems to have been at least an hour I discover a gap in the darkness in front of me. A stairwell, it seems. Only, there are no stairs, either up or down. From what I can make out—but what can I make out in that Egyptian dark?—this is just a gaping hole. For all I know it may reach down to the bottom of the earth. Meticulously I start palpating the wall again, centimeter by centimeter. Surely, if I continue this way, keeping the wall on my left, it must lead somewhere.

Once, I trip over what feels like a big box and nearly fall flat on my face.

"Fuck it!" I mutter under my breath.

For a while I squat down on the floor. There is no cause for me to get excited. There is a rational explanation for everything. This, after all, is a hypermodern building; there must be logic in its construction. No need to lose my cool. No need, above all, to hyperventilate, as my body is threatening to do. Breathe deeply, count to ten, try again.

Another hour: this time I remember to check it on the luminous dial of my watch. Then, unexpectedly, I stumble over an object in my way. A big box.

Can it be the same one as before? But if it is, I have completed a circle without passing any openings or recesses at all, and certainly no stairs or lifts.

By now I can really feel panic tightening my throat. My forehead is wet with sweat.

If only I had a cell phone with me. But that is a part of modern technology that has passed me by. (How many times has Lydia made disparaging comments about it!)

Calm down now. Just take it calmly. Count to a hundred.

And then, inexplicably, my feet find a staircase, leading up. How could I have missed it on my two previous rounds? No matter. I'm here now. I shall soon be out and on my way up to Lydia, who will be most amused. She has in recent months been teasing me about getting old much faster than she.

I keep mounting for an interminable time. Surely this is much more than a single story? I start counting the stairs. After a hundred and fifty I stop. This is bloody ridiculous.

Now what? Go down again? Most decidedly not.

Up and up. Another hundred steps.

And then, suddenly, rounding a corner, there is a glimmer of light ahead. It grows stronger. My breath is coming in unhealthy gasps, burning my throat.

The light keeps on growing stronger. After stumbling on for another eternity I find myself back on the ground floor, the lobby I know so well. The whole thing must have been a delusion. Perhaps, I reassure myself, I blacked out for a while and missed some vital clues along the way. It may not be a bad idea to have a medical checkup tomorrow. If it is still today? I look at my watch. It has stopped.

But at least there is the reassurance of the lobby. There is a row of lifts on the right. Four of them.

I enter the first, taking care to keep the door open until I have consulted the instrument panel. 2, 4, 6, 8, 10, 12…up to 20.

I'm not going to make the same mistake again.

I move on to the second lift. Uneven numbers this time, but they stop at 9 and then jump to 19.

The third lift reverts to even numbers.

The fourth has a small white handwritten card dangling from the handle. OUT OF ORDER.

So what will it be?

I can of course take the stairs. But the idea of thirteen flights does not appeal to me. Especially not after my experience in trying to get out of the basement.

Just stay calm now. Think, David. Think. *Cogito ergo sum*, or whatever.

It takes some time before it strikes me that I may, quite simply, have come to the wrong entrance. This may be southeast, not northwest. I have never made this mistake before, but there's always a first time.

Not so? Not so?

I go outside. The early evening breeze fans my over-heated, throbbing face.

I look up. From this angle the building indeed has a totally different aspect from the one I am used to.

Immensely relieved (but still with a shadow of uneasy doubt in a deep corner of my mind), I proceed along the outside wall of the huge complex until I reach the next corner, marked NORTHEAST, where I step into the brightly lit entrance hall.

Immediately I feel at home. Of course, yes, this is where I should have entered in the first place.

I have wasted an inordinate amount of time. Curiously, my first thought is not of Lydia, who must be frantic with anxiety by now. (I am such a conscientious and punctual husband, so wholly predictable. Apart from that one impulsive decision, so many years ago, when I turned down the invitation to leave the country with Embeth, I have never done an uncalculated, unpremeditated thing in my life.) The person I am concerned about right now is, instead, the strange young woman Sarah behind the blue door. She must be worried about me. And the children. The lisping Tommie, the solemnly smiling Emily with her long plaits.

I hurry to the far corner. This time I have no hesitation in opening the first lift, the one I always take.

The instrument panel is reassuringly familiar. 1, 2, 3, 4, 5, 6, 7, 8, 9, 10, 11, 12, 13…

I step inside and press 13.

The lift shoots up at what feels like a dizzying speed. I rest my right hand on the side railing to keep my balance. In the dark mirror I see my face like a pale blotch in the half-dark interior. It looks disembodied. To tell the truth, I do not recognize myself at all.

Only after several seconds do I register that there must be something wrong. We seem to be going too far. I check the panel. It has changed since I stepped inside: the sequence of numbers is quite irregular. 3, 7, 8, 11, 15, 19, 20. At 20 the lift comes to a shuddering halt, but the door does not open.

I press DOWN, but nothing happens. When I try 15 the lift comes into motion, but it swooshes right past the requested floor and once again comes to a standstill only at the last stop, the ground floor. The door remains firmly shut.

20? Once more the lift zips to the top, where it remains motionless. Then down: this time it stops at 15 and the door slides open.

Gasping with relief, I quickly step outside to take two flights of stairs down. But although this floor is clearly marked 15, and the next one 14, there appears to be no 13: the floor after that bears in bold figures the number 9.

Somewhat to my surprise—by now I am ready for anything—the rest of the sequence remains normal and in due course I reach the ground level.

Shall I try the second of the four lifts? No harm in trying.

But although there are numerous buttons on the panel inside, not one of them is marked with a number. They are all blank.

I move on to the third lift. In this one every single button sports the number 20.

As in the first entrance lobby, the fourth lift is marked OUT OF ORDER.

With grim determination I leave the monstrous building and proceed to the third entrance. SOUTH-EAST.

Once again I cannot find a single lift marked with the correct numbers.

At the entrance to SOUTHWEST I find a very old man with a bald head and a beard like a crow's nest. He seems extraordinarily interested in my actions, which alarms me sufficiently to take the precaution of asking:

"Excuse me: I have to go up to the thirteenth floor. Could you please tell me how to get there?"

"Take the lift," he mumbles indistinctly. "Press the number 13 button inside."

I go to the first, but the moment I pull the door open I hesitate. Once again the instrument panel appears defective: there are no numbers on the buttons, only the letters of the alphabet.

For a moment I hesitate, before I go back to the Ancient Mariner.

"Does it make any difference which lift I take?" I ask him.

"Not to me it doesn't," he grumbles.

"Should I rather wait?"

"Up to you," he says, with what sounds like a sneer.

"But I must get to thirteen," I insist.

"Why?"

"Because I live there."

"Do you now?"

"Look," I say, making an effort to remain calm, but aware of the tightness in my jaws and of salty perspiration stinging my eyes. "There is something funny going on here. But all I want is to get home."

"Who doesn't?" asks old Methuselah.

"For God's sake!" With a tremendous effort I restrain myself. "Could you—please!—tell me what to do to get to thirteen."

"Just be patient. Wait like all of us."

"For how long?" I demand

He shrugs his bony old shoulders. His face has noticeably withered since my arrival. "I've been waiting here since I was eight. Come next April, it will be three hundred and two years." A sigh of resignation. "But of course, you may be lucky."

I am in no mood for his jokes. With a heavy heart

and tired feet I leave the building. Outside I stop to look up at the rows upon rows of windows. I used to be able to find our windows high up without any problem. Tonight I am not sure. Somewhere up there Lydia must be waiting. Or isn't she—?

I have a distressing feeling of having left her in the lurch. Betrayal of a kind I have committed only once before in my life. This time it is different. But does it not come down to the same cowardly abandonment?

How long have I been here? The hands of my watch still stand accusingly on ten to seven. For all I know it may be past midnight. What has happened in the house with the blue door in the meantime? Are the children still waiting for me to bathe them or has Sarah taken over my chores? Why should the thought suddenly make me feel guilty, as if I have let them down? I have nothing to do with them, have I?

And the young woman, Sarah?

Why should the thought of her suddenly perturb me? I don't even know her. Although she seems to be perfectly familiar with me. Suppose, in a way I have no hope of fathoming, she really regards me as her husband? I remember the full, moist touch of her lips on mine. Her black eyes. The movement of her body, her tight buttocks as she walked away down the passage. The sucking sound of her bare feet on the tiles. And in spite of myself I feel my weary step quickening as I walk on to where I left the car. If it is still there. If it has ever been there. If I myself am here.

6

THE MOMENT THE BLUE DOOR SWINGS OPEN AND I step inside, I see them in exactly the same positions and postures they were in when I left: Sarah with the fingers of one hand thrust into her hair, Tommie leaning forward, preparing to stand on his head, little Emily holding one hand outstretched toward me. As if no time at all has elapsed since I closed the door behind me. It is a most unsettling sensation, but I seem to be the only one to find it strange.

"If you bathe them," says Sarah, "I'll get on with the food. I've already put their pajamas in the bathroom."

"Yes," I say meekly, once again rattled by the total unfamiliarity of the place, the people, the situation. But now that I have been excluded from the flat where I live, I don't seem to have any choice. And in a curious way it is reassuring to be accepted so unquestioningly. Perhaps, I think, the strangeness is not here, but in me.

I may have lost my touch momentarily. Soon, who knows, everything may slot into place again. It is better not to let on how bewildered I am.

"Let's see who gets there first," I propose, and allow them to race past me with piercing shouts of glee before I follow.

In the bathroom, round the corner in a side passage, the bath is waiting, with large, soft, white towels laid out on a stand next to the toilet, and the children are already half undressed by the time I arrive. In a flash they are in the water, their smooth little bodies as slick as baby seals. A few big splashes cover half of the floor in puddles.

"Watch out!" I warn, alarmed.

"Come on in, Daddee," orders Emily.

"In, in," urges Tommie.

I take the precaution of closing the door before I start undressing. My fingers are numb with embarrassment, but they seem not to notice anything out of the ordinary and in a few moments I slide in. Fortunately the bath is so full of toys of every description that it isn't difficult to cover myself. But anxious to be out again and dressed before their mother puts in an appearance I go through the motions of a perfunctory wash, then do my best to do a hasty cleansing job on them—which isn't easy, as they wriggle and splash like eels.

Even after I am out and clothed again, they continue to demand my attention. Tommie has imaginary cuts and wounds on his knees and toes to show me, and which have to be kissed and patted before he will let me go. And Emily manages to get her long hair wet and insist on having it rubbed and dried before she will return to her games with a yellow duck and a partially dismembered Barbie doll.

It takes a lot of pleading and rash promising to coax them out of the water again. Tommie is so busy collecting his boats and fishes and cars that it takes all my energy to dry him and stuff him into his bright pajamas. Without more ado he runs off. Then it is Emily's turn.

"I'm sure you can dry yourself," I say when I lift her out to deposit her on the only dry patch on the floor.

She shakes her head vehemently. "No, I can't," she says. "You dry me."

"Then stand still."

"You must put me on the table."

With a sigh I pick her up and stand her on the table where the towels were laid out. But after a brief bout of patting and rubbing, she insists on lying down on her back.

"You haven't done my butterfly," she says, spread-eagled and with an expression of bliss and mocking on her little face.

"I'm sure you're big enough to do it yourself."

"But you always do it."

And only after the sweet little butterfly has been lovingly attended to does she consent to being dressed, exuberantly thwarting me at every turn.

After every button has been done up twice and her long black hair thoroughly dried with a new towel, leaving her fragrant and glowing, does she take me by the hand and lead me to their room off the main passage where Tommie is perched on his small blue bed, engrossed in a humming game of cars and trains.

"Now the story," says Emily as she snuggles into her own small red bed.

"Which story?"

"You know. The one of the three little men."

"Where's the book?"

"It's not in a book, silly," she laughs. "It's your story."

For a moment I am stumped. Then I try to sidestep it: "Tell you what: tonight you tell me the story of the three little men. You and Tommie can take turns to see who knows it best. Okay?"

It takes a while before they accept.

Emily begins: "Once upon a time there was a long, thin, white house, and in the house there lived three little men. A little red man, and a little blue man, and a little yellow man—"

It is a strange sensation, an echo from a very distant past. I grew up with this story, which my father used to tell us; but I haven't heard it for years and am not sure I can remember it properly. But now I want her to go on, and it is as if the story itself is drawing me into its undulations; it is like entering a place I have forgotten and only gradually rediscover as my own.

"The little red man sleeps in a little red bed," says Emily.

"A little blue bed," corrects Tommie.

"A red bed."

"A blue bed."

"A red bed, stupid!"

"I think they only get mixed up later in the story, Tommie," I gently intervene.

"A blue bed!" he shouts, sitting up. "Just like mine."

"Red."

"Blue."

"Let's see what happens if it is red," I propose.

"No, blue, Daddy."

At this point Sarah comes in. She looks amused, but tired.

"How far are you?" she asks from the door.

"Tonight it's our turn to tell the story," Emily says. "But Tommie keeps changing it because he's stupid."

"You're stupid!"

"Let Tommie try, Emily," says Sarah. "Then we'll see what happens in his story."

"But it will be all wrong!" the girl argues, red in the face with indignation.

"Stories needn't be the same every time," says Sarah. "It's nice if you don't always know what's going to happen next."

"But I want to know what happens next."

"Why don't we hear how Tommie tells it, then you tell it your way, and then Daddy can tell it the way he likes it." She smiles slyly. "And then we can have a vote and see which one we like best."

"What's a vote?" asks Tommie.

"It's a red thing with yellow spots," says Emily. "And it gobbles you up if you don't listen properly."

"Mam-meeeeee!" wails Tommie.

"All right, you tell us about the beds," Sarah quickly suggests.

Before Emily can interrupt, he reels off with an air of impish arrogance, "The little red man slept in a little red bed, and the little yellow man slept in a little yellow bed, and the little blue man slept in a little blue bed."

And from there Emily takes over and the story runs its course, as it slowly comes back to me from childhood, with the little men building a boat and dragging it to the sea, and a dolphin arriving to take them to the other side, where they visit a little orange woman, and a little green woman, and a little purple woman in a small round black house; and then the dolphin comes to take them home, but in the dark and in their tiredness after the long day, they tumble into the wrong beds and cannot sleep—the little red man in the yellow bed, the yellow one in the blue bed, the blue one in the red bed. Until someone thinks of putting on the light and they discover the mistake, and each little man gets into the right bed, and they all sleep happily until daybreak.

"Good," says Sarah as she gets up quickly, and tucks both the children in, and kisses them. "And now you sleep in your own little beds," she says happily, "and after supper Daddy and I will go to sleep in our own bed, and then we'll all live happily ever after."

7

F ONLY IT COULD BE SO EASY, I THINK AS WE LEAVE the sleepy children and go to the dining room. There is a feeling of foreboding in me. How are we going to sort this out? The mere thought of going to bed with this striking young woman makes my spine tingle. But how can I do that? It is not only the thought of betraying Lydia that troubles me, but the idea of—

somehow, even without allowing me any choice in the matter—it may mean taking advantage of Sarah. I have done at least one reckless thing in my life by turning my back on Embeth; I am not sure I can commit another terrible mistake by sleeping with Sarah.

But how could I be taking advantage of her if in her eyes I am her lawful husband, the father of her children? It is not I who is misleading her. I may be the one misled. I may be deluded, for all I know I may be hallucinating, all of this may be happening in a dream. Her two children may be as unreal as the small blonde girls on the back of a truck as I went home to fetch them water.

Sarah has prepared a delectable chicken dish, with lots of garlic, the way I love it, and with a big salad of greens and nuts to accompany it.

"This looks wonderful," I say. "You should not have taken so much trouble."

"I know you had a hard day," she replies as she sits down. "I thought you deserved a special effort."

"Shall I open some wine?"

"Please, I'd love some."

"Red or white?"

"That's a funny question. You know I never drink white."

"One never knows. You always find ways to surprise me."

"You're the one with the surprises." She smiles. "Like the candles in the bedroom last night."

I have to make an effort to keep cool. "I wouldn't have done it if I didn't believe you deserved it." And I add, as if to test the name on my tongue, "Sarah."

"Why do you say it in such a funny way?" she asks.

"What do you mean, 'funny'?"

"I don't know. As if you're not used to saying it."

"I don't think I'll ever get used to it, really."

"David."

I look up from where I have begun to remove the lead seal from the wine bottle on the sideboard behind the table. "What?"

"You're not having an affair, are you?"

"An affair?!" I nearly drop the corkscrew. "Of course not. Absolutely not. What makes you ask an outrageous thing like that?"

"You're a bit—strange." She looks me straight in the eyes. "Ever since you came home this afternoon. As if you can't really look me in the eyes properly."

"It's just that I've been battling with my painting today, without really getting anywhere."

"Yesterday you said it was going so well, you'd made the breakthrough you were waiting for."

"That was yesterday."

"You always have an answer for everything, don't you?"

"Try the wine," I say bluntly, offering her one of the glasses I have just poured.

She gives a little sigh, tastes the wine, then smiles. But her eyes retain their shadows: sadness, accusation, disillusionment. No longer as unequivocally youthful as before.

"Please don't look at me like that," I say.

"Give me your plate," she says quietly. Adding after a moment, "I've had a tough day too."

"How come?"

"The children, mainly." She hands me my plate, helps herself to a small wing too.

"They're so lovely!" I protest.

"I know. And that complicates it all. I love them, David. But they also keep me away from what I really want to do. You of all people should understand that. You had the guts to give up teaching and paint full time. But I—"

I don't even know what kind of work she does, I think. And I dare not ask. There is a silence as she looks down into her plate. Then looks up again, a swift, jerky movement of her head; the long black hair swings back from her face. "Do you remember all the dreams we once had? Is this what we have been waiting for all these years?"

"We haven't been doing so badly, have we? Only a few years ago we couldn't even have got married. We might have ended up in jail. Now we can lead a normal life together."

"I suppose it all depends on how we define 'normal.'"

A completely perverse thought suddenly strikes me: If we have a quarrel now and go to bed full of resentment and unresolved rage, I may not have to make love to her. But is that what I want?

Instantaneously something in me rises up in revolt. What am I thinking? How can I try to reject a chance like this?

(*You rejected it once before*, a voice inside me jeers.)

And what about Lydia?

"Let us try to be reasonable, Sarah," I say gently.

"Jesus, that's so like you!" she says with a flash of real anger. "Always so damn reasonable. Perhaps life just isn't meant to be reasonable. It's got to be lived, not discussed, not reasoned. When we first met, there was so much that wasn't anything like reasonable. There was love. There was joy. There was madness."

I turn cold at the memory of words so shockingly similar to these, spoken with just as much passion, but in a different voice. Could it have been only sixteen years ago? A different world, a different life. (But that was in another country, and besides, the wench is dead.)

"We have children now," I venture. "We have responsibilities. We are older now."

"But we're not old yet. For heaven's sake, David,

you're forty-four. I am thirty-nine. We still have every-thing to live for." A long, slightly shuddering sigh. "Can you understand that?"

I put out my hand across the table. "Of course I do."

"And you will help me?"

"I will."

She takes my hand. "Promise?"

"Promise."

How little it takes, I think. But how can I live up to it? I have just committed myself to a woman I have never set eyes on before today. A very beautiful, very young, very passionate woman whose hand is at this moment holding mine. And who, once I wake up in the morning, I may never see again.

But in the meantime we have this night. Which may turn into a nightmare.

Or not—?

"I'm tired," she says, almost in a whisper. "I'm going to bed. Will you clear up?"

"Of course."

She pushes her chair back. "Don't be long," she says in a voice of shadows as deep as the night, and bends over to kiss me on the cheek.

Not, I think emphatically.

8

S HE IS ALREADY IN BED WHEN I ARRIVE, LYING ON HER side, reading, her back turned to me, the outline of her body gracefully traced by the sheet, one smooth brown shoulder exposed.

But it is quite an obstacle course before I get there. First there is the bathroom. Automatically I go to the one where I bathed the children, but it is immediately evident that this is meant for the children only, or possibly for guests. Playing Blind Man's Bluff, I have to feel my way along the main passage where the lights have already been turned off, past the bedroom where the children have been tucked up for the night, toward a glimmer halfway to the left. From the passage door I can see another door leading from the bedroom, to my right, opposite the bed. To my great relief it turns out to be the en-suite bathroom. But this is by no means the end of my problems. I decide to spend a few minutes under the shower first: although I have already had a bath with the children, that was a rather hurried affair, and furthermore I need time to reflect on my imme-diate challenges. Which of the two toothbrushes—one blue, one red—am I supposed to use, which towel is mine? And afterward, should I proceed to the bedroom naked, or with a towel around my waist, or wearing pajamas? (Which will be where?) In the end I decide not to aggravate the situation by wondering about what her expectations may be but simply to follow my inclination, doing what comes naturally to me.

So I am naked when I come into the bedroom and furtively slide in behind her back, trying to hide the evidence of my state of anticipation.

She glances over her shoulder and says, "Oh." Which may mean anything.

Fortunately there is a pile of books beside the lamp on what I take to be my bedside table, and I take the top one to page through. It is Jostein Gaarder's *Sophie's World*. I've been meaning to read it for a long time, but something has always intervened. Perhaps this is as good an opportunity as any of getting through it. But I soon put it down, all too aware of the gentle undulation of the woman's body next to me. The urge to touch her becomes hard to resist. But I am restrained by the uncertainty about what might happen if I do. And there is the pure visual joy of looking at her. For the time being I do not want to do anything except to look, and look, and look. (How I wish I could paint her as she lies there now, at this moment, so close, so real.)

After a while, from the way in which she remains almost motionless, never bothering to turn a page, I realize that she is not reading either. Waiting for me to make the first move?

I move my hand closer to her, still without touching.

I seem to detect the merest hint of a stiffening in her body. But it may well be my imagination. And it is of decisive importance that I be sure before I risk an approach. Because if not—

"What are you reading?" I ask. But my voice is so strained that I have to clear my throat and repeat the question.

"Haruki Murakami," she says, turning slightly over on her back and raising the book to let me see it. *"Sputnik Sweetheart."*

"What's it like?"

"A strange book," she says without looking at me. "I don't think it's entirely convincing, but it's very disturbing." Now she settles squarely on her back and turns her head to look at me. "In the key episode of the story the young Japanese woman—what's her name?" She flips through a few pages. "Yes—Miu. She gets stuck at the top of a Ferris wheel at a fair in the middle of the night. And when she looks around, she discovers that she can see into her own apartment in the distance. And there's a man in there, a man who has recently tried to get her into bed. While Miu is looking at him, she sees a woman with him. And the woman is she herself, Miu. It is a moment so shocking that her black hair turns white

45

on the spot." Her black eyes look directly into mine. "Can you imagine a thing like that happening? Shifting between dimensions, changing places with herself—?"

"I think that happens every day," I say with a straight face.

"What do you mean?"

"When one makes love. Don't you think that's a way of changing places with yourself? The world becomes a different place. You are no longer yourself."

"You're still an incorrigible romantic."

I am not sure if that is meant as criticism, cynicism, or gentle approval.

"Shall we try?" I ask quietly. This time I put out my hand and fold it over the gentle roundness that molds the angularity of her bare shoulder.

There is a tense moment. Everything, I realize, hinges on this. Everything. Not just the choice between yes or no, between making love or turning away, but who we are, where we are, what we are, what may become of us.

At least she doesn't make an attempt to turn away. A moment later, with a small sigh, she closes her eyes. I take the book from her and put it aside. Then I kiss her shoulder.

"David," she says, as if it is not a name but the introduction to something longer and more complicated. Monologue, soliloquy, poem, reminiscence, memoir, prophecy. Or all of it together. But whatever the rest might be, is left unspoken.

I push myself up on an elbow and pull the sheet from her. She is wearing a very thin cotton nightdress, full length, but rucked up to her thighs. I bend over, down, to kiss her knees. She utters a small sound and raises her hips so that I can pull the nightdress up to bare her pubic mound. It is very small and dense, smooth as a sable paintbrush; I touch it with the tip of my tongue.

I speak her name as she has spoken mine. But I have no idea of what it means. "Sarah." I do not even recognize my voice.

And so we move through our unspoken, unspeakable text, following its rhythms and cadences, meandering along its possibilities, reaching out toward what may be its conclusion but which continues to elude us, moving ever farther away, just beyond our reach, as we writhe and pant and moan and plead, but ultimately too remote to reach.

Exhausted, covered in sweat, my throat parched, my fingers numb, I remain a dead weight on her, my face in the fragrance of her hair.

You are my wife, I think. You are my wife. But who are you? Who am I?

I must have fallen asleep like that, and only become aware again of where I am when she moves under me and pushes me aside.

"You're too heavy," she whispers.

"I'm sorry."

"Don't be." Her fingers are moving through my hair.

"I don't know what happened," I say numbly. "Something just didn't—"

"Don't talk now," she says. "It was good. There needn't always be an earthquake. You know that."

"We just need a little time to get used to each other," I assure her, without thinking.

Sarah makes an abrupt movement to raise her upper body and look at me. "What on earth do you mean?" she asks. "We've been married for nine years, for heaven's sake."

There is a sinking feeling in my gut, but I make an effort: "In a way every time is the first time," I say. "Don't you agree?"

She stares hard at me for a while, then slowly settles back into her previous position. For a while neither says anything.

Then, suddenly she moves her head against mine. "It was good," she repeats in my ear. "Wasn't it?"

"Yes, it was. Of course it was."

"Are you going to sleep now?" she asks.

"Yes. And you?"

"Yes." And after a moment, "Will you hold my hand?"

But we lie awake for a long time. I can hear it in her breathing, feel it in the unyielding tension of her body, lithe and sticky with sweat against mine.

In the morning, I think, I shall return to her. And take my time. To inspect everything that makes her. Her eyes and mouth and ears, her hair. Her shoulders, her arms and hands, each finger separately. Her nipples. Down to her toes. Everything. Everything. I must know who she is. I must find out what it means to say "Sarah."

9

B UT I DO NOT FALL ASLEEP. MY THOUGHTS REMAIN preoccupied, thinking of what has happened and not happened. Of what may yet happen.

I know that much of what has gone wrong tonight—no, that is not it: nothing has gone wrong, it has merely not gone right—has not to do with us, here, in this bed, but comes from very far back. Memories which I had thought—hoped—had long been laid to rest. Lydia, of course. But also Embeth. Perhaps Embeth above all.

It was pure coincidence (but what is coincidence?) that we met. Initially, I had not even been selected as one of the artists invited to the South African exhibition in the new gallery at the top of Hout Street that November, but then somebody dropped out and I became a last-minute replacement, not even featured in the catalog. Two of my paintings were accepted. The first featured a young woman, the left half of her body naked, the other half clothed very formally; the second showed two women, one seen from the back, the other from the front, one white, the other brown. The pose was not erotic; it was merely a study in contrasting colors (even if I had used the same young woman as a model for both figures). My style, I suppose, had initially been strongly influenced by the Nabis and less obviously by German expressionists, Otto Mueller in particular, still one of my favorites, although by that time I think I had begun to find my own vernacular. Those two canvases actually marked a new beginning.

For me, the afternoon represented a significant milestone as it was the first time I was exhibiting with more-or-less professional artists. The swirling, milling, sweat-smelling, wine-swilling crowd on the rainy afternoon of the opening included a fair number of visitors lured from the street primarily by the free drinks.

It was a heady experience. I even sold one of my two paintings, the one of the two women, titled *Sisters*. For the first time I dared to think a thought which has not let go of me again: that, perhaps, teaching need no longer be the only career choice open to me.

Somewhere in the course of the afternoon she came to me. The young woman with the smoky dark eyes and the long lashes and the provocative mouth, dressed in faded denims and a stark white long-sleeved shirt with most of the buttons undone. Her skin a smooth, even brown that became paler where the shirt was folded back. I had noticed her earlier in the crowd—it was impossible not to—but in close-up she was devastating.

"You done this?" she asked point-blank, with a swing of her head to indicate my painting.

"I'm afraid so."

"Why 'afraid'?"

"Just a way of putting it."

"A very white way."

"Why should it be a white way?"

She shrugged, as if it would be too boring to attempt an answer. After a moment she asked, "They're not really sisters, are they?"

"I suppose there are many ways of being sisters."

"They're not the same color."

"You have no white sisters?" I challenged her.

A sudden laugh, a full-blooded belly laugh, more generous than I would have expected. But once again she did not deign to answer. After a moment she asked,

"What are you trying to say?" She gestured toward the painting again. There was something intoxicating about her presence, the unabashed challenge in her attitude, the raw femininity of her closeness.

"It's a painting, not a lesson."

"Cop-out."

"I didn't mean it that way."

"It came out that way."

An unexpected smile—these quicksilver changes of mood would become one of her most defining characteristics—and then she said, "It is a fucking nice painting." Her smoky eyes narrowed. "One would almost think they're the same girl."

"You're very perceptive. They're both the same model."

"Hm." For a moment she gazed intently at the canvas. "So which one is real, which one fake?"

"They're both equally real."

"But the model." A touch of irritableness in her voice. "Was she colored, or white?"

"Does it really matter?"

"It does to me."

I hesitated. "If you must know, she was white."

"Could have thought so." Her voice a sneer.

"Why?"

"I don't think you could handle a colored woman, mister."

Suddenly, recklessly, I took the plunge: "Will you model for me?"

Without a moment's hesitation she said, "Of course not."

"Now you are scared."

"I'm not. I'm just not interested."

"Pity."

"Pity for you or for me?"

"Who knows. Perhaps for both of us."

There was a pause. Then, with a small laugh she turned and began to walk away. I could not make out whether I had won the round, or dismally lost it. But after a moment she came back.

"Tell me," she said in her voice which was low and gravelly, "do you fuck your models?"

I met her gaze. "Not as a rule," I said. "It has happened." It took some effort not to look away. "But I prefer not to keep involved."

"And if I posed for you?"

"Then I will probably not."

"Because you're scared or because I'm colored?"

"Because it would not be very professional."

"You're too clever by half."

"I'm just trying to be sensible."

"Oh God. Please!"

For a moment everything seemed spoiled. Then I said, trying my best to keep up a pretense of composure,

"Well? Where can I get in touch with you?"

"Leave it to me," she said, tapping with a finger-nail on her catalog. Her little smile was inscrutable. And she turned to go.

But I followed her, suddenly in a panic. She could not go now!

"At least tell me your name!" I blurted out.

She looked back over her shoulder. "I'll let you know if I get in touch."

And then she was gone. I am the one, I thought dully, obtusely, who has missed his chance.

Somebody put a proprietorial hand on my arm. "And who was the miss?" asked Nelia in her sweetest voice.

10

NOW, LYING NEXT TO SARAH, ONE HAND RESTING very lightly on her smooth brown shoulder, I allow all the memories slowly to ripple over me again, and I revisit them as if they belong to an old movie I have not seen in a long time.

I remember Nelia's words, the gayness in her voice, but also the darker undertone of suspicion.

"Just a fan," I hear myself replying to her question, turning it into playful teasing. "You'll have to get used to having a famous artist for a fiancé. I have actually sold a painting."

"You've sold paintings before," she reminded me.

"But only to friends or friends-of-friends," I said. "Not at an exhibition. From tonight I am in a new league, my love."

She looked after the figure disappearing in the crowd.

"I don't think my parents will like the idea," she said, clouds covering her frank blue eyes. "Nor will yours."

"Jesus, Nelia!" I exploded. "I've just met the woman. It's not as if I'm going to jump into bed with her."

She just stared at me, hurt and incomprehension in her face. And indeed, now that I think back, that was a turning point. The turning point, for her, for me, placing suddenly at risk everything we had previously taken for granted, everything that had been so predictable and safe.

We had practically grown up together, Nelia and I. My father enjoyed reminding us, especially when we had guests, of how we had been potty-trained together, sitting on our small plastic pots, one blue, one pink, on two corners of the newly bought yellow carpet in the lounge, diagonally across, our little faces red with the effort of trying to produce something to justify the family pride. Our parents had been at the University of Pretoria together; our fathers had regularly compared notes about their weekly progress with their respective girlfriends; they had married within months of each other. And on the very day of the yellow carpet they had jocularly agreed that one day the two of us would also be joined in wedlock to seal the friendship. They had so much in common—even though Nelia's father, a doctor, was in the eyes of the two mothers a small notch above mine on the social scale, mine being a mere teacher like me (though he later became a principal, then inspector of schools). In politics, in the church council, in municipal affairs, even in the tennis club, our fathers were peers, and fiercely benevolent competitors—as were our mothers in the Women's Auxiliary, in the charity drives sponsored by the church, and in cooking, baking, sewing, knitting, or arranging flowers.

And then it was all fucked up by Embeth's appearance on the scene.

For ten days after the opening of the exhibition there was no sign of her. By that time, in spite of going to the gallery at least twice every day, I had given up on ever hearing from her again. (On the third day, coinciding with an unexpectedly glowing mention in a *Cape Times* review, the second painting was sold, and in the evening the two families celebrated together—even though they had been rather tight-lipped all the way about my penchant for nudes.) Then she telephoned. I would have recognized that voice anywhere, but it was so unexpected that I couldn't believe it; and the name, of course, meant nothing to me.

"Is that David le Roux?"

"Yes, I am. And you are—?"

"Embeth Arendse."

"Embeth?" I asked. "I'm afraid I don't—"

"Don't tell me you're still afraid?"

"You mean—?"

"You asked me to pose for you, remember? Or are there so many women crowding you that you cannot keep track of them all?"

"So that's your name?" I asked inanely.

"My parents called me Emma Elizabeth, but when I was three I changed it to Embeth and refused to listen if anybody tried to call me something else."

"Precocious child."

"You still interested in a model?"

"Not just any model. You."

A brief pause.

"And you promise not to fuck me?"

"All I promised was that I would try to behave properly."

"Which may mean anything, of course."

"Exactly."

After a moment she said, "I saw you've sold your other painting too. So you can't be too bad."

That meant that she had actually gone back to the gallery. But I thought it prudent not to mention it.

"When can you come?" I asked, trying to keep my voice neutral.

"Sometime over the weekend?"

For a moment it was difficult to control my breathing. Then I said, "Why not?" and she hung up.

She came on the Sunday afternoon, a sweltering day. My apartment, in a rundown building in a nondescript little street in Gardens, was like a baking oven, even though I'd had the fan running since early morning.

"Jesus!" she exclaimed as I opened the door for her. "You do make sure that no one can keep their clothes on, don't you?" And she had barely crossed the threshold before she stepped out of the few bits of clothing she was wearing: a deep pink sleeveless top, white shorts, tiny orange knickers, thong sandals.

As a painter I was not unfamiliar with the unclothed female body, but this took me by surprise. Not only because it happened so quickly, so casually, so matter-of-factly, but because Embeth was exquisitely beautiful. Small and frail without her clothes, like a pixie, with short-cropped hair and singularly graceful hands and feet.

Lying behind Sarah, her tight buttocks cupped by my lower belly and my thighs, my hands now pensively molding her shoulders, then her breasts, I keep my eyes closed to reimagine Embeth. Two bodies so very different—one so delicate and bird-like, the other long and lithe—and yet inexplicably, liquidly, merging with one another, like the shapes of dreams in sleep.

On that first Sunday Embeth posed for just over three hours before I wrapped it up. I had made twelve or fifteen sketches and drawn rough outlines for two paintings on canvas.

"Well?" she asked as I closed the sketchpad and put away the charcoal pencils. "Satisfied?"

"You were bloody good," I said. Now that the session was over, I found it difficult to look at her. "Shall I get us something to drink?"

It seemed as if she was going to say something, then thought better of it. When I returned from the kitchen, she had put on her skimpy bits of clothing; but she was still barefoot, dangling a string sandal from one big toe where she sat in a wicker chair much too big for her.

Over the next few months I saw a lot of her, but I cannot say I came to know her better. She kept her life to herself and simply saw no need to share any of her secrets with me. I did not even know where she lived. And yet I think, now, that this was exactly why I became so attracted to her. For the first time in my tidily defined life the future was not predictable. She was a wholly unknown factor. In her lurked, who knows, danger of a kind I could not explain. And I felt possessive about her strangeness. Here, at last, was somebody, something, exclusively—and exquisitely—mine.

There was something wild even in the rashness of the first moment. I blurted out, "Embeth, I love you!"

Her answer was shockingly matter-of-fact: "Then fuck me."

And so we did.

I still remember with painful precision, here where I lie with my hands on the breasts of a strange woman who believes I am her husband, because that was the day our lives changed. In the most melodramatic way imaginable. Nelia walking in on us. I'd forgotten that she had a key to the apartment. Her face as she stood in the doorway, staring down at the two of us on the floor. No longer joined at the hip, but still naked.

Her funny little falsetto whisper: "David—?"

And Embeth getting up—not scrambling, not furtively, but calmly, almost proudly—to collect her scattered clothes, and taking her time getting dressed. After what seemed to have been an unconscionable time, still without saying a word, she went out to the front door with its frosted glass panels, carrying her red sandals in her right hand. (That is the one image I

shall remember forever from that day: the red sandals.)
Nelia's high-pitched voice: "With a meid, David? David,
with a meid?"

The very day after the end of our world, Embeth
was priceless when she mimicked Nelia: "With a meid,
David? David, with a meid?"

But it was a dead end. By that time Nelia had already
told her parents, and her parents had told my parents,
and there was a grotesque gathering of all concerned.

I pleaded with Embeth: why should we allow our
lives to be dictated by the unreasonable reasonableness
of my family? If we loved each other—

"So what do you think we'll do?" she asked, a harsh
tone of accusation in her voice. "Pretend it's okay and
nothing has happened?"

"We can go on as before," I insisted.

"Will you run away with me?"

"Where to?"

"Overseas. London. Anywhere. As long as we get
out of this place."

"There's no call for anything drastic, Embeth."

"And suppose I'm pregnant?"

"Are you?"

"It was only yesterday you took me, David!"

"What are you trying to say?"

"You want children with me? You want to go and
show them to Oupa and Ouma?"

"Embeth, please! We can sit down and discuss this like grownups."

"Like hell we can." And again she mocked in that high-pitched voice, "With a meid, David? David, with a meid?"

"You're scared. I told you that very first day—you're scared."

"Of what?"

"Of making a decision. Of choosing, for once, what you want to do, not your fucking family."

"Why should we be in such a hurry? We can take our time."

"I can't see the point of letting this drag on and on."

"Let's just see what happens."

"No. You make up your mind. Like now."

"It's not fair."

"Then just fuck off."

Then she left. This time she was wearing the red sandals, not carrying them in her hand.

Through the intervening years I have put the whole memory of Embeth safely and securely out of reach. But tonight it is suddenly back, flooding my conscience and my consciousness. As if, with me, it had slipped in through the blue door that once seemed so familiar.

11

I N THE EARLY DAWN, WHEN THE FIRST LIGHT COMES
filtering into the bedroom, I start caressing Sarah,
whose body is still half-folded into mine. I lie
against her tracing her outline with my hand. The
rounded sweep of her hip, moving over her ribcage to
trace the arc of a breast, feeling the nipple stir and
stiffen under my touch. I am aching with desire. Most
of the night I have floated on or just below the surface
of sleep, not wanting to awaken her, but hardly able
to contain my urgency, to resume from where we have
left off last night. Even before my eyes can scan her
face to see again what I have seen before, only more
intensely now, more assuredly, more possessively, I
recall the images of the first time, the very dark eyes
half closed, a thin snail trail of saliva running from the
corner of her ample mouth, a small frown of concentration between her eyebrows.

Half awake, she stirs, first moves as if to turn away,
then shifts to her back to make herself more acces-
sible, one leg drawn up. A small sigh. The hint of a
welcoming smile.

"David—?" she mumbles.

"I'm here," I whisper.

My hand moves across the crinkly roughness of her mound, two fingers probe the entrance to her sex, feeling for the minuscule slick puckering of her clitoris. With one hand she pushes the sheet down to her thighs.

And then there is a low thundering of feet and two ululating whoops of joy as the children come charging through the door and hurl themselves onto the bed, landing right between us. Instinctively we both roll away to make room for them, as we frantically try to cover ourselves. They do not even seem to notice our nakedness as they wriggle and writhe and roll over us and choke us with wild demonstrations of love and small wet mouths cover our faces with saliva and snot. Tommie, especially, is wheezing and snorting most alarmingly.

"You got a cold, lovey?" asks Sarah as she gathers him in her arms and presses him against her. His nose leaves an oystery smudge on her cheek.

Tommie nods fiercely, then breaks into a wide grin. "But you know what? The wind got a cold too, I heard him sniffing outside all night."

"Tonight we'll put out a big handkerchief for him, then he can blow his nose. Okay?"

"And a blanket," proposes Tommie, "so he won't get so cold again."

"The wind doesn't need a blanket, silly," Emily sneers with a puckered nose. "He's got the clouds."

"When I was a grownup," says Tommie, "I also slept under the clouds."

"We don't want to be late for school," says Sarah, swinging her legs out of the bed. My eyes dwell on the curve of her back. "Come on. Daddy can help Emily, I'll dress you."

"I can dress myself," Tommie says. "I'm big enough."

"You can't even tie your shoelaces," Emily jeers.

"I can too."

"You can't."

"I can!"

"Let's see who gets done first." In a flash the little fairy girl is out of her tiny nightie and running down the passage.

The next hour is a whirlwind of comings and goings, running and jumping, teasing and taunting, laughter and tears, chasing and fleeing, hiding and seeking, all of it with a total commitment to every new moment, an energy that leaves me breathless. At last everybody is clean and fed, and Sarah prepares to drive them to crèche and preschool.

"You want me to come with?" I ask at the kitchen door, thinking it might be an easy introduction to the morning routine—and the route to school, in case I have to take over sometime.

But Sarah shakes her head. Imprinting a brief kiss on my cheek, she says, already on her way to the small red

Corsa parked under a lean-to behind the kitchen, "I'm going to have tea with Brenda afterward. And I know you have more than enough to do before the exhibition."

What exhibition? I wonder.

From the kitchen door I wave and spontaneously call, "Bye. Love you."

Unexpectedly, she stops to turn.

"I love you, David!" she calls back. Then she unlocks the car door for the children and they scramble in, scrambling and whooping.

To my own surprise, I ask, "Why do you love me?"

Sarah comes the few steps back to me. She reaches out and puts her hands on my shoulders. With unexpected seriousness she says, very softly, "Because you make me possible."

And then she goes back to the car. I watch them as they drive off.

Please come back! I want to plead. But I do not speak the words.

At last they are gone. An almost eerie silence descends on the house.

Where shall I begin? There is a whole world waiting to be discovered, probed, registered for future reference. And now that I am alone, the place feels precarious, menaced from all sides. Will it not suddenly cave in under me? Will all kinds of new doors swing open before me, leading to God knows what unpredictable spaces, what new threatening or welcoming strangers?

As a precaution I return to the front door where it all started yesterday. Hesitate with my hand on the doorknob, then turn it. I am conscious of a tightness in my chest. The door swings open. The outside is the same deep blue I first painted it, and looks exactly as it has looked for years. The bit of flaking paint, the two parallel scratches near the keyhole. I remember the feeling of exultation with which I painted it. My declaration of independence. My door. My space. Mine, mine only. In which I could do whatever I wished without anybody else—not even my own wife—knowing where I was or what I was up to. I remember how I first set upon the surface (a dreary, ordinary brown, a kind of civil service brown, at the time), covering it with wild and uncontrolled strokes in all directions. How I imagined strange faces, shapes, animals, humans looming up from the mysterious ultramarine depths, appearing and disappearing, changing, transmuting. All of it mine. That was before Lydia followed me here and colonized my space.

Back inside. Closing the door meticulously behind me. First to the master bedroom. It is all still there. The clothes strewn on the floor, the cupboard door ajar, the bed crumpled. I kneel beside it, push away the blankets and press my face into the sheets. They bear a faint odor of bodies, of sex, us. Unless I am imagining it all; unless I have imagined it.

I tarry there—scared, perhaps, of what I may find in the rest of the house? This room, at least, is a space I know by now. I close my eyes to call up again the image of the strange, beautiful, young woman who thinks of me as her husband and who believes that I am the father of her children. Anxious to savor the moment, I stay to make the bed. Then turn to face the built-in cupboards and work systematically through all the shelves and hanging space. One whole section is taken up by men's clothes, presumably mine. On the whole I approve of the taste they reveal, although there are a few rather disreputable old jeans and shirts among them. Rummaging through them I discover a shirt I recognize. It gives me a strange sense of belonging, even though I don't have the faintest idea of how it ever got here. Then a few more shirts. Two pairs of trousers. Some underpants that can do with mending or throwing away. They must indeed be mine. I shrug, hesitating between relief and alarm.

After that I inspect the women's clothes, mostly with approval. Excellent taste, particularly in casual dresses and underwear, erring on the side of youth: minidresses, sexy sandals, thongs and G-strings. In one drawer, a large collection of jewelry, flashing and funky and fun. I like this person. I could live with her. I do live with her.

From the bedroom I proceed to the en-suite bathroom, still in delightful disarray, presumably from Sarah's ablutions last night before I used it and came to bed. But then I become impatient. The rest of the house is waiting. God knows what lurks behind each new door.

There are pictures in the passage. A couple of my paintings: I do not recognize them individually, but the style is familiar. It has taken me a long time to arrive at this point. In the beginning my work was eclectic, perhaps even haphazard. At one stage I moved into abstraction. Fun, but immensely frustrating in the long run: I felt threatened and oppressed by the limitless freedom it implied, the tyranny of freedom. What I needed was discipline, some kind of framework—even if only to challenge it with the possibilities of breaking out of it. That was when the Nabis began to point the way. At least it made me feel safe. Even though I always remained conscious of an urge to break free more radically, to take risks, to place my certainties at stake, I could never quite abandon the need for the reassurance of the familiar.

There are other pictures in the passage too. A few, unmistakably, done by the children. Also a couple of large framed photographs. Black and white. One portrait of a woman: her head draped in a dark cloth that hangs loosely over one shoulder, leaving the other exposed; and with a nipple visible in the bottom left corner. An intriguing face, largely in shadow. It takes a while before I recognize her. It is Sarah. My immediate reaction is jealousy, suspicion: who was the photographer? But there is no clue to his identity at all, except that I sense it must have been a man. Only a man could have insisted so darkly on the eroticism of that nipple.

The second bedroom is the children's. No dark surprises here. Once again I linger to make the two small beds and tidy up the mess.

There is a third bedroom. On the wall, another of my paintings, and two photographs, starkly stylized, and once again in black and white. No signature, no clues; but for some reason I have no doubt that they must be the work of the same photographer. For a moment I catch myself wondering whether it could be Sarah's husband—until it strikes me that I am her husband. Supposed to be.

Lounge. Dining room. Kitchen. The second bathroom, where I bathed the children last night. Another, shorter passage branches off from the main one. What immediately strikes me is the series of photographs on the wall, ten or twelve of them, quite close together, all in black and white, all of doors, some ajar, most of them closed. Wonderfully textured shots, printed in heavy grain, all divorced from the buildings to which they must have belonged. Just doors, doors. And the cumulative effect is overwhelming. A sense of secrecy, of secretness, doors not only to the unknown but the unknowable, their mysteries forever out of reach. I cannot make out whether they are ominous, louring, threatening—or simply blank, unsettling in their very ordinariness. They force me to look round to where I have just come from, expecting perhaps to see some stranger on my heels, man or alien, or even the woman of the house herself, the one who goes by the name of Sarah and who first opened the outside blue door to me to invite me into her secret space. Which turned out to be merely a house. Her house. Presumed to be mine. The house where I live. Where I may have been living for years.

After the series of photographs there are two more doors in the side passage, one open, one closed. A door in natural dark wood—not plywood but solid, impressively solid, forbiddingly solid.

Should I risk it? But how can I not?

For a long time I remain standing in front of the closed door. A very, very ordinary door. So ordinary that it makes my skin turn to gooseflesh.

I don't want to go in here. What are those famous words that still make men cringe after six hundred years? *Abandon all hope, ye who enter.*

Bloody ridiculous.

This is my house. It should have no secrets for me.

I push it open.

The door opens to a very untidy room. Quite big, probably six meters by seven or thereabouts. It is a studio. A photographic studio. Two large-format cameras on tripods. Several others, 35 mm, strewn across two trestle tables, almost as if a very hectic session has been interrupted midway. Against the far wall, a wide roll of black paper, some three meters across, hanging from a beam. Various items of furniture: easy chairs, a swing suspended from the ceiling. Bits and pieces of clothing draped everywhere: scarves and shawls, dresses, tops, stockings, panties, bras.

There are photographs on all the walls. These are not framed, but pinned haphazardly to large softboards. On both the tables are stacks of other photographs, some threatening to topple over.

After wandering about in some bewilderment I decide to start from the door and work my way anti-clockwise around the studio.

The photos are of an astounding variety, cityscapes, landscapes, trees, groups of people, cats, individual faces. Yet it does not take long to acknowledge that they must all be by the same person. The majority are studies of women, their faces and bodies obscured, but also dramatically molded, by shadow. Still intrigued by the anonymity of the photographer, I start hunting for clues.

I am halfway round the room before the answer becomes obvious. There is a whole collection of intimate shots, a number of them nude, others with underwear in the process of being put on or taken off; some of which show only parts of the body: an elbow, a shoulder, a torso in three-quarters profile, a ribcage, a breast, a stomach with the indentation of the navel staring like a vacant eye. All of them obviously taken in a mirror, which is incorporated in the composition. One mirror in particular is used to astonishing effect: an art nouveau design, the contours of the frame formed by an undulating young woman with long hair and gracefully curved arms, the glass shaped like a harp. Sometimes there are two mirrors, or even three, in such a way that an endless dialogue between reflections is triggered. The series concludes with several shots of the photographer in close-up, distorted by the mirrors, either with a fragment of the body visible, slightly out of focus, below the face, or showing the face only, the single-reflex lens like a huge Cyclops eye peering at the spectator. It is not a man after all. It is, every time, Sarah. No doubt at all.

After facing this disturbing series I cannot absorb much more; and the rest of my tour is more cursory. I can, after all, always come back.

Moving down the passage to the last door in the side passage, I start feeling less agitated. Already I have a presentiment of where this will lead to. And my hunch turns out to be right: all the signs point to it being my own studio. The studio which, as I remember it, used to take up most of my rented cottage with the blue door. But it is still not without surprises: quite a number of the paintings are ones I am sure I have taken home long ago. A few, I remember very clearly, have been sold. What is most unnerving is that two of them are the paintings which were shown at the very first group exhibition where I met Embeth. The one of the girl split in two, one half immaculate and formally dressed, the other half naked; the second of the white and brown girls, one approaching, the other going.

I close my eyes for a moment. I must not lose my head now.

Finding it unbearable to face that pivotal moment from my past any longer, I return to the main passage and head for the kitchen. Time for a cup of tea, a few minutes of rest to gather my thoughts and plan my day. But there is a sense of inconclusiveness about the morning. Something continues to bother me.

From the kitchen I go back along the side passage to the first of the two studio doors. Impossible to avoid them, most particularly the first one, behind the closed door. I must see more of Sarah. I must come closer to solving the riddle she poses in her work—as a pointer, perhaps, to the riddle of herself.

The first thing that strikes me as I open the door to her studio again is that the sequence and configuration of the photographs on the walls appear to have changed. Several I do recognize, but now they are in different positions—that is, if I remember correctly; if my memory is to be trusted. But I realize that I may indeed be mistaken: except for that one series of self-portraits and nudes I may simply not have paid enough attention on my first visit. Suppressing the anxiety that I can feel building up inside me I start going round the walls again. This time my first—and worst—suspicions are confirmed: although I do not expect to recall every detail precisely, surely it is unlikely that so many of the photographs should appear altogether new this time round? The uneasiness persists.

It grows worse when I become aware of the fact that with every new round I make along the walls I seem to notice different things—not only in the configuration of the pictures, but in the images themselves. I remember specifically studying the portrait of a woman with a mantilla covering half her face, with a beauty spot prominent on the exposed cheek. It is mounted next to a rather shocking study of a girl doing a cartwheel. But on my next round they have shifted: the woman with the mole on her cheek has moved farther along; the cartwheeling girl is no longer there.

75

I can feel a coldness quivering its way down my spine. I do not want to be here any longer.

But I must make one final round, to be absolutely certain. I advance one slow step at a time, trying to memorize as much as possible of each individual photo.

This time there is no doubt at all. The discovery comes when I reach, once again, the spot where I first saw the girl doing the cartwheel. She is still missing. But in her place there is a portrait of a face I know only too well.

Embeth.

How can I ever forget the contours of that face, those sad and ominous eyes, the mouth half open, the way I saw her in the throes of making love?

I have to go. Impossible to linger here a minute longer.

As I approach the door, my hand already outstretched to grasp the knob so that I can close it the moment I go out, another photograph, immediately to the left of the doorway, brings me to a standstill.

Lydia.

Her eyes—even in black and white I recognize their luminosity—gaze straight at me in what looks like accusation. And I can hear her voice as she said yesterday when I prepared to leave for the studio:

"Please don't forget to get the things at the supermarket. Have you got the list?"

"In my jeans pocket," I said.

And then I left. And went to the supermarket after I'd finished my day's work. And returned to find myself here, at the blue door of this house. And when, later, I tried to go back to our apartment building, there was no way in.

I am terrified to stay in this room surrounded by these photographs, yet I cannot move, unable to tear myself away. I cannot leave before glancing around the room one last time.

Faces, faces, unmasked, stripped bare, stare at me. The others—the cityscapes, the figures, the group studies, the cats—have all disappeared. Only the portraits remain. The staring faces with their eyes, their mouths, their foreheads, their eyes, their eyes. I know them all. In one way or another they have all played a part in my life.

I must go. First of all, I must find Lydia again. I cannot stay here. I have never felt so exposed, so threatened, in my life.

12

THERE IS SOMETHING INEVITABLE ABOUT THIS trip, back to Lydia. The city surrounding me has an air of detachment, of remoteness, as if it is waiting for whatever is to happen, without intending to interfere or get involved in any way. I drive along Eastern Boulevard, with the sea and the harbor below on my left. In the middle distance, a brownish smudge in the cerulean cobalt blue and turquoise and ultramarine of the ocean, lies Robben Island. Now almost irrelevant, canonized by history, no longer a defining presence, unless one chooses to remember. What is past is past. Or isn't it? Is returning to Lydia not in its own way an attempt to retrieve the past?

Lydia. But, behind her, Embeth too. The day she left with her red sandals in her hand. The day she kept them on. The utter finality of that good-bye. Even in dreams she was canceled, enclosed behind a door no one and nothing could open again.

Yet it was not a complete return to the bosom of my family either: we would never feel quite comfortable with one another again. They forgave me for my "aberration"—but the very fact that they believed I needed forgiveness drew an invisible screen between us.

It took a long time to adapt to the new phase of my life. But the curious thing about knowing that Embeth could not form part of it, was also a kind of release. Something deep inside myself had closed for good. For good or bad. Something would remain forever unfulfilled, unrealized, unthinkable. But I was also free. To move on. To whatever lay ahead.

And perhaps—no, not perhaps, but undoubtedly—that was one of the reasons why I was ready to meet Lydia when she made her appearance in my life a few years after Embeth disappeared from it.

I remember going to the shop selling artist's materials in a somewhat messy side street off Lansdowne Road. I needed a few camel-hair brushes and some tubes of paint—cobalt blue, vermilion, cadmium yellow. I'd known the manager and his wife, the Laubschers, for years, ever since they'd moved from the old shop in Long Street; but this morning was the first time I'd met their daughter Lydia, who had then just finished her degree in architecture at UCT and was helping them out during the holidays. A rather stormy meeting in the happy confusion of the little shop which had always been a tranquil little refuge in the past (and known for the fine, freshly ground coffee they served to old customers). This time there was a lot of shouting going on, an altercation between a very big customer with an untidy mop of hair and large stained hands, and Lydia, whom I'd never seen before, petite and delicate behind the counter, her red hair flaming in a shaft of morning sunshine that slanted through the side window.

"Don't you tell me about what green to use!" the customer was shouting. "I wanted sap green, not this stupid cobalt green."

"Why didn't you check the tube before you left? And anyway, you said you were painting a eucalyptus tree, and sap green is too bright for that."

"You turned my painting into a bloody mess and I had to come all the way back. Is that the way to treat an artist?"

"Nobody who uses sap green to paint eucalyptus trees is an artist's backside," sneered the young woman. "You should paint walls, not canvases." Her eyes, I noticed immediately, were themselves a most intense cobalt green, with touches of amber.

"That's what comes from putting a woman behind the counter in an artist's shop!" stormed the burly man. "I demand a new tube of green."

"And I won't exchange it because you've already used up half the tube."

"One little squeeze, that's all I used," he raged.

"This is not one squeeze. Look!" She grabbed the tube from him, unscrewed it in a single deft flick of her wrist, and pressed.

Neither of them could have expected what followed: a long, slimy green worm of paint came flying from the tube and hit the customer in the face.

"You clumsy clot!" he bellowed, reaching toward her across the counter.

I am not a big man, certainly not compared to that bellowing beast; and I usually avoid anything remotely resembling public brawls or tussles. But this was an emergency, and the two of them were so grossly mismatched that I had no choice. I grabbed the big man's arm from behind and pulled him away from the counter. He was off balance already and the unexpected jerk caused him to stagger back to the door. At that moment another customer came in, accompanied by the girl's father. The situation was defused. The new customer moved in between the counter and the aggressor; in spite of the young woman's protests, her father offered a tube of paint (cobalt green) to the bearded, gesticulating man, who decided to leave, still dabbing at his smudged face with a dirty handkerchief and muttering imprecations under his breath.

It took a few cups of very strong coffee for the tempers to settle down, but soon both Mr. Laubscher and his daughter could laugh about the outburst. Both of them had a delightful sense of fun, of humor, of generosity. And in due course Lydia and I discovered more and more reasons to spend time together. She was very busy at that stage of her life, involved as she was with several community projects in which her skills as an architect and her strong sense of civic responsibility stood her in good stead, so we did not always have much time to ourselves. But I was attracted by her warmth, her spontaneity, her passion about "doing something" after the drastic changes that had occurred in the country. And I suppose she made me believe that, through her, I, too, could do something to atone for the way in which I had let Embeth down.

We were married just over a year after the day in the shop. For her, it meant finding a firm foundation to do what she really wanted to do. For me, it was a return to normality—no, not normality, but, but the mere possibility of a normality interrupted by Embeth.

As it turned out, for neither of us there was happiness ever after. Only on rare—and relatively unimportant—occasions did I see further signs of her delightful, unreasonable temper, her uncontrolled passion; marriage seemed to bridle her and restrain her, curbing her natural exuberance in anticipation of motherhood. Whereas I—? I really just settled into the predictabilities of matrimony. The old dream of giving up teaching and painting full time was continually postponed—no longer because it was regarded, as Nelia and her parents had done, as unworthy and romantic, but because I myself felt the need to be a provider, not an escapist. On the other hand, I would never again feel free either. I had made a move, but not far enough. I had never arrived "on the other side" of whatever it might have been. An in-betweenness would be the most I could hope for. But it was better than nothing. Wasn't it?

Lydia's dedication to the projects she was involved with—a school in Crossroads, a crèche in Khayelitsha, a vast housing scheme in Delft, a recreation center in Lavender Hill—made it difficult to lead a relaxed life together; but the fulfillment she derived from her work made it worthwhile. And I was happy to support it while I kept the back door to my own ambition open. Of course, what was really missing from the marriage was children. Both our sets of parents were pressing for grandchildren; for various reasons—many of which we could not even bring ourselves to discuss—we, too, wanted a family. But it just didn't work out like that. It was not for lack of trying! But it never happened. At one stage I suggested that we go for tests, but Lydia—strangely—refused. It didn't "feel right" to her. We learned to adapt; but there was the emptiness of an ache between us, and in time it grew more, not less, urgent. I could see the difference it gradually made to Lydia, how her green eyes began to lose their spark; and we both started filling the gap with other activities, with social obligations, with money. I learned to paint what the market wanted. Lydia accepted contracts that had less and less to do with the community, more with increasing her visibility.

I don't think it really bothered us all that much. And perhaps that was the worst part of it? A "good life," a "working marriage." Security.

Until, suddenly, yesterday, if it was only yesterday, a blue door closed between us. And now I know just how important it has become for us to talk. To talk properly about it all.

I remember how she once told me about her love of swings when she was small. How she loved to go higher and higher, and then suddenly to shout at her father to run and catch her, and then to let go, wildly, madly, irresponsibly, absolutely confident that he would arrive in the nick of time to pluck her from the air and press her against him; and the smell of green grass when they fell down together, and laughed, and knew that the world was a good place to be in. And how, in later years, she started having nightmares about it, with her father arriving too late, or not at all. And feeling how that early faith and trust began to be eroded, and filtered away. From then on there was the need, ever more urgent, to find other forms of security. In her work, in me, in friends. She became almost paranoid in her fear of the unpredictable. The very wildness, the freedom, the ecstasies of her early years slowly turned into a terror of the things that had made life worth living before.

I don't know why all of this should be coming back to me now, on this radiant early summer morning.

But I do know that I have to get back to her, to have
and to hold her again, tightly, securely. I must return
to that huge building that so unexpectedly let me down
last night. I still have no explanation for what
happened. It can only have been some kind of delusion. But today, in this unequivocal sunshine, I know
it will be different. She will be there. She must be. And
this bizarre dream I have been imagining since
yesterday, since the moment I stepped through that
blue door, will be over.

(But where will Sarah be then? Sarah with the
graceful curve of her brown hip, the empty eye of her
navel in her pale belly, the round perfection of her
breasts, the deep gravelly sound of her voice? And the
two lovely children, our children, Emily and little
Tommie? And the photographs? All those unsettling
faces, those shadows and brushstrokes of light?)

I turn off from Edinburgh Road, move into the
smaller streets, head for the gigantic building I know
so well and which changed the aspect of the whole
suburb when it was built.

But it is not there.

I could not possibly have been mistaken!

I find parking on a yellow line and set out on foot.
Double-check the street names, even though I know
them by heart. Everything exactly as—and how—it is
supposed to be. But the building is missing. As if the

suburb has reverted to what it used to be, long ago, before planners and builders and developers and architects (Lydia among them) moved in. Claremont Towers is no longer there. Not there at all.

After half an hour of increasingly desperate searching, I approach a group of bergies on a sidewalk. Some are drinking from bottles wrapped in newsprint; one or two have passed out.

"Excuse me," I say hesitantly. "I'm looking for a block of flats. It's called Claremont Towers. Could any of you guys tell me how to get there?"

For a moment they interrupt their drinking to stare at me, then start conferring heatedly among themselves. But the verdict is negative.

"Never seen a place like that," a spokesman informs me.

"Are you quite sure?" I demand.

"We been coming here to this place for years, sir. Mandela was still in jail, like, when we first come here. You sure it's not in Newlands or someplace?"

"I am absolutely sure." After a brief, embarrassed hesitation, I say, "I live there."

They go into a huddle again.

"Sorry, Master"—for greater emphasis the spokesman has reverted to an obsolete form of address—"but Master must be a little bit mistaken. No such place in these parts."

Before it becomes more humiliating, I move off. Stop at one or two houses where brown gardeners in blue overalls or pink ladies in broad-brimmed straw hats are pottering in flower beds, and repeat my inquiries. No luck.

With ferocious determination I stride toward the shopping streets of the area. Printing shops, florists, household stores, antique dealers. Then right into the heart of the suburb. Cavendish Square.

Not a single person has any knowledge of the building. And yet I live there! (Don't I?) I was there last night. True, I couldn't find my way into the building, but it was there. For God's sake!

Back to my car. A pink ticket fluttering from the driver's window. I tear it off without looking, crumple it into a ball, chuck it away.

My building no longer exists. My apartment, number 1313 on the thirteenth floor, has disappeared like a boat in a fog. Lydia is no longer there.

There is nowhere else to turn to, nowhere at all. Except back to Green Point, where I have just come from.

Back to the blue door which I painted myself.

13

BACK ALONG THE BOULEVARD, UP STRAND STREET into the High Level Road, then a little way down and right, to where I used to park when I went to work in my studio. Now the place that is to be my home. There is a feeling of resignation, perhaps even desolation in me. This is it. Will have to be it. But there is a touch of inexplicable joy too. At last to have something definite to come back to. As if, after years of dithering, of living a suspended existence, I have taken something resembling a firm decision. Now I want to be where I am.

A strange thought: the arrogance of the presence. A presence that dares to affirm itself, to be what it is, without being attached to, or defined by, past or future. No guarantee of duration. That is excluded from now on. But to be here is already much.

I feel suddenly weary, the weariness that the little men in the children's story must have felt upon returning to their long, thin, white house after the dolphin had brought them back from the other side of the sea.

In my dream, it occurs to me, I lost wife and children. Here, today, I have found a new family. It makes sense after all.

I get out of the car and lock it. Open the side gate of the property and walk through it. Down, and then around to the front door. Where, for once, I know exactly what will be waiting behind the blue door.

Except that this time the door was not blue. It was, I noticed as stopped in front of to take out my key, a deep and uncompromising cadmium yellow. I stood and stared for a minute, struggling against the numbness that threatened to engulf me.

But at last I took a deep, sad breath, inserted the key into its deep hole, and leaned with my full weight against the door to push it open.

MIRROR

This could be the lead for his story, he thought:
waking up to the recognition of the habits
of his mind like the same old face
in the shaving mirror.
—Nadine Gordimer

An event becomes such as it is interpreted.
—Marshall Sahlins

1

I HAVE NEVER NOTICED ANYTHING UNUSUAL ABOUT the mirror before today. It was Carla who bought it for the bathroom, very soon after our wedding, which was twelve years ago. Not my kind of mirror, really: her taste is older than mine, although she is six years younger than I. I suppose I would have gone for something more rectilinear and functional (except where a curve is clearly more economical), but she has always liked art nouveau.

"Steve is the architect," she usually explains—or excuses—it to friends. "He likes clean, unambiguous lines. I prefer curves. That's why I'm the potter."

Which gives me the opportunity to come in with the obvious retort, "Nothing wrong with your curves. You know I've never been able to resist them."

Even after twelve years of marriage, and two daughters born from it (Francesca, 10, and Leonie, 7), I am still in thrall to her curves.

Not that there is unlimited opportunity to indulge the kind of desire she provokes: with two children as inquisitive as squirrels underfoot, a man has to step carefully. And most mornings Carla has to go to work at the women's magazine where she is the fiction editor (nowadays, pottery is strictly a hobby). But there are weekends, when the girls often go out for sleepovers with friends; and during the week, over the last few months, we have had the live-in au pair Silke from Stuttgart whom Carla hired to take them off our hands. (Silke, as blonde and silky as her name, has other virtues too, I have sensed, which one can imagine merging into delectable vices; but that is territory I have not allowed myself to trespass on.) So it is possible, more often than before, to prevail on Carla to lie in for a while longer in the mornings. And over the past twelve years the inventiveness which first drew me to her has not in any way diminished; if anything, she has become more resourceful, more imaginative, more deliciously outrageous.

It happened this morning too. My body was still tingling when she bent over to kiss me good-bye, and it was hard not to grab her long-fingered hand and draw her back into bed. But in her playful, graceful way she eluded my grasp to go to the door and wave at me from there.

"Now don't lie about too long," she remonstrated with a teasing smile, her face still flushed with the afterglow of shower and sex.

"I won't. I have to be on site for a meeting with the developer and the project manager at ten."

"The new mall?"

"Afraid so."

"It's time you moved on to something else. They're exploiting you, Steve."

"Only an hour," I assured her. "I warned them yesterday. I want to get on with that new development in Khayelitsha."

"The one you're doing with Lydia?"

"*Ja.* Not that there's much money in it—"

"We don't need the money. It's the kind of project you should get into more often."

"Because it's for 'the people'?"

"No need to be cynical about it, Steve."

"I'm not, my love. I promise you. But this country doesn't need more charity. It needs bloody hard work. And commitment. And some sense of responsibility."

"Yes, Mr. Minister."

"I wish more ministers would say that kind of thing. And mean it."

She quietly came back and leaned over me for a last kiss. I tried to cup a lewd hand between her thighs. She laughed, and pulled the blankets from me, dropped them on the floor, and ran out. A few minutes later I heard her car pull out of the garage deep under the house. In my mind I followed her, through the high streets of Fresnaye, down to Beach Road, gliding expertly above the glittering morning sea, and round the Lion's Rump to the grid of city streets. The same fluid movements I have so often watched, spellbound, as she whirls a pot on the wheel with exquisite balance between free flow and utter control, or smoothes it into shape from coils of glistening clay.

He likes clean, unambiguous lines. I prefer curves.

I can understand why she was excited about the mirror. As art nouveau objects go, it is a beauty, shaped like a harp held by a languorous naked girl with long hair streaming down her face, her arms with the curves of a swan's wings tapering off into elongated hands with delicate fingers that conjure up images of sensual caresses. Too beautiful, really, for a bathroom; but I had complained from the beginning about the old, cracked mirror above the basin in the rambling Victorian home in Kenilworth in which we'd begun our married life. (We'd bought the old place on her insistence; but after a few years this high plot against the mountain slope above the sea became available and I jumped for it: an investment opportunity not to be missed; and in addition it provided a chance to make a dream come true: designing my own house.)

"Now you can shave in style in the mornings," she'd insisted.

"You know I shave only every other day," I pointed out.

She pulled a mocking face. "My poor deprived husband. I suppose you were never really meant for Africa, were you?"

"You're not exactly made for summer and sun and surf either," I mocked. "With that red hair and those freckles and that skimmed-milk skin. We'll always be misfits, my darling. The little lost white tribe of Africa. And proud of it."

"The rainbow nation is supposed to accommodate us all," Carla reminded me. "If it doesn't, I can always dye my hair."

"Don't you dare."

For it was her hair that first seduced me: dark red and rust-hued, like Cabernet Sauvignon, thick and abundant and generous, luxurious, down to the curve of her buttocks, an unmistakable sign of generosity and passion.

"We'll just try to make it together," I said in mock solemnity, as if proposing a toast. "If all else fails, from now on we'll always have a mirror-mirror-on-the-wall."

"Oh you're a survivor all right, Steve," Carla said with a straight face.

"What makes you say that?"

"Because you can play the game. And beat everybody else at it."

Was that a compliment or a backhanded swipe?

Yet I suppose it was true. Still is? Right in the beginning, it often seemed I had begun with a disadvantage, compared to other students whose fathers had already paved the way with the right kind of money or politics. My mother, whose family liked to rub it in that she'd married "beneath" her, became more complaining and venomous as she grew older, starting her career as a typist and rising to the post of secretary at the Divisional Council. My father worked on the railways and made it to a conductor on the Trans-Karoo train. What in my early childhood had appeared to me as the epitome of glamour, slowly dwindled into something to be ashamed of. But in its own way, that might have been a good thing, as it meant that I always had to work twice as hard as all my friends, and that made people pay attention. It was possible, even if there was a touch of condescension in the attitude, to regard poverty as something of a virtue. And when all was said and done we were never really poor in any dire sense: at worst, I suppose, we belonged to the mass of the "less privileged" the dominie invariably mentioned in the second-last line of his Sunday prayer, giving due warning to the younger member of the congregation to stop fidgeting in preparation for the triumphant arpeggios of the singular grace of "Thy Everlasting Mercy, Amen."

Certainly, during those dark years, when I was still struggling to prepare for entering the world of architecture, it was a matter of sinking or swimming. But in the end, swimming was unexpectedly easy. The important thing was not to rock the boat, ever, but not to play along too conspicuously either; and then to make sure you were good enough at whatever you chose to do to attract attention, to make them interested, and finally to make them want you. Because as apartheid became more sophisticated (however crude the underlying principles might have remained) the more important it became to the men in gray shoes who wielded the power to perceive you as somehow up-to-date—with technology, with social planning, with economic engineering, with strategies for the future—in short, with everything in which architecture had, or could have, a role to play. Look at what architects like Albert Speer achieved even under a monster like Hitler. Or less damningly, controversially, in the work of a Niemeyer, or a Frank Lloyd Wright, or an Alvar Aalto. Look at the Paris of Haussman, or more recently of Renzo Piano under Pompidou or men like Johann Otto von Spreckelsen under Mitterrand. Do not forget Tokyo. Or Sydney. Or Berlin.

To start with, I needed to be, politically and morally, wholly transparent, a "man without qualities," deviating neither left nor right. In politics I found it very easy. It was not a matter of calculation: I simply was not interested. The ideologues would say, I know, that especially in a country like South Africa, this was in itself a political choice; but I honestly did not think of it like that. I just could not be bothered. Of course I had feelings of—and on—right or wrong; but it seemed to me useless even to think of "doing something about it." It was beyond the reach of individuals, I believed. So I preferred to stay out of it. Having made up my mind about this, I then had to ensure that in one way or another, either in my work or in sport or some other extramural activity, I made an impression. I've always liked sport (cricket, tennis, a bit of rugby), but without being in any way remarkable. So that had to be ruled out. In music or drama or art I suppose I was what one could term "talented," but in this country, at that time, that would put no one's ears up. In the domain of culture, nobody in a position of power really cared, one way or the other.

All that remained, was my studies. Very calmly, very focused, in a very methodical way, I planned my moves. What was at stake, after all, was nothing less than the rest of my life. But I must confess that in the end it was just as much a matter of sheer good luck as of calculation.

In my semifinal year I handed in a portfolio with designs and projects so bold and innovative that the head of department, flanked by two external examiners, was obliged to grant me an audition. There was a long, and at times quite heated, discussion about my presentation. But I was prepared for it. I avoided all hint of provocation or confrontation. I remained respectful, but not subservient; ready to discuss, but not to argue. I tried to project myself as intelligent and original, not arrogant or cocky. I wanted to learn from them, and from my mistakes, not lecture to them. And they liked that. No, I certainly did not win all my points, not even close to it. But I did make them rethink their own positions. And this was carried over into my last year. After our final examinations and presentations there were offers from no fewer than three top firms in town to choose from. And that was how it all began.

There was also an unexpected windfall. My best friend at university, Martin Coetzer, became a lawyer, but our shared interest was music, especially opera. Then one day in our final year, on my way to a lecture on town planning, some stupid bastard came hurtling over a stop sign and nearly wrote off the little car I'd just bought—and then had the audacity to blame me for it. When Martin heard about it, he insisted that I overcome my reluctance about litigation and that instead of just paying for my own repairs and the damages the culprit demanded, I go to court. He unofficially steered me through the proceedings, which ended with the offender having to pay for everything. At about the same time, during one of many weekends I spent with Martin at his home, there was a discussion about renovations his parents were planning for the house. I was drawn into the conversation and offered some ideas which I then presented to them in a series of drawings, and much to my pleasure and surprise I was commissioned to handle the project (more, I think, because I was Martin's friend than anything else). Martin's father—portly and affable in appearance, generous to friends and family, but with a reputation for ruthlessness—was a prominent man in the Party, and I knew what might happen if he could be persuaded to offer his approval, let alone his enthusiastic support.

It turned out better than anything I could have hoped for. I think something of the way-out inspiration that had fired me in that famous portfolio rubbed off on the new project: it was solid and reliable, but—if I say so myself—with a flair of unexpected inventiveness. The whole family was delighted, and couldn't wait to show off to their friends. Several of whom then approached me with projects of their own—not only renovations or additions to their houses, but new homes altogether. And new offices. And even a church, for a congregation in Johannesburg that just had to outdo their nearest neighbors. But the cherry on top, to coin a phrase, was a towering new building for a major insurance company, a firm that was then in need of redefining its image: most of its buildings dotted throughout the country were at the time a functional gray, as reassuringly staunch, and as unimaginative, as the po-faced leaders of Party and Church, which were two sides of the same coin. What the firm wanted now, was to move into the vanguard of original (if still staunch and reliable) thinking within the Party.

It was a first step toward what I still regard as my proudest achievement so far: Claremont Heights, the controversial flat building despised by some as a latter-day version of Brueghel's Tower of Babel, but praised by others (the more knowledgeable ones, I daresay) as something in the class of the Chrysler Building in New York, or some of the more recent structures along the Thames, or in Leipzig, or even in Dubai (though mine was obviously on a more modest scale). I managed to land the contract on behalf of one of the first top-range consortiums established under the banner of Black Empowerment.

All of this I have done, I am proud to say, without rocking anyone's boat and by staying in step with all the changes and upheavals on the country's political and social scene. During the apartheid years, while avoiding any overt political overtones, I'd started making some cautious moves toward cooperating with black architects and civil engineers and social planners, which I firmly believe persuaded the government that they were "moving with the times" and working "at the cutting edge"; and once the move toward democracy gathered momentum, I was ready to "show my true colors" and get into step with the movers and shakers, as the saying goes, of the new regime.

This morning, spread-eagled in the wide crumpled bed still damp with our lovemaking, I could not suppress a feeling of deep contentment. At forty-two years old, I have not done too badly, have I? The house on three levels on the high slope of Fresnaye, all glass and polished steel, with solar energy and underfloor heating and every square centimeter of it designed by myself, overlooking the sweeping ultramarine panorama of the Atlantic. Partner in one of the top firms of architects in the city, and a name in my own right. (In my study on the middle floor of the house there are several framed scrolls and certificates of awards earned over the years.) A wife who is the envy of my friends and all the clients who have had the good fortune of meeting her. Two lively and lovely talented children: this past December little Leonie danced in a ballet in the Artscape; two years ago, when she was still only eight, Francesca had a painting chosen for a Sanlam calendar of children's art. (If I must be totally honest, I would have loved to have at least one son; but it is of course not yet too late.) In the spacious garage, in estate agent's parlance, there are a silver Volvo for family outings, a Ranger 4x4 for weekends on the farm near Paternoster, Carla's small Merc (her choice, although what she really wanted was a battered old Volkswagen which I managed to talk her out of), the spare second-hand Renault—Carla's old car which we keep for Silke's use—and of course the nifty little red Porsche for my own indulgence.

The interior decoration of the house is largely my father-in-law's handiwork: we've worked together for so long now that he knows my taste inside out. Carla herself had a big hand in choosing the paintings, although I did make a few contributions, particularly the two Irma Sterns, the Maggie Laubser, and—more recently—the Gerard Sekoto, but also some of the newer pieces by up-and-coming youngsters. It is not, I must insist, a matter of materialistic gloating, or a desire to accumulate, to own. I do believe in spiritual values (I have a whole collection of Paolo Coelho's books, which I had bound in leather, one of them inscribed by the author: *Be a warrior of the light*). It is rather, if I have to attempt an explanation, a wish to live life to the full.

How fortunate that Carla and I are still young and vigorous enough to make it work. What with her duties at the magazine, she doesn't have all that much free time, even with Silke now available, but I try to go to the gym three times a week. No more, no less. One's body needs attention, perhaps even some pampering. And I must say, when I do happen to look into a mirror—often the art nouveau one Carla bought for me, for shaving—I am content with the reflection. Even the touch of gray at the temples has, I dare say, an enhancing effect. I can imagine that, like most of the men I associate with, I should not find it too difficult to engage in the odd affair. No lack of opportunity. And there have indeed been occasions when a young woman made a pass. But I am happy to say that since I married Carla I have never yielded to an urge to stray. I do believe in some old-fashioned values like monogamy. That said, let me confess that I have been conscious of a certain attraction in the young and nubile Silke. I have caught myself wondering about how her breasts would look. And, more brazenly, her pubes. Would she be as blonde down there as the silky brightness of the hair on her head? Or perhaps she shaves? I remember one girl in our office soon after I entered the firm, and before my marriage. Stephanie. The sense of frankness, of shamelessness, when she undressed for the first time: the upfrontness of her slit, the bold curve of her lips.

When, not long afterward, I met Carla and in a moment of boldness suggested that she also shave her mound, she refused, without fuss, but firmly. And I did not insist. It would have been silly anyway. She was, as she still is, beautiful enough without adding or removing anything. I did not even need to close my eyes, where I was still lying in our bed, to conjure up that bewitching patch of dark, deep-red hair, uncommonly soft and long, covering her mound, but so sparsely that it seems from a distance like a tentative little smudge, no more, revealing as much as it conceals. (I have seen this same effect on some of the paintings by the artist David le Roux;

I've even bought one. Given the present state of the market, it should soon be worth a packet.) To see her, to smell her, to taste her.

It may seem far-fetched to jump from Carla's cunt to her ceramics, but the link is direct and intimate. I cannot think of making love with her without seeing her hands. Those long, thin, sensitive, delicate fingers with the unexpectedly square tips. And those same fingers would move in what I can only describe as languorous energy across the slithery, smooth surface of a pot in the making: movements that are deft and infinitely sure, as if she always knows exactly what she is doing, and why—though at the same time, she has assured me, it is all wholly tentative, literally feeling her way toward the final product (a word she would never use).

The first time I saw some of her pots was in The Yellow Door, the gallery in the Gardens Centre. They were from her Blue Period, when she mixed a liberal dose of cobalt into her slips and glazes; and the pots were usually bulbous, with fat calabash bases tapering into delicate necks, or otherwise starting slim at the bottom and swelling into globular fullness, like mushrooms. Sensual, sexual shapes. I immediately bought all the work on display; and I asked the gallery for the potter's address. Which they refused to divulge. They offered, instead, to pass on my address to her and leave to her to decide whether she wished to contact me.

Strictly the correct procedure, but it peeved me no end; and it was aggravated when she took three weeks before sending me a hasty scribble with her number. By which time I was so pissed off that I deliberately kept her waiting for another month.

After that, everything developed much faster. At our very first meeting (inevitably in The Yellow Door in the Gardens Centre) we started a conversation which may be said to be still continuing. And the main impetus in it was, strangely enough perhaps, not her work but her father's: it turned out that he was the interior decorator with whom I had been working on several of my projects for almost a year already. She had never come up in our conversations: our relationship was strictly businesslike, even though he had been to my home several times to discuss ideas and plans. He mentioned that he had asked her to make some large jars for a socialite's house in Llandudno on which he'd just started working with me. But Carla had refused, saying that she was not interested in working for that kind of person, and that both the client and I could go and fuck ourselves. (Her turn of phrase has never been delicate; and it still from time to time surprises me to hear such language coming from a woman with her kind of seemingly fragile beauty. On our second date, when she came home with me for a liqueur after dinner, in the middle of a very intense and erudite conversation about an exhibition we'd been to earlier in the day, she suddenly asked, "Why are you eyeing me like that?"

"I'm not eyeing you, I'm listening to what you're saying."

"Bullshit," she said. "I think what you really want to do is to fuck me."

I started stammering like an adolescent: "Carla! How can you say such a thing? I assure you—"

She gave an almost prim little smile, an unholy light in her angelic emerald eyes, and said, "Just do it, Steve. You'll feel so much better afterward." The briefest flickering in those challenging eyes. "And so will I.")

She remained hesitant about accepting the Llandudno commission, refusing to commit herself before she felt she was "ready" for something like that; but shortly before the house had to be handed over to the client, she relented. "Okay, I've thought about it and I need the money. I'll give it a go. But no more than five jars."

"We'd really planned for at least a dozen, Carla. You know, the whole house has to be—"

"Then get another whore to do the rest."

"How can you insult an artist like that?"

"Because at the end of the day we're all the same." Her—by now—familiar little deprecating smile. "At least some of us do it because we like it."

As I lay in our crumpled bed this morning, fondling memories, I heard a car arrive downstairs, then the front door slamming, and footsteps. Silke was back from the school where she'd deposited the children. It really was time for me to move on into the day.

I threw off the still-fragrant sheet, swung my legs over the edge of the bed, and remained sitting like that for another few moments, allowing my eyes to gaze through the wide window across the sweep of the bay far below before I walked across the deep pile of the carpet to the en-suite bathroom opposite. There were puddles on the white tiles, and Carla's dark green towel lay crumpled in the middle of the floor. I stooped to pick it up and drape it over the chrome rail, then removed my own, which I put on the thick white mat in front of the shower cubicle, and stepped inside, bracing myself against the copious spray of steaming water from above.

I took my time to work my way through the strict routine of the daily shower: soaping and washing and rinsing my hair, then up the lengths of my arms and down under them, my chest and stomach, lingering with satisfaction along my genitals, then my buttocks, and finally down my legs to my feet: all of this with my eyes closed to protect them against the foam. A few last minutes of pure cold water as I gasped for breath and yodeled with shock and primitive pleasure, before I stepped out, picked up the towel, and vigorously dried myself until my whole body glowed with replenished vitality.

It was my shaving day. I took the razor from its shiny container beside the elegantly shaped double basin, ran in hot water, tested the temperature, then luxuriously lathered my face and prepared to proceed from there.

This is where I stop.

I stare into the art nouveau mirror, into the harp shape of the glass held up in the gracefully curved arms and hands of the nude pewter girl with the flowing long hair.

Uncomprehending, petrified, shivering in a sudden rush of coldness, I keep staring.

Then lean forward until my forehead touches the steamed-up surface of the mirror.

I see my eyes, stricken and wide, then screwed up into thin slits.

With one wet hand I stroke across the mirror, trying to clear the surface.

The nude girl embossed in the pewter frame stares back at me. Is there a grimace on her shapely face which I have never noticed before?

I drop the razor, bend down to rinse all the lather off my face, before I straighten up again.

Once more I peer into the mirror. It is a face I have never seen before in my life. Involuntarily I bring a hand up to my cheek. The reflection in the mirror does the same.

I can feel the astonished touch of my fingers on my cheek. It must be me.

Yet it cannot be. It cannot possibly be me.

The face staring at me from the mirror is black. So is the hand touching the cheek.

And as I turn away from the reflection to look down at myself, across my chest and stomach, the vulnerability of my penis still half distended from the exuberance of the shower, along my legs, all the way to my feet, my whole body is a clear, clean, shiny, deep, dark brown.

2

THERE IS SOMETHING PRIMAL ABOUT THE SCENE. I think of Adam and Eve surprised in the Garden and hiding away among the leaves because they are naked. I have never felt so exposed before in my life. In the bathroom where I still find myself, conscious of sounds elsewhere in the house—Silke who must be moving around, presumably barefoot, her blonde hair in a ponytail behind her small head; the more substantial housekeeper, Alida, bustling about in her voluminous overalls—I crouch, covering my groin with my hands, looking about in panic. (Steve! What have you done?) I cannot remain in this position indefinitely. I must get out. I must go somewhere. But where can I possibly go? This is my house, my bathroom, my bedroom, it is supposed to be the holy of holies of my life, for God's sake. If this is invaded, everything will be relentlessly exposed, and forever. I am naked. I am black. Where can I hide? They cannot see me like this.

Whoever they may be.

The house is full of sound. And fury. I will be pursued to the ends of the Earth, hunted down, bludgeoned to death, a messy pulp.

Now stop the melodrama, I tell myself. Nothing has happened yet. I am still here. I am in control.

But I am black and naked!

I have to be practical. Do something. To begin with, I can close the bedroom door and put on some clothes.

Taking a deep breath, I cross the floor to the inside door and close it, then turn the key. At least this will buy me some time.

I return to the bathroom. It is tempting to avoid the mirror altogether, to deny it, to move into the day without trying to confirm what I know by now. But I realize it will not let go of me so easily. I have seen myself. I must probe this discovery, test it, examine it, explore it. Leaning over

forward as before, I start studying once more the unfamiliar dark face behind the smooth untroubled surface.
The dark-brown eyes, the nose, the mouth with its stark
white teeth. The shoulders—are they broader than
before? no, it must be my imagination—the open hands
with pale palms pressed against the glass, the square,
short-trimmed nails. The chest with a few sprigs and
whorls of hair. Then I lower my eyes to the stomach, the
dense patch of coarse pubic hair, the penis resting on the
testicles gathered tightly in the scrotum. This holds a
special fascination, as in the early days of my adolescence.
The shape and size appear reassuringly unchanged, but
the color is drastically different from the way I remember
it. Unlike the rest of me, which I can still acknowledge,
though in a different, darker hue, this thing doesn't seem
to belong to me at all. I push the foreskin back to examine
the glans, a virulent purple. The scrotum, contracting
and extending as always, but very black. Then more
familiar territory again: legs, knees, ankles, feet. Pinkish,
yellowish soles. Small marks and blemishes that I suddenly
recall from earlier times, some from childhood—this scar
across the big toe, this spot above my heel left by an
ember that fell into my shoe, this indent in the cuticle of
a middle toe. I recognize them all. They spell me. And
yet not the same me which I thought I knew.

I return to my face, pull it into a variety of grimaces,
mocking and taunting myself. It is I. It is not I.

But I cannot remain here all day. There is nothing more about my body to discover. Even if this is temporary, I have to make my peace with it. For now. There is no other choice.

In something of a daze—For God's sake: This cannot be!—I force myself at last to turn away.

In the dressing room next to the bathroom I slide open the louver doors. Somewhat to my surprise, all my clothes are still there. Everything looks familiar. Perhaps it is all right after all.

But when I turn to face myself in the full-length mirror opposite the walk-in wardrobe, the stranger is still there, lurking like an intruder, a thief, a would-be assassin.

Involuntarily I go down on my haunches again, and it takes a few moments before I can slowly rise up to full length once more. Controlling my breathing like a woman in labor (I was present at the births of both my daughters), I wait for the excessive beating of my heart—fluttering like a trapped wild bird in a cage, knowing instinctively that sooner or later it will be found by a man with a gun—to subside. Then I begin a methodical inspection of my clothes. Which is easy: I have always been an organized person. And it is comforting once again to see everything exactly as it should be, as I had arranged and hung or stacked it myself.

White jeans, a striped blue shirt. Bright red underpants (I always like a streak of the unexpected, even the reckless, provided it is well covered, not visible from outside). Socks and running shoes. No tie. It is not a formal meeting after all, only a small on-site gathering with Gerald and Derek. And both of them are very conscious of my standing, my seniority. (Even the developer, Gerald, is in no position to throw his weight around: he needs this project more than I do; it was I who contacted the minister to get the go-ahead when there was some contractual hitch about rezoning early on.) If anyone can pull rank, it is I.

Theoretically, my new appearance could even be an advantage. This is the New South Africa. Color is (once again) important, even in an altered paradigm.

But this is not a theoretical situation. What has happened to me—a new, furtive glance in the mirror confirms it—is very real and practical. And urgent.

Or should that be in the past tense? When this project started, I was white. I no longer am.

I put on my clothes, deliberately trying to stretch it out as much as possible, stopping from time to time just to make sure. The mirrors in both dressing room and bathroom relentlessly confirm what I already know by now.

Turning away from what I can see of myself, if it is I, my eyes rediscover our bed. In a rush of urgency I return to strip off the love-sheets and bundle them into the polished steel laundry bin in the bathroom. It is something I would not ordinarily have bothered about, but today I find it embarrassing to leave undisturbed the signs of our early-morning encounter.

Even though I realize this country has become a different place from the one I'd grown up in, I still know how it must feel to have "evidence" like this exposed to other eyes. During my student years, my friend Martin had a brief and surreptitious fling with a brown girl. She was studying law with him, one of the star students. And strikingly beautiful. They were trapped by the police. Six burly men bursting into the outroom where they'd arranged to meet for their clandestine trysts. It was a week before the final examinations. I remember how he told me about the eruption into the little room. How the sheets were pulled from them, and one of the men spread an open palm over the damp patch on the bottom sheet. How one of the others ordered Martin to stand up so that he could be photographed with his half-tumescent penis. How the girl—usually so sophisticated and self-contained and smart—kept on sobbing uncontrollably throughout, while they pulled her arms and legs apart and forced the back end of a torch up her vagina, and the things they said about her.

As it happened, everything turned out well. Martin's father, Party stalwart that he was, had a word with the minister (if one had the right connections, there was nothing that could not be "arranged"), and the case never came to court. Both Martin and the girl—Valerie, her name was, I remember now—passed their finals with distinction. But it was the end of the affair. She refused even to speak to him. And before the start of the summer vacation she quietly left the country, and joined a legal firm in Dublin where a friend-of-a-friend of her father was able to find a place for her.

This is a world of which, over the years, fortunately, I have caught no more than unsettling echoes and unhappy glimpses. But in a sense we all grew up with it, and were scarred by it. Even when, from time to time, there was a touch of black (?) humor involved. A random recollection: a young woman, Nelia, whose father, a leading cardiologist, was one of the first to offer me a major contract after I'd joined my first firm. I had to design a house for Nelia and her husband (an insipid young man lodged firmly under her shapely thumb). I worked very closely with her, as she was the one in charge of the whole project. A spoiled brat, but very attractive. And she was only too aware of it. As she was of her body, particularly during the summer months. I no longer remember how our conversation one day turned to pain and suffering, but she started telling me about what she'd had to endure in her young life. Most especially when, in a previous relationship, she'd walked in on her then-fiancé and caught him in flagrante with a colored girl, which had practically ruined Nelia's life. ("With a meid, Steve!" I can still hear her shrilling. "Can you imagine? With a meid!") For many months, she assured me, she had to bathe between three times a day, just to cleanse her of the memory. For me, the worst of sweet Nelia's brief appearance in my life was the way she tried to use the account of her suffering to get me into bed. Which I turned down as tactfully as I could. But what would she do if we were to meet again today and I confronted her with it? ("With me, Nelia? With a kaffir?") Through all these years there has always been, behind everything, the awareness of them and us. And today, suddenly, I find myself one of them—.

In the welter of tumbling thoughts in my mind, there is one that takes shape more urgently than anything else: the need to talk to Carla. I must talk to her, hear her voice, get close to her, draw reassurance from her. Reaching out to my cell phone on the glass bedside table I instinctively dial her number at the magazine. But she is in a meeting, the receptionist tells me in her melodious, customized voice. Can she take a message? For a moment I consider it, then decline. In a way even this comes as a relief. What could I possibly have told her if she'd been there? What is there I could say that wouldn't sound preposterous?

In spite of everything the failed call imposes some kind of direction on the morning. I cannot stay in hiding here any longer. Even though I have no idea yet of how to handle it.

Leaving the safety and the damp memories of me and Carla behind, I venture into the passage. It is a strange sensation, as if I'm moving from one kind of space into something utterly different: the kind of radical change one would associate with a dream, like walking through a mirror. But I keep clinging desperately to what ought to be familiar: the three levels of the house, with all the carefully planned interruptions along the way—water features, a small patch of lawn under a high glass roof, mosaics, tiles from Mexico, several of Carla's large blue urns, like ancient Greek amphorae, strategically placed.

Near the ground level I stop to check on the whereabouts of the women. Alida in the kitchen (no doubt about that: she has a cheerfully clamorous and clanging way of indicating where she is at any given moment). Silke—? She is more surreptitious and more sly, as she whispers along on her soft feet. But after a few moments I do detect the sensuous sucking sound of bare soles in the living area: she must be going out for a swim. (I wonder if, when we are out, she skinny-dips?) But I resist the urge to reconnoiter. I cannot risk being discovered like this. Imagine her finding a strange black man in the house! Would she activate the alarm immediately as we have taught her? Summon the police? The security company?

My hand relaxes on the banister. I rapidly steal down the last few stairs. On the very last one I catch a glimpse of myself in one of the perfectly placed rectilinear mirrors on the opposite walls. They are interspersed with openings in the wall, allowing fleeting views of other rooms and snatches of garden behind, which sometimes makes it difficult to orientate oneself: are you inside, or out? Here, or there? It is like getting lost in an Escher drawing, much more intricate and sophisticated than old-fashioned trompe l'oeil.

Avoiding the kitchen, I hurry to the side door on the right to move directly into the wide garage, open the driver's door of the bright red Porsche, and slide in. As the muted, reassuring growl of the engine envelops me I press the button to turn the revolving floor so that the car now faces the tilt-up door, which is raised at the same time, and drive out. Half a block farther on I turn left, out of our peaceful side street into the avenue that runs all the way down to the sea. From there driving usually becomes almost automatic, but I find that today I concentrate ferociously on every turn, every set of traffic lights, every change of lane—anything to avoid thinking of what has happened, and what is likely to happen at the on-site meeting. It may be the end of my career. In all probability Gerald and Derek may not recognize me at all. And if they do it may be worse.

My stomach has turned into a solid lump, like cold porridge. Perhaps I should simply turn back. Telephone Carla, or my PA at the office in Dunkley Square, and ask them to cancel all my appointments till further notice. Until I can think of something to help me face the world again. A world irrevocably changed. Because I am no longer who and what I was.

But who knows what I was, what I used to be? Perhaps my memory has crashed the way the hard drive of a computer does, always at the worst imaginable moment.

How can I even tell who and what I am, right here, right now? Am I a white man in a black skin? Or a black man? What makes a black man "different"? Or is there no real difference? Does it depend on who you "are" or purely on the way others see you? Am I being determined from outside (my image in the mirror), or am I black in and of myself? Or is all of this merely part of the hallucinations of this time and this country?

In the Main Road, just after Giovanni's Italian delicatessen, I turn into a side street. A friend of mine has a studio just up the road from here. David le Roux. The painter. I could drop in for a cup of tea. Or a whiskey, why not? Perhaps he can help me find a way out from my dilemma, or at least of an explanation to offer Gerald and Derek. He is an artist. I'm sure he will understand.

But how can I be sure? Who, of all the millions of people in this crazy country, can conceivably hope to understand what has happened, is happening, to me?

I find a place to park, and turn off the ignition. For five minutes I sit without moving. Not a prudent thing to do, in this city. On a lamppost almost next to the car a newspaper headline proclaims:

MINISTER OF SAFETY AND SECURITY SAYS WHINING WHITES SHOULD LEAVE COUNTRY

I recall photographs of the man on recent front pages, flashing his uneven teeth in a broad, uncomprehending smile at a world of which he clearly has no understanding. The blunt eyes, the untidy little tufts of beard, like a mealie land in the Free State in a bad drought.

Somebody knocks on my window. A drunk is leaning precariously against the car, waving vigorously to attract my attention. In a moment of consternation I mistake him for the face from those newspaper pages. But this face is white. Bloated and distorted and gone to ruin, but unmistakably white, with bloodshot, pale blue eyes. One of God's own people. With an effort I pull myself together and mutter, "Scoot!"

He keeps on gesticulating. Now he starts fumbling with my door handle.

"Fuck off!" I shout. And start the engine in a rage.

He loses his balance and stumbles as he tries to get

out of the way, but without the support of the car he is hopelessly unsteady. "You blarry people think you can drive fancy cars and take over this country!" he bellows in incoherent rage. Then, in a last vociferous explosion he suddenly bends over and vomits in my direction. A grayish, purplish eruption splashes against the window. Then I race out of reach, tires wailing. The last I see of him is when he staggers a few steps back and sits down heavily in the street. A passing car narrowly misses him, hooting furiously. Trembling with anger I drive up to the next street, then left, and down again. I have no choice. I'll just have to face whatever comes.

3

THEY ARE WAITING IN FRONT OF THE SPRAWLING building which is propped up by scaffolding like a reconstructed dinosaur skeleton in a museum. Both of them are wearing yellow hard hats. I take a deep breath, open my door, and step out to face them in the fierce sun. Gerald, who is the developer, still lingers in the shade of a stunted syringa tree that was spared, for the time being, by the bulldozers when they prepared the site. Then he removes a half-smoked cigarette from his mouth and stubs it out underfoot, straightens the floral bow tie he wears with his crisp white shirt, and takes out a handkerchief to wipe his brow where beads of perspiration catch the light on his dark skin. Derek, the project manager, comes striding on ahead, bulging from his safari suit like an overgrown schoolboy. In his usual jovial way he puts out his hand when he is still a good ten meters off. (It will be a clammy, steely grip, I know from previous experience, putting into it his whole reputation as a provincial prop forward, expected to live up to his sports-page fame of fifteen years ago.)

"Hi, buddy," he bellows with his customary exuberance. And then, the moment he grasps my hand in his great tanned paw that bristles with blond hairs, he seems to freeze. "What the fuck has happened to you?" he asks.

Here it comes, I think. But I try to meet, as stoically as I can, his horrified gaze.

Only then do I realize that he is staring, not at me, but past me, at the splotched window of the red Porsche. "Somebody took your car for a bloody toilet bowl?"

"Some stinking drunk," I stammer, not yet recovered from my shock.

Without letting go of my hand—it will be numb with pins and needles for the rest of the day, I fear—he shouts back over one of his massive shoulders in the direction of a foreman, "Bennie! Get one of the boys to clean this bladdy car!"

"No need," I mumble, managing what must be a pretty wan smile.

Then, to my relief, Gerald catches up from behind and joins us. Did he momentarily wince at Derek's terminology? But I suppose he is too experienced in this kind of thing—not a novice like me—to show any reaction. Having wiped his face he looks as natty and prosperous as ever. "Morning, sir," he says, also taking my bruised hand. "Glad to see you. I think we've got some interesting stuff to show you."

"Everything still on track?" I ask, still somewhat tight in the jaws.

"I think we're gaining on schedule," he says. "Derek tells me the new foreman is giving them hell."

Not a word about my appearance. As if nothing untoward at all has happened. Yet my hand, as I can see with a glance the moment he lets go, is the same color as his. As black, in South African parlance, as Derek's is white.

I have no idea of what is happening: have they always regarded me as black? or do they still regard me as white? or are they just pretending, for the sake of propriety? or am I the one still suffering from a delusion? Whatever it may be, at the moment it suits me.

But it still doesn't clear up the mystery. If anything, it compounds my confusion.

I am aware, especially, of a curious sensation that imbues the morning with something quite new: as if I am observing, not only my two companions but myself: as if I am acting in a play of which I am also the director. I am aware—not mechanically, not passively, but critically—of every move I make, every word I say. As if I am running the risk of betraying myself with every word, every move. At university, both Martin and I were keen members of the theatrical society; we went on tour with student productions a few years running, until our academic work became too demanding. I even became interested in writing plays myself, and tried my hand at it a couple of times. There was one play I never wrote, but which kept bugging me for a long time: a play dealing with a group of friends invited to a party. Upon their arrival at the house of their host, everybody in the group has to draw the name of one of the guests from a hat—the idea being that for the rest of the evening every person has to act the part of the name she, or he, has drawn from the hat. An opportunity— a challenge—to take the mickey, or to show how well you know that person, or what you imagine her or him to be deep down, even to be satirical or bitchy. But the real challenge, inducing a kind of existential angst, comes when one member of the party happens to draw his own name and then has to pretend to be himself. And this is exactly the kind of experience I am having today, here, on this building site. I am not the Steve I have been—effortlessly, inevitably—all my life. I am somebody pretending to be that Steve. I am acting Steve. I have to try and conjure up everything I remember about this person, everything I have ever observed, everything I can imagine—and then to project my understanding of him through interacting with these two unwitting companions. I have to convince them that I am Steve. I have to convince myself that I am Steve. And it does not come naturally, for at every turn I discover that I actually do not know this person as well as I have always assumed: certainly not well enough to give a convincing performance of his life, his behavior, his thoughts, his being. I have to work very hard at it. And the more persuasive I appear to them—that is, the more persuaded they appear to me; the more persuasive I appear to be to myself as a result of their reaction to my acting—the more I become aware of the hard work that goes into the attempt to persuade myself that I am persuading them of being who I am: that is, to be who I am not. And the more convincing they appear in conveying to me that they really believe I am who I am, the more unnervingly I doubt their performance, since they may just be acting very persuasively in trying to make me think that they have not seen through my own deception. They may just be as good in their pretense, in their acting, as I am. Or better.

One of the laborers brings me a yellow hard hat like theirs; then, carrying a bucket of water toward my car, he proceeds to wash the soiled window. Together with Gerald and Derek I leave on our tour of inspection. They provide information to bring me up to date as we move on; I put in questions, make some observations: at least, I soon discover to my relief, I am still the architect I used to be, even if I may no longer be the same person. (But why should I have presumed that a change of skin color could have turned me into a different person?) From time to time we stop to compare our plans or consult notes. Once or twice there is a pause when I point out a deviation from my specifications, demand an explanation, raise an objection, express dissatisfaction or surprise, register annoyance or misgivings. And as we continue, more and more of these pauses begin to occur. There is no longer the relaxed smoothness of our previous encounters, as I remember them. Perhaps we are all a bit more testy than usual. The reasons may be varied: it is Monday morning, the weekend has brought in its wake a reluctance to return to routine, there may be the last clouds of hangovers to contend with. But apart from these factors—we regularly meet on Monday mornings after all—there seem to be other variables in the equation today.

They are very subtle, almost imperceptible to begin with, and I cannot be sure that they are really manifest or exist only in my imagination. But they seem to grow larger and become more weighty, and more irksome, as we continue. And as I apply my mind more consciously—that is, as my perception of them, and of myself through them, becomes more acute—they do impress themselves more definitely on my mind. For example, I have always got along very well with Derek, because large, bear like men, particularly with a reputation as top rugby players, tend to elicit feelings of bonhomie and camaraderie from me. I feel like slapping them on the back or pummeling their biceps, even if only metaphorically. I certainly tend to trust them implicitly. Almost always they have my full and easy confidence. But I find that I am a tad more reserved with Derek today, to the point of impatience; for once, his ebullience does not inspire reciprocity; instead, I'm beginning to suspect that his easygoing bluster may be a smokescreen, a cover-up perhaps for slipshod work. I find that I am not prepared, as perhaps I was in the past, to toady for the sake of relaxed relations. Because today I am black. (Am I not?) I cannot allow him to boss me around. To use his whiteness as an excuse, a too-easy confirmation of his imagined superiority, or my blackness as the sign of an underdog. So I enquire more meticulously than I may otherwise have done (but how can I be sure?) into why he has done certain things—changing, however slightly, the ratio of sand cement in the mortar, removing supports for the scaffolding a few hours earlier than before—and when he reacts with a show of pique I promptly insist on parts of the work being done over from scratch. If rank is to be pulled, I shall do the pulling.

With Gerald I have always had very correct relations, respecting him as the developer, while not allowing him to deviate from specifications to save on costs or cut corners here and there. But today I find (even though I am myself surprised by it) that I am more inclined to argue with his decisions. At one stage—for the first time during our collaboration—the tempers flare. He is in charge of this whole project, he points out, raising his voice: at the end of the day it is his money that is involved, he will make the final decisions. That makes me blow my top. He has selected me as the architect, I retort; he cannot now argue with my instructions. That makes no difference to the fact that this is his project, he insists. In that case, I tell him, calmly but firmly, he can have it his way, but that will cost him, in time and in money. I am happy to leave the project right now so that he can appoint another architect, provided he pay my full fee plus the penalty provided for in clause 73.2(c).

While the argument is still going on, the unnerving feeling persists that it is all playacting; that I am looking on, astrally, at the two of them going through their motions, and—more disconcertingly—at myself going through mine. And I get the distinctly unpleasant impression that even though the acting may be good, the play is bad. Someone should think about rewriting it.

Unless the acting is all that matters, irrespective of the sound and fury.

As I walk away at last—much later than I have planned to—I am conscious only of a deep disgruntlement. If my initial doubts have turned out to be quite unfounded—I have, have I not, survived the first ordeal?—I have achieved nothing of importance, and proven nothing. I've fucked up the good relations I have had with my project team. On the surface we have parted, if not as friends, at least as sound colleagues. But something has shifted between us, something has been lost, our mutual trust has taken a knock.

Reaching for the handle of the car door—the spattered window now cleaned of its mess; but with traces still remaining—I stop to look back (Stop, two beats, turn round, remember to draw back your left leg or it will look awkward). They are still standing as I left them, at the main entrance to the sprawling gray building hemmed in by its scaffolding. Wearing their hard hats, they look like Lego men. From habit, or prompted by a too-late surge of goodwill, I raise my right hand to wave. They do not react.

Then fuck you, I think as I get into the car.

At least I've passed this hurdle. I can face the rest.

Except that I know the toughest is yet to come. I must still confront my family. They will have to face what I faced in the mirror this morning.

4

I REMAIN SITTING IN THE CAR FOR SOME TIME. MY first impulse is to telephone Carla once again. It is even more urgent now than before, to draw from her the assurance without which I cannot proceed into this intimidating day. I key in her number on my cell phone. But just as I am preparing to activate it, I freeze. Dare I really risk talking to her now? How can I try to explain anything to her before I myself have any clear idea of what is going on?

I try to gather my thoughts, but there is nothing that makes sense.

My first reaction in front of the mirror, I recall, was shame. But why? Surely not shame about being black, but rather shame for not recognizing myself.

There was nothing in that mirror with which I could identify, nothing I could even recognize. To discover that I was no longer me. Yes, that must be it. No longer to find anything in myself I could hold on to. And if I could no longer recognize myself, then there was nothing in the world I could presume to know any longer. An awareness for which I have just begun to find confirmation.

I cannot go home now, not right away. It is unlikely that Carla will be there—Mondays at her magazine are hectic; I'm not expecting her before five or thereabouts in the afternoon—but I cannot take the risk. At least not before lunchtime, when Alida leaves. The girls will not be home before four, as they usually stay at school for a supervised homework session, followed by music lessons. Silke is not much of a factor: she goes her own secret ways, and usually avoids me. Even so, the house, right now, is a place where dangers lurk.

If my own private self can no longer be trusted, I shall have to find it outside and beyond myself. And immediately I know where I should go.

I cancel the call to Carla and turn on the ignition. Almost mechanically I steer the car in the direction of De Waal Drive to get out of the city and round the mountain, toward the Southern Suburbs. Then down toward Paradise Road and on to Claremont. From close up the magnificent building obscures even the mountain. Claremont Heights. My magnum opus so far, not the slightest doubt about that. And over the last three years, every time I felt worried or anxious or in doubt about anything, every time my confidence needed bolstering, this is where I have come to. There is something almost Biblical about the way the building encompasses me, spreads its eagle wings around me, welcomes me, comforts me. It is majestic, it is awe-inspiring, it is magnanimous, it is outrageous, it is fun.[1] Not at all, as far as I am concerned, the Tower of Babel some critics have called it, nor Fort Knox or Gormenghast, nor a cousin to the Guggenheim Museum in Bilbao, or a resurrection of a Maya temple or Angkor Wat, or a film set from *Raiders of the Lost Ark* or *Star Wars*. My inspiration has been Escher, more than anyone else. It makes my spirit soar every time I come here. I feel like a child who has finished his first own Legoland. It makes me laugh. It comforts and soothes and inspires me.

I park in a back street near by, preferring to enter on foot rather than driving in (although the driving is sheer pleasure too).

A hundred meters or so from the northwest entrance, where I usually go in, a small cluster of bergies are huddled on the sidewalk, playing dice, drinking blue-train from bottles wrapped in newsprint, partaking of glue or tik, smoking dagga, arguing, laughing, cursing to high heaven. So they're back. I haven't seen them around for quite some time now: I thought I'd finally scared them off. The trick, a colleague of mine had once enlightened me, was absolutely foolproof: one afternoon, driven to despair by their presence so close to my block—the noise, the litter, the drinking and carousing on the pavement, the pissing and shitting in public—I paid them a visit, stood around for a while, then squatted on the edge of the pavement near them, offered them some chips from a large packet, then started up a conversation without looking at anyone in particular, as if I were talking to myself. At first it went haltingly, until a bottle of Old Brown finally loosened the tongues.

"You chaps living around here?" I asked.

Lots of shoving and poking and thigh slapping, before someone hesitantly volunteered that yes, they're from the area.

"You been here a long time?" I pressed on.

"Sort of, you may say so."

"Why you asking?" one young man snarled, glaring at me suspiciously with bloodshot and yellowed, pinched-up eyes.

"I'm just interested in the history of the place."

"What history?" Mistrust was spread in a palpable layer across his slurred speech.

"I want to find out about the old days, you see."

"Now why you want to do that?" This time it was a woman. She had a classical triangular Khoi face, bruised and battered like an old avocado, and wizened more with alcohol abuse than with age: she looked ninety, going on thirty. No teeth to speak of. Her dress, or the assortment of tatters that represented a dress, left one breast exposed, shriveled up like a crumpled brown paper bag, the scaly, purple-black nipple resembling the head of a lizard.

"What I heard, was that in the old days there used to be a cemetery right here where this building is now standing. They say there were hundreds of graves here."

Even before I could finish my query they were gone. One moment they were all still around, eyeing the Old Brown bottle and the packet of chips, the next they had vanished. Just vanished. No sound, no nothing. And nobody from the building has ever seen them since. It's only very recently that some of the tribe have been noticed in the vicinity again, presumably a new lot who know nothing about the past.

The real irony is that my story was not a lie at all, as it had been in my colleague's experience. Toward the very end of our excavations on the site for the massive foundations, we had actually unearthed some old unmarked graves. I felt my heart contract when the foreman called me on my cell phone with the news. Barely two years earlier the same had happened to a developer in Green Point when the graves of a number of slaves from the early years of the colony had come to light during excavations. Historical and archaeological and conservation groups pounced immediately and all work was summarily suspended until extensive research could be done. It took an unconscionable time. I was horrified at the prospect of something similar happening to my project in Claremont.

It is not that I underestimate the value of historical research. I have as genuine a feeling as the next man for our cultural heritage or whatever they may choose to call it. But we were working against time. The winter had been excessively cold and wet, which caused interminable delays. An enforced stoppage to dig up and authenticate the old graves under my building might just be the coup de grâce. I stood to lose not only several millions of investors' money, but the contract itself.

There really was only one solution: all evidence of the graves had to disappear. Literally overnight. The foreman was in complete agreement. The untimely discovery could cost him a considerable bonus. As it happened, only two graves had been unearthed by the time he'd called me, and no more than a handful of workers were aware of the find. We conferred well into the night. Then the bulldozers were brought in. At the first glimmering of daylight the excavations were complete. The few bags full of human bones that had been found, were reinterred in a hastily dug grave right on the boundary of the property. The few trusted men involved in the operation were paid substantial cash rewards—not for disposing of the evidence, but for being willing to work overtime through the night to meet a fictitious deadline. Apart from the few of us in on the secret, nobody was any the wiser. Much later there were some rumors and I offered to do everything I could "to get to the bottom of it." The two clandestine graves at the edge of the property were dug up, the handful of bones presented to archaeologists from UCT, and in a touching little ceremony we were lauded for our commitment to honoring the country's past. It was concluded that the human remains of several skeletons from unmarked graves may have been those of slaves once attached to the refreshment post once known as Papenboom, established for the comfort of travelers from Cape Town to Constantia or thereabouts. A small brass plaque was attached to a wall in one of the foyers, and that was that.

There is a touching corollary to the event. Within the first year after the building was opened, rumors started doing the rounds about a ghost haunting the basement and the ground floor of the southwestern entrance. It concerned a disheveled old man with a moth-eaten beard and old-fashioned clothes stumbling about at night, wailing and moaning and mumbling, allegedly looking for his lost home, accosting anybody who happened to turn up and directing them to places where they did not want to be. It seems that on a few occasions when Good Samaritans offered in good faith to take him to his place, he enticed them to enter a lift to the roof, where they said he tried to make them jump twenty floors down into the void. But these rumors could—of course—never be substantiated. It has now become one of the endearing urban legends of the Cape and adds considerably to the reputation (and, in effect, the value) of my block.

Today, finding the bergies back after an absence of—what is it?—six or so years, I toy with the idea of bringing up the old graveyard story again. But something in their attitude makes me hesitate. There is none of joyous, mischievous banter I remember from the past. They sit there sullenly, glaring at me with naked hostility. When I mutter a good morning, they glower without answering. I am sure that if I approached them, today, with my bottle of Old Brown, they would refuse to take it. Today I am not a benevolent whitey trying to ingratiate myself with them. Today I am black: I have been promoted from the bottom of our contemporary social scale to the top, leapfrogging over these who once used to be in the middle and have now been demoted to less than before. (What is the cheapskate old truism? *Yesterday we were too black for the whites, today we are too white for the blacks*.)

With the bergies no longer offering an excuse for lingering, there is little reason for me to spend more time at the massive apartment block. But it occurs to me that I may still pay a quick visit to my colleague, Lydia le Roux, who has drawn me into her community project in Khayelitsha. She and her husband, a teacher and artist, have been living here, on the thirteenth floor, from the beginning. Together with him and Carla, the four of us often go out together of an evening, or over weekends. In fact, we are supposed to come over for dinner this evening. It may not be inopportune to drop in on her now, although it is doubtful that she'll be home. Lydia is over-energetic, if anything. A redhead, too, I may add; and rather attractive, although her hair is less striking, less beautifully affirmative, than Carla's.

By a curious coincidence (although that is something we discovered only much later) I was actually present in the small shop specializing in artist's materials when Lydia and David first met.

I had known Lydia's parents, the Laubschers, since their shop was still located in Long Street, before they moved into a little street off Lansdowne Road. Their daughter did architecture at UCT. She was a few years after me, but we met at some end-of-year function in the Department and some time after that we started going out. I was attracted from the beginning by her manner: she never took nonsense from anyone. There were stories circulating about how she'd even given some of her lecturers hell. I found her alluring—the athletic quality of her figure, the sardonic expression she often had on her face, the way in which she wore her red hair in little plaits all over the place. But it was tough going for any man showing the slightest romantic interest.

The first time I asked her out, after we'd spent many lunchtimes together in the Students' Union cafeteria or simply having coffee and sandwiches on the steps of the Centlivres Building, she asked point-blank, "Why?"

"I'd like to have a good meal with you. We never seem to have enough time to talk."

"You sure you just want to talk?"

"Absolutely."

"Right. Then it's a date."

It was the first meal of many. She always insisted on paying her share, which in the beginning I found something of an insult—but it was either that, or no date. And it was certainly worthwhile talking to her. It wasn't only architecture that interested her: she could go on, brightly, incisively, challengingly, on painting or sculpture and music, also on social issues. Apartheid and its aftermath, inevitably (things were always moving too slowly for her), but also the deterioration of American politics, the turbulent transition in Central Europe, Blair's sly cover-ups, the innumerable betrayals of Africa by the West and by its own leaders. An evening with Lydia could be exhausting. But always worthwhile. Only when it came to the "soppy stuff," as she called it, there was no headway to be made. The odd brush of a kiss, if I was quick enough to catch her off her guard; otherwise our meetings always began and ended with a firm handshake. (And that impenetrable look in her eyes.)

It changed without warning, late one night when we were in the Department together. Often there would be any number of students working after hours on their projects and portfolios; but on that blessed night there were only the two of us. I was working on a major design. Lydia had come to keep me company. Which I found generous and stimulating, but also frustrating. Because she started commenting—not merely incisively, but outright scathingly—on everything I was doing. For a while I tried to keep my cool. But she was, after all, very much my junior; yet she seemed intent on cutting me down to size all the way.

Until I could take it no longer and told her, curtly, to shut up.

She stared at me in disbelief. "You're telling me to shut up?"

"Yes, I am," I said.

"And may I ask why?"

"Because you've been interfering and disruptive all night long and I just cannot take it anymore."

"You don't want me to tell you the truth?"

"I don't want you to keep on dishing out advice on things you don't know anything about."

"Excuse me," Lydia said, bitingly. "From the stuff you've been doing tonight, I get the impression that you're the one who doesn't have a clue."

"Lydia!" I made an effort to control myself. "You're a third-year. It's bloody cheek to think you can keep on correcting me and insulting me."

"I think you're too big for your fancy boots, Steve," she said, unruffled. "You need cutting down to size, otherwise you're going to make a balls-up of your project."

"And you think you're the one to do it?"

"Yes. Because no one else seems to have the guts to tell you the truth. Not even the profs."

"I see. You know the truth, the whole truth, and nothing bloody but?"

"No. But I care."

"You what?"

"I don't like seeing you messing up something which could be so much better."

"I'd prefer you to you keep your third-year opinions to yourself!"

"You're a spoiled brat, Steve. And I'm not going to let you get away with shit."

"What the fuck entitles you to pretend you're an architectural genius?"

"You're not the only genius around. Even though that seems to be what you think."

"Oh, buzz off, Lydia!" I suddenly shouted, unable to take any more of her impertinence.

"That's exactly what I'm going to do." And she stomped off.

I stared after her, at a loss for words.

She seemed set on marching straight off, through the dark building and into the night. But at the door to the passage she turned back, slowly. She was livid too, I could see. But she managed to control her anger.

"I'm so bloody disappointed in you, Steve," was all she said, after a long silence.

I was still too angry to talk.

"I never thought you'd be so unsure of yourself that you can't even take criticism from me."

"And what makes you so special?"

"I told you," Lydia said, very calmly. "I care about you."

"You what?" I had clearly not grasped earlier. I gaped at her.

"That's not any kind of invitation," she snapped, annoyed.

"Then what do you want?"

"I don't want to hurt you or break down anything. But if you're willing to give me a chance, at least I can show you what I would do if it was up to me."

I gazed at her through narrowed eyes. Then stood aside. "All right, show me."

"Feel free to criticize," she said with a straight face and sat down on the high stool in front of my drawing board.

It was not perfection. Her sketch was marred by flaws (the kind of flaws, I thought, one might expect of a third-year student). But the idea was brilliant, much better than mine.

When she was done, I remained standing behind her for a very long time, without a word.

"Well?" she asked at last, turning her head to look up at me.

"It's—" I was ready to trash it. But something stopped me. Something in the limpidity of her eyes. "You're bloody good, Lydia," I said, chastened.

I put my hands on her shoulders. Then, after a moment, lowered them to her breasts. Her nipples reacted. She wasn't wearing a bra under her cotton blouse.

She put her hands on my wrists. "No," she said quietly.

"Yes," I said.

It was a steady, wholesome affair, and it lasted for two years before it blossomed into a brief period of stormy fireworks that came to an abrupt end. Lydia fell pregnant. We should have foreseen it: we were pretty reckless and couldn't stomach the idea of curtailing our lovemaking with petty practical considerations; we both loathed condoms. At the same time a baby at that stage would have wrecked our lives. Her parents, warm and generous and loveable as they were, were old-fashioned people. They would insist on marriage. That would, at the very least, have forced her to suspend her studies, if not end them. There were nights and nights of talking. I wanted to go through with it. I promised her that I wouldn't leave her in the lurch. Together, we would find a way. She just had to complete her degree. All that talent and energy and enthusiasm could not possibly go to waste.

But Lydia was adamant. "I cannot go on studying and have the baby, Steve. Not right now. In a few years perhaps, but not now."

"Then what—?"

"You know what."

"We cannot do that."

"We have no choice."

"I won't allow you to!"

"This is not for you to decide, Steve."

"We did it together. The responsibility is ours."

"But the choice is mine."

"You cannot do that to me, Lydia!"

"You will just have to trust me."

The arguments went on and on. At last we reached a point where she seemed to relent. She insisted that I give her a break so that she could think it through, lucidly, and alone. I agreed, reluctantly.

Three weeks later she nearly died. She had gone through with the abortion, after all. On her own. An old woman in Retreat. Lydia knew several other students who had gone to her. One or two hadn't come out of it too well. The others had. She was the unlucky one. Something really went wrong, very badly. She had to go to Groote Schuur for an emergency operation. Only after that I was told.

I still don't know how she managed to keep it from her parents. The fact that they were in Europe at the time, on a trip they had been planning for years, did make it easier, of course. Even so I was amazed that she never let on to them after they returned, that her resolve never faltered, that everything could be masked as a botched appendectomy.

But it was months before we could try to resume the friendship. There was no chance of being lovers again. In a moment of weakness—the only one I can remember from that dark time—she told me that she would never be able to have babies. That was the lasting scar of her ordeal.

"In a way it may even be a good thing," she said with a brave but crooked smile. "I can concentrate on my work from now on."

But I couldn't handle the new hardness, the residue of bitterness, in her. Still, gradually, we managed to settle into a more relaxed kind of comradeship. We were good colleagues rather than sharing friends. It was, undoubtedly, one of the real losses of my life. And if it didn't sound so melodramatic, I may be tempted to think that after that there was in me a somehow diminished capacity to love quite so unconditionally, wildly, absolutely as with Lydia. But yes, time has a way of smoothing these things. A process of attenuation. The scars heal, even if they still tend to ache on rainy days. Life goes on, as they say. We went on. And after Carla came into my life there were no raw feelings between Lydia and me. I never told Carla about what had happened before her. Sometimes I get the impression that she suspects, in the way a woman knows these things, that there had been "something" between Lydia and me before she turned up in my life. But it has never threatened her, and so it quietly subsided. No need to call up anything that had been so firmly laid to rest. And so Lydia and I could even go on working together. Criticizing each other's work with no punches pulled. But with mutual respect. Carla found it easy to be friends with both of us; the best of all possible worlds. As they say.

Then Lydia met David. A match, I thought from the beginning, destined for a breakup. Yet they are still together. And happily, it would seem. Perhaps being childless has something to do with it: they have to dig into themselves to keep on finding enough to share.

The day they met I'd gone to Lansdowne Road to have a cup of coffee with her. Her father had always been a mean hand at brewing coffee. A mixture of Mocca Java and Blue Mountains and some others which he kept secret; I believe there are a few more unorthodox elements in the mix as well. Perhaps a hint of cinnamon? Even the merest suggestion of orange peel? But Barend Laubscher refused ever to give anything away.

On this particular morning I met Barend a block away from the shop, and we started talking. Only when we came to the front door, which was standing wide open—it was a bright, hot summer's day—we heard a commotion from the inside and went closer to investigate. We found Lydia standing behind the counter, caught in a fierce argument with a loud and bulky customer who seemed apoplectic with rage, advancing with outstretched arms, as if to attack and strangle her. Another customer, a rather pale academic type was preparing to intervene, making frantic, ineffectual gestures as if to grab the fat man from behind, but too timid really to do anything. Both Barend and I rapidly moved in between Lydia and her unsavory aggressor. Clearly taken aback by the new turn of events, he started to back up—the skinny young man still making furtive movements in his direction, like somebody trying to swat a bee, but scared of getting stung—and that was the end of the matter. Some kind of a mixup about paint, if I remember correctly. In his jovial, cajoling way, Barend soon put an end to the aggression. He even invited Lydia's attacker to share a cup of coffee with us, but he refused and left, still muttering and mumbling like a bee trapped in a bottle.

No longer feeling in a mood for coffee, I excused myself and also left, leaving father and daughter and the recently arrived stranger—clearly a well-meaning but limp young man—to their coffee. It was only a week later, if not more, that Lydia told me, strangely uneasy and blushing, that the man was a painter, one David le Roux, and that the two of them, well …

It was only after we'd both got married, Lydia to her David, I to Carla, that everything settled into the delicately balanced foursome relationship we're having now. And now, on this hot and brazen day where everything seems to be exposed and unambiguous, I am on my way back to her. Not for a business consultation of the kind that usually brings us together, but for a cozy cup of tea. Except, of course, that today I am not the man I was, the man she last met, whenever that was.

What would have happened that distant night in the Centlivres Building, if I had then been black? Would I have dared—? Would she—? How very differently everything might have turned out.

Perhaps that is what I have come to look for in Claremont Towers today. Some form of certainty. Of reassurance. A place where I can start to go in search of who and what I am. Because Lydia may be able to guide me.

And yet I already know that even if she were home and we could talk, no one but I can provide the answers, or make the decisions. Everything inside and around me has started stability and definition. I have to go somewhere. But how? And where?

To be black is no longer what it used to be in this country. In many respects it may have turned into the opposite of what it once was. Surely it can only work to my advantage?

But the mere thought annoys me. This is not what I need to explore. Advantage or disadvantage has nothing to do with it. I want to find out what it means to be black. I want to know what it means to be me. And right now there is at least the possibility—or merely the hope—that Lydia may be able to help me.

I stop in front of 1313 and put out my hand to press the bell.

5

B UT NOTHING HAPPENS. LYDIA IS NOT HOME. A pity, but I should have realized from the outset that I could not have expected her to be home in the middle of the day.

It will have to wait till tonight then. But I would really have liked to discuss our project. We have thought it up together. I cannot even remember which of us first came up with the idea: it was a joint effort from the beginning. Ever since our first night in that lugubrious building on the Upper Campus we have learned to batter out projects together. Sometimes with much shouting and argument. But always with underlying respect.

A simple plan, basically. Trying to speed up the backlog of black housing and the government's apparent inability to do something quick and effective about it.

We cannot, we decided, simply set up a new housing project (with Scandinavian money, Chinese money, Canadian money, whatever), get thousands of little boxes built after half the money had been siphoned off by project managers and their wives and cronies, ministers and their wives and cronies, executive officers and their wives and cronies, facilitators and their wives and cronies, consultants and their wives and cronies. All we proposed to do would be to build a wall. A long wall. A sturdy wall. With electric wiring built into it to supply a specific number of outlets. And water pipes and sewage pipes built in to supply a specific number of outlets. Then to invite displaced people from informal settlements to come and build their own houses backed up against our wall. With help from our consortium: not as handouts, but in the form of loans, following the Bangladeshi model of Muhamad Yunus. And then to repeat the exercise ten or twenty or a hundred times, in the same township or in different ones.

The night we finally came up with this blueprint, after innumerable cigarettes and whiskies and other beverages, was another occasion, like that remote night on campus, which might have debouched in a No, followed by a Yes and a raging bout of lovemaking. But we are somewhat older now. Hopefully wiser. And both married. Lydia to David, I to Carla. And neither of us inclined, or prepared, to stray.

Today it is even more important. If I am what I am beginning to suspect I am, it concerns me even more urgently than before. It has to do, after all, with "my people." Even if I have no idea of who "my people" are. For the simple reason that I don't know who I am.

I let go of the buzzer and turn away from the door. Along the wide passage to the lift landing. It arrives without a sound. Everything in this place works perfectly.

Down to the ground floor. For a moment I am tempted to go round to the southwestern entrance. Who knows, I may meet the wandering old Methuselah. But today I am already contending with enough other ghosts inside myself.

Outside, the bergies are still scattered like laundry on the sidewalk around two Shoprite shopping trolleys piled high with what must be all their earthly possessions. One woman with an eye like an overripe plum is squatting against the wall of Claremont Heights, her skirts hoisted up to her thighs, peeing copiously. Two of the others are engaged in an argument that can be heard several blocks away; but they break off abruptly when they see me coming. The silence is embarrassing. To break it, I attempt a hearty greeting, "You chaps still around?"

They just stare. As I come past, a man from the group suddenly shouts, *"Jou ma se swart poes!"* (Your mother's black cunt!)

If this had happened on any other day, I am convinced, I would hardly have paid any attention. It might, at most, have provoked a grin. But today, without any warning, I feel totally exposed. Today it is much, much more than the immemorial taunt of the Cape Town streets. It is as if he has very specifically directed it to me. As if he knew exactly where it would cause the most hurt, the most damage.

Even this is not the end of it. Just before I go round the corner to return to my car I hear a voice from the huddle of malodorous, dilapidated bodies calling loudly, to no one in particular, "I say! These kaffirs think they own the place nowadays!"

I can feel my ears throbbing. Briefly, I lose all control. As I turn round to face the small crowd of wretched humanity they scramble to get up, jeering in a raucous chorus, taking up threatening postures. I start striding back toward them. I have no idea of what I will do when I reach them, but in my blind rage I am ready for anything: I know I am capable of launching myself into their midst to hit out at anyone, anything, within reach. Not since my schooldays have I ever been in a physical fight: although I may have come close to it on several occasions, sense— or pusillanimity?—has always prevailed. But this time it seems inevitable; and I find myself prepared for it.

As I approach, the jeers and taunts rise to a cacophony. On the far side of the street passersby are gathering to watch. Some join in the shouting, but in my overpowering rage I cannot make out on whose side they are. The bergies still appear to take it as a game of bluff. But as I get to the first man, who has just scrambled to his feet on the curb, they seem to realize that I am serious. The jeering breaks up into a multitude of separate sounds, like a mirror shattering. I grab the man closest to me by his tattered shirttail and jerk him back toward me. He falls down, now blubbering with fear, while all the others retreat helter-skelter to a safe distance, half a block away.

"*Ag*, please, man," the wretched man in the gutter is sobbing. "Please, man, I didn't mean it nasty like, man, now don't do something reckless, man, *ag*, please, man, fuck it, *tog*, man!"

I pull back my leg as, in my student days in a rugby match, I would prepare to take a drop kick at the posts.

All the other bergies have now subsided into a slobbering near-silence of confused wails and groans.

At the last moment I rein myself in, overtaken by sudden disgust. At this clown in front of me. Above all at myself.

Taking a deep breath, I turn away from my would-be victim who is now lying in a bundle of misery, knees drawn up, elbows protecting his head.

"Kick him! Kick him! Kick him!" some of the bystanders are chanting.

Other voices do an accompaniment in the background: "Shame! *Foeitog!* Blarry kaffir! Give him hell, *ja!*"

Without looking back I stride off toward the corner, away from my building, the pride of my career, to get back to my car.

Behind me there is silence. But the moment I round the corner I hear the wild shouts breaking out again—although I'm sure, without looking, that should I turn to face them, they will subside into abject moaning once more.

I press the remote control to my car. The brief double sound is deeply reassuring. Without waiting, I slide in behind the wheel and drive off.

But a mere block or two away I stop again, turn off the ignition, and remain slouched in the driver's seat, my head against the steering wheel.

Anger, revulsion, rage assail me in a blinding headache.

But disgust above all. A feeling of total shame. What the fuck has happened to me? What have I done? What would Carla say if she were to hear about it?

I have lived in Cape Town for most of my life. I know bergies. Their taunts and wisecracks, their unbridled jeering, their wretchedness, their exuberance. What, then, has made me snap today? I feel filthy. I want to hide somewhere. For God's sake, I just want to get away from here. Forever.

It is no comfort to know that I have restrained myself in time. I haven't really done anything. I gave the man a good scare, but no more. And he bloody well deserved that. But I know there is no solace in realizing that I managed to stop before it got out of hand. It was not the action, or lack of it, in itself that mattered. It was the unexpected readiness for violence that shocked me. The excess of violence I so briefly felt capable of. Where did it come from?

Your mother's black cunt! One hears that on any street corner every day. With or without the black. (Or could that really be what made the difference?)

These kaffirs think they own the bloody place. In front of my own building, for God's sake. But wasn't that funny, more than anything else? Excruciatingly funny. Nothing to cause this feeling of humiliation and shame.

I lift my head. My face is running with sweat. My hands on the steering wheel are trembling as if I'm in a fever.

But that man, that bloody little shit—!

No. No. No. If there was humiliation in it, it was my own doing. No one else can be held responsible. And all because of a look in the mirror this morning—? Nothing that has happened to me all day has exposed me so numbingly to the discovery of my blackness.

I cannot go on reasoning with myself like this. This is something I cannot explain. Least of all to myself. For the moment I suppose I should simply learn to live with it.

But that is precisely what I am least prepared to come to terms with.

All I know is that I am exhausted. And ashamed. And filthy. I must get home to rest. Have something to eat.

I haven't touched food or drink since I had my tea this morning. I need a swim. Literally, to cool off.

I must go home.

6

DRIVING BACK, THE CAR COMPLYING WILLINGLY, obediently with every slightest movement, I gradually feel some peace of mind return. I am still in control. This was just a momentary aberration, an unpleasant but almost irrelevant reminder of a world that is gone forever. (Isn't it?)

My mind once again on automatic pilot, I glide round the mountain, down to the sea, and up again to the symmetries and aesthetics of my eagle's nest.

In the garage there is no sign of Carla's car yet. And by this time Alida will be gone.

I feel relieved, although I realize that it can only be temporary. At least there will be some respite. Unless there is still someone at home and I am discovered as an interloper with criminal intentions in my own house—!

There is a brief interruption as I enter the house from the garage. In the wide entrance lobby I meet our cat Sebastian, short for Johann Sebastian, who is really a female but had to be named after Bach, on whose birthday—21 March—she came to live with us. She was one of two—the other was Vivaldi, but he met a violent early end under a passing car. So now Sebastian has to bear the often effusive demonstrations of love from the whole household. Especially from the girls.

She is always eager for a rough-and-tumble and when she has decided to be part of the game, under no matter what circumstances, nothing will keep her out of it. There was one memorable occasion when she joined Carla and me in a bout of lovemaking: after a long preliminary session, at the moment when I was ready to enter her, kneeling between her parted thighs, I suddenly became aware of an intrusive presence between my legs—and looking down, past my erection, there was Sebastian's mischievous little face thrusting itself past my balls and crawling lengthwise onto Carla's lower belly, purring loudly. We both collapsed in laughter, and that was the end of that particular threesome.

Which doesn't mean that she always insists on being a member of the party. As cats do, she very calmly and efficiently knows when she has had enough and wishes to remove herself from our mundane goings-on to withdraw to an altogether higher, rarer sphere of being.

Today she has, it seems, already retired to that place to which we lesser mortals have no access. It goes beyond haughtiness. She becomes untouchable, unreachable. When I go down on my haunches to greet her, Sebastian draws her slender, pitch-black back into an arc and hisses at me. She has never, never done this before and it leaves me hurt and flabbergasted, insulted.

"Sebastian—?" I say gently.

This time the cat actually spits at me as if I am an intruder in my own home, a stranger, a threat, an enemy.

I utter a few purring sounds, but it only makes me feel foolish. Sebastian archly turns her back, tail raised defiantly, and moves away in an elegant, dignified, stiff-legged way, like a drunk pretending to be sober.

It is ridiculous that this should affect me so. But I really feel denied, rejected in a way I would not have believed possible. You are my cat, I want to say. This is my home. Everything in here belongs to me. You cannot treat me like this.

She can. She does.

Who am I really?

I can pretend to shrug it off, even though I know this will rankle for some time. But I know my superstitious mother would have seen this as a "sign." And in the light of what this unsettling day has already wrought, it makes me feel most ill at ease. I am pissed off. Also nonplussed. Has Sebastian sensed something which

Gerald and Derek missed? Or were they simply covering up their true feelings? Only Johann Sebastian Bach cannot be duped. But if her reaction—which certainly was as unequivocal as they come—means that what the mirror showed me this morning is the unadulterated truth, then how am I really going to handle it? Is this a charade and can I go through with it? Or is it reality—my own, new reality? What does that make me? Who does it make me?

When will I find out—how can I find out—who I am? Who I have been? Who I may yet be?

For a moment I want to follow the cat. I need to get something out of her. Confirmation or denial, whatever. Anything. Something.

But she has gone. And will not come back, unless she herself decided to do so.

I must go up to my study. In the top right-hand drawer of my broad, streamlined, glass-top desk, I know, I will find my ID. A very obvious, even silly, thing to do. But at the very least it will give me a clue. A photo. To show me what I used to look like. In my newly shaken world, I need assurance. I need proof. At this moment, after the cat's reaction, anything will be better than the bewilderment in which I find myself.

As I reach the second terrace and start proceeding up to the bedroom floor, there is a slight, whispering sound behind me. I stop and turn round to look.

It is Silke, coming in from the pool. Her wet blonde hair is untidily draped over the tanned smoothness of her shoulders. She is naked, trailing a large bright beach towel behind her. The colors are bold and primal, red, yellow, blue. My first reaction is to look around for somewhere to hide. I have momentarily forgotten about her presence in the house. She has obviously not been expecting me either. But she must be blinded from the dazzling sun outside, for she doesn't stop or hesitate but comes straight on toward me. She is humming a little tune.

She already has one foot on the bottom stair when she stops.

Yes, now she has seen me.

To my surprise—my sudden, uncomplicated pleasure—she does not crouch in the immemorial defensive position. She does not even think of raising the colorful towel to cover herself.

She looks up at me, gives a little smile, makes a melodious, half-formed sound which may be *I'm sorry*, or *Hello*, or simply the continuation of her hummed song.

I stand aside to let her pass.

I can smell her as she lightly steps aside. Not so much suntan lotion, or shampoo, or whatever she may have applied to her skin or her hair, as the sun itself, womanness itself. The smell of light.

She stops. I am aware of inhaling strongly, deeply. Not to lodge her fragrance in my lungs, but to inhale her.

"You are very beautiful," I tell her. My voice sounds surprisingly calm.

Her little smile is back on the provocative roundness of her lips. Perhaps it has never left them. From so close up they have the slightly swollen appearance of one of those actresses who are suspected of enhancing their natural curves artificially. But there is nothing artificial about Silke. She is all nature, all youth, all woman.

"Thank you," she says, almost formally. For a moment—she is German—I expect her to dip into a curtsy. Instead, she drops her towel. Accidentally, perhaps. Perhaps not.

I bend down instinctively to retrieve it. But instead of offering it to her I drape it over my own shoulder. Everything is happening in slow motion. Once again I am aware of observing us, myself, from a vantage point outside both, slightly higher up, as if I have already preceded her up the stairs.

Her eyes—impossibly blue, I realize—are intently probing my face.

Just for a moment panic hits me. She is looking at me. She is seeing me. As I am now. As I am.

But there is no shock or disapproval in her face

This is when I raise my hand. And she takes it in hers.

In fascination I look down at them, clasped. Hers slim and small, yet sinewy, strong; and white. The light tan is irrelevant. She is white. My hand black.

We look each other in the eyes. I raise her fingers to my mouth and kiss them, smell them.

It is at this moment that she says, "Your skin. I like how it feel, how it look."

And suddenly it is as if something gives way in me. This is the one thing I do not want to hear. The one thing she should not have said.

I let go of her hand. I am aware of drawing in my breath very sharply as I move in behind her and start pushing her up the stairs ahead of me. She makes a sound, perhaps the beginning of a question, or a protest. But I do not let go. Almost violently, my hand pressed against the small of her back, just above the swollen whiteness of her buttocks, I shove her up before me.

I follow her up to her small but airy room at the end of the passage that runs from the master bedroom with the endless sea view to this end, which looks out over the mountain range. It continues, I know, beyond the visible, to Cape Point, to the southernmost tip of the continent, and then on and on, across the stunning black-blue of the Atlantic, all the way to Antarctica. Coldness, whiteness, absolute pureness.

It is the notion of absolute that determines everything.

I bring my hands up to the top of my shirt and start undoing the top button. Then the second.

"No," she says and moves my hands away. "I do it, yes?"

But I shake her off with a kind of growl in my throat. If this is what you're after, this is what you're going to get. Fucking little white bitch.

"*Bitte,*" I hear her say, her voice caught in her throat like a moan.

I tear off my clothes. My shirt literally comes off in shreds. I drop everything on the floor.

For the first time I become aware of what is happening inside me. Not passion, not lust, not ecstasy, but rage. A terrible and destructive rage. The only words I can hear careering through my mind, round and round like a fucking merry-go-round, are *Bloody black stud!*

The bed is narrow and has a bright and innocent look about it, covered with a white, tasseled spread. Next to it, on the bedside table, is a small pile of magazines and books. Strange what one can focus on, and how absently, in a moment of pure rage. The one on top is Hesse's *Steppenwolf.* (Pretentious. Who does she think she is? Who does she think I am?)

She turns away briefly to pull, with German correctness, the white spread from the bed, tucks one end under her chin, and swiftly and precisely folds it into a rectangle; then, with her back to me, bends away—briefly displaying the cleft that divides her buttocks—

and neatly places it on the carpet that is dark red like old blood.

But I can no longer contain my anger. Each of her tidy, calculated movements seems designed to provoke me with their controlled poise. While she is still bent over, I grab her from behind and hurl her on the bed.

In my mind a senseless jumble of images. The drunk vomiting on my car window. Gerald and Derek in their hard hats. The bergies. Their strident voices reverberating in my throbbing head. *Jou ma se swart poes*. I feel again the shame burning in my face. *These kaffirs think they own the bloody place.*

We couple on the narrow bed. I see it, intently observe it, my blackness and her whiteness, every limb, every angle and curve and indent, every movement, some smooth, others jerky, becoming more and more insistent, thrashing and hammering and battering, tearing and raging, with a violence I have never known myself capable of, attacking her, assaulting her, forcing helpless sounds from her mouth against mine, feeling her open lips crushed against my teeth, as I go on and on in a frenzy that possesses me, possesses both of us. I feel all her ferocity battered out of her, feel her grow helpless as she subsides and begins to sob. And as it goes on, I can feel, can see, how she changes, her very body changes. In the beginning she reveled and celebrated and defied and dared—Yes, yes, yes, fuck me, please fuck me, *ja, ja, fick mich, fick mich*—but now it is turning into pain, she becomes terrified, and my very discovery of her stokes up my rage, inspires me to greater excess. Her head is swinging left and right on the stark white pillow beneath it, like the head of a rag doll, all the stuffing beaten out of it, while I feel myself growing in strength and rage and fury, making and breaking, destroying and devastating, without beginning or end, and all of it is me, me, bellowing and thundering, almighty, taking her as I have never taken any woman before, in all imaginable and unimaginable postures, in every orifice she savagely or unintentionally offers me, while she goes on whimpering and moaning, sobbing, slobbering, in a passion in which rage and agony can no longer be distinguished, screaming like a creature beyond hope or redemption. I hear her gasps and sobs in my ear. But as it rises to a crescendo the utterance changes. It begins, and continues for a long time in German—*Fick mich, mich, mich, mein Gott, mein Gott, mein lieber schrecklicher Gott, du bist...du bist*—but then it mutates into something else, a scream distorted and shrilled by madness: Fuck you—fuck you—fuck offffff...! And we collapse in a tangle, wounded and plundered, smeared by the spit and sweat and the fluids we have fucked from each other's bodies, in a final stuttering and shuddering and sobbing whisper, discarded like two lifeless, drowned things from a shipwreck on a remote, apocalyptic, godforsaken beach at the end of the Earth, beyond all limits and frontiers and boundaries, with the cries of goddamned seagulls overhead. Somehow, sometime, she must have torn herself from the bed and gathered an armful of stuff—the brightly colored towel, a sheet, bits and pieces of clothing—and scrambled out of the room, leaving me behind in a numb descending silence. (And even in this moment I hear that strident voice shrilling somewhere: *Jou ma se swart poes!*)

Much later, from my own room awash with afternoon light through the wall-wide window, I go to the en-suite bathroom. There is a sudden jolt when I face my own reflection in the art nouveau mirror. Every time the same shock, and every time reaffirmed, branded into my mind.

I step into the shower and move in under the jet, which I have opened to the full. The impact on my raw skin is almost painful. But I relish it. The kind of glee with which, I can imagine, a medieval monk might have relished flagellation. I want this forceful stream of water to cleanse me, to wash everything from me that is not essentially me.

Only very gradually, slowly, do images and memories begin to filter back into the vacuum of my mind. What has happened? What have we done? What have I done?

And why, for God's sake?!

169

Your skin, was what she said. I like how it feels. I like how it looks. That was where it all began.

The water splashes and streams over me like a cataract. Wash me, and whiter than snow I shall be.

Gradually, as the heat drains away whatever reserves of energy I may still have, I become aware of just how tired I am. This day has all been too much for me. Not that I am black, but that I am not myself. That I am other. If this is what I am now, how will I bear it into the future? And what kind of a future?

And what has happened to her? Where is she now?

I cannot stay here under the shower while she—

Hurriedly, breathlessly, I start drying myself. Then rush out into the passage, still leaving wet tracks all along the carpet.

She is not in her room or her bathroom. I want to call out but cannot find my voice. For a moment I have even forgotten her name.

I go downstairs, make detours to every corner of the house and garden, but I can find her nowhere.

In the garage her little white Renault still stands, like a poor relative, next to the Porsche. So at least she hasn't left.

Except on foot?

Once more I go through the whole place, but there is no sign of her. I am just tired, tired, worn out. With a blinding headache.

And Carla may be home soon.

I need out. I need, at the very least, a rest.

I am about to sprawl on our big bed—immaculately made up, with fresh sheets, by Alida since this morning's gymnastics: was it only this morning, a few hours ago?— when I remember something and go out into the passage to my study. It is on the floor below.

Everything is exactly as I left it last night when I came to bed. Alida is not allowed in here. Even Carla does not dare to tidy the place. When anything has to be done, I do it myself. Rarely, but still. It is my space. My ultimate space. Where I can be me.

Who am I?

But this is exactly why I am here. After all that has happened I need, at last, some assurance.

I hurry to the wide desk. Leather, stainless steel, glass of a centimeter thick.

Only when I pull open the right-hand top drawer do I remember: I have applied for a new ID. I handed in the application a month ago, after we had a burglary—God knows how anyone could get into this redoubt; may have been an inside job (resulting in the firing of housekeeper and gardener, who had both been with us for years: but one cannot be too careful). It will be another month or so before the new one arrives. The Department of Home Affairs is not built for speed.

Chagrined, I close the drawer again. I can go in search of my passport, which must be somewhere. But that is locked up elsewhere. All our papers and monthly bills are kept downstairs, in Carla's pottery studio: that is her domain.

I am simply too tired now to be bothered. (Too tired to find out who I am?)

I return to the master bedroom. (Master, indeed!)

As I am about to enter, the hint of a sound behind me makes me swing around. In time to see Silke emerge from her room at the far end of the long, wide passage, ready to go down. She is wearing white thong sandals. Very small white shorts. A blue and white striped top. Not a blonde hair in her ponytail out of place. As if nothing has happened. (For one wild moment I think: Perhaps nothing has happened. Perhaps it has all been part of the madness of this day.)

I am still naked. In some consternation I seek refuge behind one of Carla's large pots. Perhaps Silke has not noticed me yet. Perhaps she cannot care less.

But at this moment she calls out, "Hello!" Not exactly brightly, but evenly. Neutrally. Which is better than silence. It is too late.

I poke my head out from behind the pot. "Silke—?" I say tentatively, my voice a croak in my throat.

"I go fetch the girls from music." She moves fluidly down the stairs.

I wait until I hear the bottom door slam, followed by her little car starting up.

Then I go into the bedroom, close the door behind me—the children have been taught long ago what this means—and fling myself down on the matrimonial bed.

7

I AWAKE WITH A START, FOR A MOMENT NOT KNOWING at all where I am and why I am there. All I am aware of is that something has happened, something violent and sudden. It is, I discover, the cat Sebastian who has jumped on my knees, not to join me on the bed but to try and drive me away. The first I am aware of is her fixed stare. Her eyes gleaming with animosity. That she has just rudely intruded into my dreams is of no concern to her.

Shreds and wisps of those dreams begin to waft back to me, airy and incoherent, ungraspable. But I want to catch hold of them: all of a sudden this is of immense importance to me. If I miss them, I will have lost a vital clue. But under Sebastian's ferocious gaze—

until she decides to decamp again and leave me to inchoate memories—nothing coherent or conclusive takes place, and I am left only with a sense of unease and disgruntlement, a hint of sadness or melancholy at something that has slipped out of reach and will not come together ever again.

I know I was making love to a woman. There was something very beautiful and very terrible about it. I was getting closer and closer to a discovery, an illumination, that might change my life, or the world. But what was it about? The woman—yes, I seem to remember now, was Silke. Or am I simply reaching back to what happened just before the dream? Where, exactly, did the dream begin? Did Silke belong to the world before the dream or in it?

Reaching out, groping, grasping, I try to sift out some possibilities of memory and dream. Silke is memory now. Yes, I remember that. My body remembers her, all right. But she was also part of the dream. I recall that distinctly now. We are making love here in this bed. I am deep inside her, with the full length of a finger probing the smooth depths of her rectum. But then—yes, that is it—I look down and realize that the woman is not Silke after all. She is Lydia. The Lydia of years ago, when we were young and irresponsible and she—yes. But then it isn't Lydia either. I raise myself on my outstretched arms to look down at her and see that it isn't a woman at all, but a cat. A very big cat, with a taunting smile, like the one in *Alice in Wonderland*. And then it is no longer a cat, but Carla. And I am not making love to her but masturbating, and she is looking at me with inscrutable eyes. They may be commiserating, or questioning. They may be damning.

I hear myself saying, "It isn't me, it isn't me, I swear, it isn't me."

And, reflected in Carla's eyes as in a mirror, I see myself and realize that, indeed, it isn't me. It is somebody else who has been making love: I have only been watching, not part of it at all, at all. And then I lose my grasp on it and cannot put anything together anymore.

From somewhere outside the room—on the stairs? in the passage?—I hear a rattle of footsteps, and shouting voices and arpeggios of laughter, followed by peremptory hisses and shhhhs.

The children are back. I can hear them arriving right outside my door.

"You think Daddy is home?" asks one of them. It must be little Leonie.

"Don't go in," Francesca hushes her. "If Mummy is with him they may be making love. You know that is what they usually do when they close the door. And then they don't want to be interrupted."

"What will happen if we rupt them?"

"I think they get a terrible sickness, like AIDS, and they die."

Leonie sighs audibly. "Then we better let them be, I suppose. And I so wanted to tell them about the music lesson."

"It's late enough, I'm sure they won't mind."

"But you said we mustn't rupt them."

"But that is only on Sundays. And anyway, people don't make love in the daytime," says Francesca in her most schoolmarmy voice. "They only do it in the dark when no one can see."

"That can't be much fun," protests Leonie, with the accumulated wisdom of her seven years.

"They don't do it for fun," Francesca pointedly corrects her. "They do it to make babies. That's why they had us. You know that, stupid."

"You mean Mum and Dad actually did it twice?" asks Leonie in her high-pitched, incredulous voice. "But that is gross."

Flushed with warmth for my daughters, I feel an urge to embrace and cuddle them. But I cannot face them now, not like this. I am not prepared to see the shock on their innocent faces. First, I'm naked. I am also black. The nakedness should be no problem, we are all used to walking about without clothes at home; sometimes, in exuberant mood, all four of us even have a bath or a shower together. But today I feel self-conscious. After what has happened, it feels as if they can find Silke's imprint all over my body. Her smell—even in spite of the drastic shower. However, that can still be remedied without too much effort; and while the discussion is still continuing just outside my closed door, I hurry to the dressing room and start putting on clothes—without any of my usual fastidiousness about matching the various items.

But how do I handle my blackness? I know that children miss nothing, mine least of all. Certainly not anything as definite as the color of my skin. It will be hard enough to face Carla soon; but she may yet be prepared to handle it with tact. Not these sweet savages. How often have they embarrassed us in public: *Daddy, why didn't that man button up his fly? Daddy, do you think that lady has false teeth?* It is not color in itself that would attract their scrutiny: for all their lives we have had visitors of all creeds and colors. But to expect them not to comment when suddenly confronted with a father who has changed his color overnight—? This is not just a test, as the meeting with Gerald and Derek was this morning, but the ultimate litmus test.

Dressed, but still barefoot, I stand inside the door, my hand on the stylish steel doorknob. It is now or never. I can feel my heart jumping about like a slaughtered chicken.

"You think we can knock?" Leonie asks outside.

I close my eyes, take a deep breath, pull the door open. There is a moment's silence. Then they hurl themselves at me, Leonie with utter abandon, Francesca with perhaps a touch more propriety. (She is ten, and the senior, and has to live up to it.)

"Daddy! You are back! I told her we could come in!" shouts Leonie, burying her face in my belly with such enthusiasm that I am nearly winded.

"I hope we didn't wake you up?" asks Francesca.

I try to disentangle myself, ruffling their hair, red and dark respectively. (Why do they look the way they do? These two sweet white darlings. Why hasn't my color rubbed off on them? Unless all of this is a delusion. But if so—?)

"Of course you didn't wake me," I say, choking back a lump in my throat. I still cannot believe that they are accepting me so unreservedly. (But what does it mean? What does it make of me?) I sit back on the bed, facing them. "Now what is all the excitement about?"

"We're going to be in a concert!" announces Leonie.

"Both of us," Francesca specifies. "I'm going to play 'Für Elise.'"

"And I'm playing a lullaby. It's by"—she whirls round to her sister—"what's that man's name?"

"Brahms," says Francesca patiently. "In a simplified version."

"What's a simplified whatsisname?" asks Leonie.

"It's specially written for little kids like you."

"I'm not a little kid. Daddy! Tell Francesca I'm not a little kid anymore. We're going to play in the Artscape. That's where all the grownups play, isn't it? Mr. Hugo himself has played there. Many times, I think."

"Derek Hugo," Francesca makes the point. "Our teacher. And he's very good, isn't he, Daddy?"

"He's one of the best pianists in the country," I confirm. "That's why we're sending you to have lessons with him."

"One day when I am big," Leonie announces, "I am going to marry Mr. Hugo."

"Oh, I'm sure he's already asked you," Francesca bitches witheringly.

"We are just waiting for the right time," retorts Leonie. "I think I am still a bit too young now. But I'm growing up fast, aren't I, Daddy?"

"Much too fast," I agree.

"You can't marry Derek Hugo," sneers Francesca. "He already has a girlfriend."

"He doesn't."

"Does."

"Doesn't."

"Does too."

"That's just to keep him busy while he's waiting for me to grow up," Leonie says tartly.

"And who is this girlfriend?" I inquire.

"Her name is Nina Rousseau," says Francesca. "She

is a soprano. A very famous soprano."

"The Nina Rousseau?" I ask.

"Do you know her then?"

"Everybody knows her," I say. "Or knows of her. I've heard that she's not only an amazing soprano but very, very beautiful."

"When I'm big," Leonie interposes quickly, "I'll not only play the piano, I'll also be a wonderful soprano. And by that time this other one will be old and ugly, so he will kill her and marry me."

Francesca snorts in a most undignified way. "Suppose she kills him first?"

"I won't allow her to," Leonie cries. "I tell you, I'm going to marry him!"

"Let's try to arrange all this without any unnecessary violence," I intervene. "I'll tell you what: when the time comes I shall have a chat with both Derek Hugo and Nina Rousseau and we'll arrange everything peacefully."

From a distance comes the sound of a car door slamming.

"That's Mummy!" cries Leonie, all wedding plans forgotten. "She's home!" She rushes out, nearly tripping over Sebastian who is haughtily poised in the doorway, her back fastidiously turned to me.

Francesca also turns to go, then looks back forlornly and returns to me. Her big green eyes are brimming with tears.

"What's the matter, darling girl?" I ask, pulling her to me.

She starts talking, but for a while the emotion is too strong for any coherent utterance. At last she sobs wetly against my chest, "Daddy—please—you mustn't tell anybody—but I also want to marry Mr. Derek Hugo. You can't let Leonie do this to me."

"I promise you we'll all sit down together and we'll find a solution that suits everybody."

"Like what?"

"Perhaps you can take turns," I say randomly.

She stares hard at me, then asks hesitantly, incredulously, "But can one do that?"

"Many people do, my lovey. You just have to keep it very quiet."

"I'm not so sure—" she says. Then looks up at me. "But you will think of something?"

"Oh yes. I will."

"Promise?"

"Promise."

She slobbers kisses all over my face. Ten is not so much older than seven after all. Then she runs out in Leonie's turbulent wake.

I am left behind to face my own destiny.

8

CAN HEAR THEM APPROACHING FROM FAR BELOW. IT is like a small whirlwind of sound. The children's voices babbling nonstop, claiming simultaneous attention for their two versions of the afternoon's music lessons, interrupted from time to time by a remark or a comment from Carla. Halfway up, they appear to peel away from her, presumably to go swimming. I can imagine their small, smooth otter bodies gliding and cavorting, glistening in the silky water. (Followed, in due course, by their shrill voices clamoring for towels, because I'm sure they have jumped in without bothering to change into bathing gear.) I wish I could be there with them now; wish I could be anywhere in the wide world except here, now, in this bedroom, waiting for Carla.

What will she say when she sees me? What will I say?

At the moment I am more concerned with the latter. No one else has remarked on my changed appearance: not Gerald or Derek, not even the children. Only Silke, in a way. (*Your skin. I like how it looks.*) But that did not reveal whether she'd seen it differently before. How utterly different her reactions had been, compared to those of the pleasant but strictly correct au pair I had known before.) And this is where my unease, my dread, is lodged at this moment. Is it possible, is it conceivable, that Carla will not detect a hint of our afternoon together when she faces me a minute from now? I cannot be the same man as before. It is not even the act of betrayal as such that most perturbs me, but this fact of something inside myself that has changed. I feel out of touch with the person I used to be. I can no longer be sure of reactions, perceptions, thoughts. It is not just the color of a skin. It is me. The innermost core of me. Or is that, ultimately, the cause of my bewilderment?—that I no longer have a core, a something that defines me, something that is me?

Perhaps, and this is even more disturbing, I have never had anything one could call a core, a me. It was just a convention, a way of thinking, because it fitted in with all the circumstances of my life. From one moment to the next, I may always have been a fluid thing, in motion, gliding between somewhere and somewhere, never fixed, never anything to be, reassuringly, called I.

In my university days: how carefully and meticulously did I plot what I could be, might be, one day. Not wishing to offend anybody; wishing to please anybody who might at some stage be of use or service to me. Gliding from shell to shell like a hermit crab, from persona to persona, something of a chameleon. And afterward, having once found my "niche" in a solid and reputable firm, still gliding from client to client, meta-morphosing into the fulfilment of their expectations, their wishes, their commands and demands. I believed myself to be the rectilinear man, the architect of predictabilities and certainties. Whereas, deep down—who was I, who have I been, who the fuck am I?

I remember an argument I once had with Carla. It was, in fact, soon after she had given me the art nouveau mirror of the girl with the flowing hair, holding the harp. It must have been in the time I was working on Claremont Heights. That amazing building (if I say so myself) in which each of the four entrances appears to open up into a new space, a new kind of space, a new and ever-changing dream space.

"What are you trying to do?" Carla asked. "What are you trying to say?"

"Perhaps I'm not going to say anything," I jokingly replied. "I'm just telling stories in my buildings."

"But are they the stories your clients want to hear? Or something you are imagining from inside yourself?"

"Is there so much difference?" I asked, still in a teasing, playful mood.

"I'd like to know who you are," she said, unexpectedly serious, her voice more urgent than I think the occasion warranted. "I'd like to know who I am in bed with when we make love."

"I am a multitude," I said.

"That is not even original," she answered, annoyed.

"Of course it is original. I've just thought it up."

"No you haven't. It was written by Walt Whitman more than a century ago."

"I have never read Walt Whitman."

"You must have," she remonstrated. "These things cannot fall out of the air."

"Who knows?" I argued. "Is that not where all stories come from?"

"No!" She was most adamant. "Stories come from other stories."

"Then there is no originality anywhere."

"Does it matter? Perhaps our very idea of originality is overrated. And unoriginal."

"This is original, isn't it? These eyes, this mouth, this breath you're breathing, this lovely red hair."

"I have my grandmother's eyes, my father's mouth, the air I'm breathing has already been breathed out by hundreds and thousands of people and trees and flowers. And my hair is my mother's."

"Come and kiss me," I said and took her in my arms. She tried to resist, but succumbed to my caresses, and the lovemaking that ensued seemed to confirm everything that was good in the world.

Except that, afterward, as we lay intimately together, my face in the dark red tangle of her pubic hair, she suddenly pushed herself up on one elbow, pensively drawing a finger along the outlines of my face, my arms, my chest and stomach, my flaccid penis, she suddenly asked with a vehemence that surprised me, "Who are you, Steve? I know—my lover. I know you are my husband. My all-in-all. But who are you? Will you please tell me?"

There is a turmoil of thoughts inside me clamoring to break out. I have no control over them. The need to understand. Not just the self I am, the selves I was. But the link between them. The continuity. That is what I miss. Without it, I am lost.

Overwhelmed by memories, I walk to the vast window that overlooks the sea. It seems to have no substance: there is no water, no beach, no clumps and clusters of trees, no houses, everything is reduced to color, pure color, and to lines and patches, shapes, an uncontrolled and uncontrollable design.

"Steve," she says behind me.

Although I have now been waiting for this moment throughout the long, turbulent day, a deep undertone to everything I have been thinking and remembering, it comes as a shock to hear her voice. After all the doubts and dreads and evasions and fears—at last to be confronted with the simple fact of her being here. With me. Opposite me.

"My love," I say, wondering absently—once more as if at a distance from myself—why my voice sounds faltering.

"Am I very late?" she asks, coming closer.

"Not at all. To tell you the truth, I fell asleep and lost all track of time."

"Good. Then you're not resentful and angry."

"Am I ever resentful and angry with you?"

"More often than you think." She smiles. I catch her smell. (Can she smell me?) She comes even closer, right up against me, gazing up intently into my face.

"Why—why are you looking at me like that?" I dare to ask, but only after some time, when further silence would become unbearable. (Now she is going to tell me.)

"You know, sometimes when I look at you, I get the strange feeling that I've never seen you before, that I'm meeting you for the first time."

"And what do you see in me today?"

(A traitor? A husband who has been fucking another woman under your own roof? A total stranger? A black man?)

"I love you, Steve," she says.

"Tell me one thing," I ask in a sudden rush of urgency. "Just one thing."

"What is it?"

"What do you see here?" I hold out my hand and press it against her.

Carla looks at my hand, into my face, then back again. "Your hand, of course," she says.

187

"But what does it look like to you?"

"A strong hand. Well-shaped. A hand I trust. A hand that has done lovely things to me over the years."

"Is that all?"

"Isn't that enough?" She kisses my hand, takes it in hers, presses it against her breast. "Are you pushing your luck? We haven't got all that much time, you know. We're going out tonight—, have you forgotten? I still have to shower and get ready."

"I can wait," I say, trying to smile, suddenly relieved, as if an unbearable weight has been lifted from me. I cannot possibly make love to her now. Not after this afternoon. I don't know how I'll get over this, but I shall try. As long as she does not expect me to prove anything to her—or to myself?— tonight.

At the same time I cannot just drop the matter here. We're in it now; we've got to see it through. Wherever it may take us.

We are still standing close together. I am now looking her straight in the eyes. Those deep green eyes that contrast so perfectly with her hair.

"Tell me," I say gently, "have you ever been sorry that you married me?"

"Oh, many times," she says mischievously. "Every time another man proposes to me I think what a bloody fool I am. But it's too late to change now, don't you think?"

"I'm serious, Carla," I insist. "When you married me—did you ever think it might come to this?"

"This what?" she asks. "We have two really special children, we have a good life. What more do we need?"

"Have I—" I try to think of the words, but they do not come easily. "Have I been—what you expected of me? Have I ever let you down?"

"Letting each other down is part of a good marriage," she says. "It's the making up afterward that makes it worthwhile."

"You really don't want to answer me?" I know that I am really pleading, yet I dare not admit it outright.

"I'm not sure I know what you are asking, Steve."

"We're living in a country where color has always mattered," I say, averting my eyes. "It has always been decisive. In everything, in every way."

"Are we talking politics now?"

"We are talking person to person. We love each other. I've got to know."

"But what, exactly, is it you want to know?"

"I told you: color."

"It's supposed to be a new place now. Nothing is the same anymore."

"But is it? Can we really be sure? Are you sure?"

"We have talked about this so many times," she says with a small sigh.

"Have we? Have we really—really?"

"Steve!" She takes my face in her hands—her lovely, sensitive, long-fingered, white hands speckled with small freckles—and forces me took look straight at her. "What in God's name is bugging you today?"

"White and black," I tell her to her face. "I want to know about that."

"We live in a gray world, Steve. Or a mottled world. Whichever you prefer. That is what matters in the end. We're agreed on that. Aren't we?"

"I'm not talking about the world. I'm talking about us. About you and me."

"So am I. And I think we're agreed on that too. We are what we are. We don't want to be different. We are happy like this. We've always tried to accommodate others too, to make room for others, to allow space for everybody. But we're not going to be weighed down by any guilt, real or imaginary. We are prepared to take responsibility. But not to bear guilt." There is a very long pause. Her eyes do not waver. At last she says, "This has always been enough for us. Let's just keep it like this." Carla raises her face and kisses me. "Then let's go."

I sit down on the edge of the bed, trying in vain to sort out what has been said, what not. I watch her as she moves to the far side of the room, where she turns half away from me to undo the buttons of her blouse. She drops it on the chair in front of her art nouveau dressing table, moves her hands to her back and deftly unclasps her bra, then leans forward to shake her breasts free. Their immaculate, vulnerable whiteness makes my throat contract. She must be aware of it: I see her long nipples stiffen. Then she unzips her tight black pants and kicks them off. Raises one leg, then the other, and slides her small red panties to the floor. Her clothes now litter half the room.

She stands up, looks at me, her hands now resting on her hips.

"You're watching," she says. It is not an accusation or a question, just a tranquil observation.

"Yes, I am."

(Am I comparing, even without consciously wanting to, Carla's body, as I see her before me now, with Silke's, as I saw her earlier this afternoon?)

For a moment she looks self-conscious. She half turns away from me, then back. Her most forthright, unambiguous smile lights up her face. "Feel free," she says. "It's all for you. If you're prepared to wait."

Then she goes to the bathroom, and the next minute I hear the powerful jet of the shower splashing over her.

After that, time gets diverted in a multiplicity of ways. We both get dressed for dinner. We meet the girls in the dining room, where Silke has prepared supper for them. (She has, mercifully, retreated to her own room just before we enter to take over.) I read them a story in bed. There is much cuddling and giggling and running away and jumping back into bed. But at last the household judders down to rest.

Carla and I are just preparing to leave when the telephone rings.

"You take it," says Carla.

It is Lydia. A rather distraught Lydia.

"I'm sorry, Steve," she says. "I know this is the worst of bad manners. But will you ever be able to forgive me if we cancel tonight's dinner?"

"Of course, no problem," I assure her, trying to imagine what could have caused this. "But why? Has anything happened?"

"No, no," she says. "At least I think not. I hope not. But David has not come home yet and I cannot get hold of him anywhere. He was supposed to be here with groceries and stuff for our meal, but he never turned up. I waited as long as I could, but now it's too late."

"Have you tried his cell phone?"

"He doesn't have one. I've been nagging him about it for years now, but he refuses. Says it disturbs him when he's painting."

"He can turn it off, surely?"

"Of course he can, but he doesn't want to be bothered."

"You want me to go and look for him?"

"No, no, I'm sure he is all right." She hesitates. "I have already phoned the police—you know what crime is like nowadays, one isn't safe anywhere anymore—but they couldn't tell me anything. In fact, they treated me—when they answered after keeping me waiting for more than ten minutes—as if I were just a nuisance."

"Is there anything I can do?"

"Not really." I can hear that she is making an effort. "I know everything will be all right. I'm sure he just got stuck in a painting. You know what he's like once he gets carried away. He will turn up. But it's already too late for dinner, I'm afraid. That's why— Perhaps some other night? I really feel bloody awful about this."

"Don't you worry. We're terribly sorry to miss this, of course. But we can always catch up."

"Sure. Thank you, Steve."

I hesitate for a moment. Then ask. "You sure you're all right, Lydia?"

"Of course I am. Please don't give it another thought." An old, almost forgotten warmth returns momentarily to her voice. "Bye, Steve."

"Bye, Lydia."

Carla has followed the conversation from a distance. "So David has gone AWOL?"

"Held up at the studio, she thinks."

"Perhaps he has a new model," she jokes.

"David is not the type."

"I'm afraid not." She looks at me. "Well, what do we do now? All dressed up and nowhere to go."

I shrug.

She comes toward me, briefly presses herself against me. "I could make a few suggestions."

On many other nights—on most other nights—I would have reacted immediately. But tonight there is something intimidating about the thought. (She will find out. I cannot let her find out. Not tonight.)

"So what will it be?" she asks, a husky undertone to her voice.

9

THE RESTAURANT IS A SMALL FAMILY PLACE IN Oranjezicht. Carla's first choice was Blues in Camps Bay, then The Restaurant in Green Point, or Five Flies in town, but I feel threatened by the idea of anything busy or showy. I cannot very well explain my reluctance to her, but she does accept my somewhat exaggerated account of exhaustion following an unusually hectic day (which was, strictly speaking, true). That is when she comes up with Chez Alice, run by a Swiss family, where it seems she recently went to interview someone for her magazine.

Along the way, in the silver Volvo, Carla fiddles with the radio. Not much to listen to. A few music stations, all hell-bent on scaring off anybody over the age of thirteen. A brief snatch of news: President Mbeki has lambasted unpatriotic people who harm the image of the country by saying that crime is out of hand. The government, he reportedly insisted, has the situation completely under control.

"Good to know," she says laconically, and switches off.

From Somerset Road we turn toward the mountain in Buitengracht, where we dip down and curve toward De Waal Road. Soon afterward we park the car and walk toward the dimly lit entrance to Chez Alice, accommodated in an old church hall.

We enter through a curious doorway which might be either futuristic or art nouveau, wholly out of keeping with the rest of the building: it is like entering through an ornate frame, decorated with suggestive willowy shapes that may be over-stylized naked sylphs or figures from the Kama Sutra or musical instruments. It is like entering another dimension, another world, and it gets my hackles up.

"I wonder what architect perpetrated this," I grumble.

"Promise me you're not going to bitch about all the other architects in town again," hisses Carla.

I shrug. I take her elbow and put on a conciliatory smile. "At least," I say, "we don't run much risk of finding anyone we know inside."

As it turns out, our children's piano teacher is there too, Derek Hugo, with the soprano who poses such a threat to Leonie's marriage prospects. Nina Rousseau. And I must say she is exceptionally beautiful. Very tall, unusually slim for a singer, with long, startlingly blonde hair down to the middle of her bare back, expressive hands (I have always had a weakness for sensitive female hands: they tend to set me fantasizing about lewd and secret caresses; and this evening I cannot help remembering, of course, Silke). She is wearing a long, very dark blue dress, with a low neckline that flatters her neck, which is accentuated by a striking aquamarine on an exquisite, very thin gold chain. Hugo beckons us over and introduces us to his companion—even from the few words she speaks I can make out that she indeed has a beautiful voice— and invites us to share their table. Carla, I can see, is eager to accept. But I am still not in a mood for company, and I get the impression that the two musicians prefer to be alone together anyway.

"Bad news," says Carla when we sit down at our own table, right at the back.

"What are you talking about?"

"That woman with Derek Hugo."

"The one that has just dealt our Leonie the coup de grâce?" I briefly fill in the background for her: it turns out that she already knows.

"Never mind Leonie," says Carla. "I don't think this woman is going to be good for Derek."

"And why shouldn't she? I think she's beautiful. Utterly beautiful."

"I don't find her anything special at all." Carla's voice sounds unnecessarily sharp to me.

"Then why were you so eager to accept Derek's invitation to join them?"

"Because I'm curious," she says with disarming frankness. Then makes a dismissive gesture with her deep-red head. "Perhaps I'd like to find out what really turns you on so much."

"I was just saying what she looks like to me."

"And since when are looks a criterion for talent?"

"From what I've heard she's one of the best sopranos in the country."

"In the land of the blind—"

"I really think you're being quite unreasonable, Carla. I think Nina Rousseau is beautiful and talented."

"You're a man." An uneasy pause.

I try again. "There's something about her eyes—"

"What about her eyes?" she asks aggressively.

197

"Mysterious eyes. Exotic. Smoldering. That faraway look."

"Like a dog shitting," she sneers crudely. "If you ask me, she has the eyes of a witch. There's a mad streak in them."

"Now you're being ridiculous, Carla. Or are you jealous?"

"Just intrigued." She pulls from her evening bag the small notebook she always carries around with her. "I think I should interview her for our magazine." She jots down a note. "Did you know that there are some very dark stories doing the rounds about her past?"

"Like what?"

"Not sure. I'll try to find out tomorrow. But some really scary things."

"Come on, Carla. This is gossip-column stuff. I thought you were into more challenging things."

"We'll find out," she says, opening the large menu the waitron has put in front of her. "Let's order. I have heard that their vichyssoise is to die for."

"Then let's die together. And what we will have to celebrate will then be a resurrection."

How can we know that only a few hours from now everything will look utterly, utterly different?

The evening meanders on like a wide, placid stream, forming a small detour here, the hint of an eddy there. I can slowly feel my tension subside. Memories of the day's events recede, lose their hard edge—even Silke no longer seems real; she may have retreated into the domain of dreams and wishes and unrealizable desires from which she came—and fail to disturb any longer the even flow of our dinner and its easy accompaniment of conversation. A few new customers turn up and are shown to their seats. At some tables the patrons who arrived early finish their meal, call for the bill, and leave. For a last moment they are molded by the light on the stoop beyond the preposterous frame of the door, then they disappear into darkness, as if a drawing has been suddenly erased.

It is only when I look down momentarily from time to time and notice my hands manipulating the cutlery or resting on the tablecloth that I remember this morning in the bathroom, that devastating look into the mirror. This one event cannot lose its edge, cannot merge into anything else or subside into dream. It will take time before I get used to it. If ever. Surreptitiously I look around me, making an inventory of the people at the other tables. All of them white. Unusual, for Cape Town. I must be the only black person here tonight. That is, if I am black. Something about it makes me uneasy: not merely the fact of the blackness, but the suspicion that it may be a delusion. That is what gives such a sharp edge to the recollection of this morning. But I clench my teeth. I'm working on it. (Sounds like the authorities at the Koeberg power plant when there's a blackout in electricity supply. They're always working on it without ever really solving the problem.) For the moment, I must try to avoid looking to closely at my hands. It must get easier if I do not remind myself of it all the time. It must. I will. I'm sure it is already better than it was. Perhaps, I resolve with grim—too grim?—determination, I am beginning to cope after all.

The evening becomes a confirmation, not only of our day—together or apart—but of our shared lives together, the merging of our separate histories, the way in which we have learned to live together, to survive together. We have shed old friends, previous lovers; some have emigrated, some have just faded away—or, in recent years, disappeared with a bang in violence of one kind or another. (I remember Derek saying at one of our recent conferences, "Yes man, this is not a country for sissies.") We have folded inward, like sea anemones, to protect what we share, to cherish our children.

Carla gets up once to go to the bathroom. I go outside twice to check on the car: these days one never knows.

We finish our espressos, and our last round of drinks: a Vin de Constance for Carla, Port for me.

At the small table near the entrance I notice Derek Hugo and his blonde companion preparing to leave.

She checks her lips in a small pocket mirror, he pats on the pockets of his jacket, presumably to make sure he has his wallet.

I take it as a signal and push my own chair back. "Well, shall we go?"

"What about a last drink?" Carla, always impulsive, proposes.

"We can have a nightcap at home."

"Yes," she says, with a sudden gleam of wickedness in her eyes. "Naked? In bed? By all means."

This is the moment when everything changes.

We are aware of an irruption from the front door as a bundle of bodies come hurtling inside, shouting incoherently. It takes a while for five separate men to disengage themselves from the group and spread through the restaurant. They are wearing khaki balaclavas over their heads. Designer jeans and T-shirts or sweaters. Nikes. These are not down-and-outs driven by need. This is the New South Africa. Thugs smelling of expensive aftershave.

Everything splinters into chaos. Some of the patrons are jumping up, overturning their chairs, falling over tables. Women are screaming. Somehow it all appears to be happening in slow motion, as in a film. But it is a very bad movie. Not to be recommended. Only the screams and shouting—from the intruders, from the patrons—happen very fast.

Two shots, three, suddenly explode into the turmoil. Only now do we realize that all five men have guns. Mostly pistols; one semi-automatic rifle. That brings sudden, total silence. Except for one middle-aged woman with a made-over face and unbelievably awful hair, who keeps on giggling hysterically as she whines in a high, monotonous voice like a mosquito: "Ohmygodohmygodohmygodohmygod."

One of the balaclava men moves back toward the over-elaborate entrance, facing us. He makes a motion toward the door. Two of his men, quick as cats, move past him and slam it shut.

The man with the rifle, presumably the alpha male, raises his weapon in one hand. Must be an AK-47. "You all—!" he shouts. "Hey, you all—"

Nobody moves. Now he points his gun downward. "On the floor!" he shouts. "You all, on the floor. You sleep."

There is a scramble as we all fall down. It's like a kid's party game. Everybody tries to be the first to be prostrate. (Look what a good boy I am!)

All thought seems to petrify. I am unable even to register precisely what is happening. The only thing that sticks in my mind is a silly, endlessly repeated line: This is it. This is it. This is it.

For a while nothing happens. The five appear to be conferring in low whispers. Our fate is undoubtedly being sealed in this rustling silence. All we can make out is the single repeated command shouted over our heads: "Sleep! Sleep!" The whispers continue. Why this ineptitude? Did they not plan everything meticulously beforehand? Surely one cannot rely on improvization in a situation like this? Unless it really is a chance event, thought up on the spur of the moment? But how come they had the guns all ready?

The discussion is over. "Now you wake up!" the leader shouts. "Wake up! You all wake up!"

We scramble to our feet.

As I roll over to get up, behind our table at the back, a single clear thought strikes me. I plunge my hand into my jacket pocket, get hold of my cell phone, thrust it into my sock, down the side of my shoe.

"You wake up!"

I must be one of the last to get up.

"Now you give us everything," says the leader with the AK-47. (If it is an AK-47.) "You give us watch, you give us cell phone, the jewels, the money. Everything, you hear?" I am trying to place his heavy accent. For some wholly illogical reason I feel that it would be more acceptable if they were Nigerian, Congolese, Rwandan, whatever. Anything but our compatriots.

The four cadres, if that is what they are, the ones with the handguns, start threading their way slowly through the tables, starting from the front. Holding out their hands to accept whatever is offered. One of them has taken a black plastic bag from under his sweater and all the loot is dropped into it.

As I watch in morbid fascination, I see Derek Hugo's companion removing the delicate pendant from her long white neck and dropping it in the bag. She looks deathly pale, her face taut as a mask. Behind her loom the ambiguous shapes of the doorframe. No longer able to bear watching, I look away.

A woman at one of the tables near the middle of the room protests. She will not hand over her watch. The man nearest to her jerks back the hand in which he is holding his gun and pistol-whips her in the face. She screams, and folds double. Blood comes pouring from her nose and spills down the front of her pale blue dress. A murmur of protests, angry and fearful, ripples through the place.

"*Tula!*" shouts the leader. "Shut up!"

The woman keeps on howling. Two of the other assailants come hurrying past tables in their way, knock down a chair. One grabs her by the hair from behind, pulls back her head, as the other jerks up a knee into her face. She gives another scream, then subsides into smothered, snotty sobbing.

"You all hear me?" the leader calls out. "Last time now. You give everything. Everything."

A small, wiry, elderly man standing next to the table where the woman has been assaulted makes a move toward the leader. "Look, we will give you whatever you want, but please leave the women alone!" he calls out with controlled rage. Adding, under his breath, "Bloody animals!"

Not a good idea. Instantly, as if obeying a command, the four cadres converge on him, leaving only the leader with the AK-47 standing at the door. What follows is sickening to see. While the old man is half-strangled in the crook of someone's arm, the others set on him with flailing arms. He drops to his knees. They start kicking him from all sides. His protests turn into grunts and moans, then a pathetic wailing.

"You see now?" the top man calls out from the front. "We want no talk, no nothing. You just give everything."

The four attackers let go of the old man at last, leaving him on the floor in a small crumpled bundle as they proceed with their business. The early impression I had of chaos, as if they were acting randomly, without any plan, has long worn off. This looks more like a military operation.

I become aware of Carla clinging urgently to my arm, trying to say something.

"Don't talk," I hiss out of the corner of my mouth.

She brings her face closer to my ear. "I'm not giving them my wedding ring," she says.

I press against her. "For God's sake, don't provoke them. You saw what happened," I whisper back. "There's no way out here, my love."

"I won't."

"Please, Carla. Don't."

For a moment she is silent. Then she says, "You must talk to them, Steve."

"You want me to be beaten up like the old man?"

She is breathing unevenly. "You're the only one in this place who can talk to them."

"How come?"

Then it hits me. In the pit of my stomach.

She nods against my shoulder. "You're—" She hesitates. "*You're one of them.* If there's anybody here they may listen to, it's you. Please, Steve. You've got to."

I can understand her logic. Obviously. Yet what she is saying is perhaps the most terrible thing I have ever heard in my life. You're one of them. This cannot be what she means: but it is as if she is swiftly, but very definitely, closing a door between us.

From this morning, when I first saw my face in her mirror, the earth has been unsteady under my feet. I have felt it heaving and swaying, like old film footage of the earthquake in San Francisco. But at least I've kept my balance. Until this moment. Now I can feel nothing firm underfoot at all. There is just darkness. A void. A sensation of falling, of tumbling through endless space in free fall. I am sick, sick. Vertigo.

"Please, Steve," she whispers.

"Shut up!" a voice rings through the semidarkness of the restaurant where every flickering candle on a table seems isolated in its own private sphere of light, no communication between them, each utterly alone, enclosed by darkness.

Carla is pushing against me. And I know she may be right. It is now, or never.

I cough to clear my throat. I am aware of some of the patrons looking at me. Perhaps they are thinking the same as Carla. Slowly I take a step forward. "Excuse me," I say in a voice I do not recognize as my own.

"You! Do not move!" shouts the man in command from the front door.

I raise my hands high above my head. For a moment I stand motionless.

"Please let me talk to you," I say quietly.

To my own astonishment I no longer feel as weak and trembling as a moment ago. A curious, unnatural calm has taken hold of me, as if an invisible capsule has suddenly closed around me, shutting me off from the world. This is not heroics. This is desperation. Perhaps it is, simply, madness. But I now know that Carla was right. There is no one else in this obscure silence who can do this. It may still be hopeless. But there is only me.

Between this moment—and whatever else may come.

"What is it?" the leader asks with a sharp edge of impatience. He comes a single step closer.

From nowhere a line filters into my mind. Be a warrior of the light. The mere thought makes me cringe.

"Please do not kill us," I say, as calmly and steadily as I can. "We all have small children at home. Like you, perhaps. We shall do what you want. But do not kill us." It is their balaclavas that make me say this. If their faces had been open and recognizable, we might still have had a chance. As it is, they must realize that tonight they are free to do absolutely anything without having to hesitate or reflect. They can literally get away with murder.

"*Tula!*"

I feel hope ebbing away from me.

But I persist, unable now to stop myself. "Listen," I say, "I know what you feel. I know what you're thinking." I am now speaking very slowly and quietly. "We all live in this country together. We are all in this thing together. I am one of you. Listen to me and let us go. Please!" It sounds so wretchedly limp. But what else can I say? What is there I can possibly do?

The commander stares at me through the gloom. I see the other four turning to face him. They appear to be conferring. But in silence, without a word.

"Please," I say again.

He comes another step closer, but now the movement is definite, unequivocal.

"*Awungomnye wethu,*" he says in a firm, even voice. And suddenly I realize that it is Xhosa and that I understand what he is saying: *You are not one of us.* I do not know how it comes that I can understand him, but I do. I also understand what it means, beyond and behind all the words. An ultimate denial, ultimate rejection.

The man comes still closer. He seems to be growing taller as he approaches, until he is towering above me, above everybody, he is huge. He is a giant. And his shadow spreads across all the walls, the ceiling, the whole place.

He makes a gesture toward the surrounding tables. "*Uhlelinabo,*" he says. *You sit with them.* He stares unwaveringly at me. Then he adds, as if he is spitting out a mouthful of bad food, "*Ungomnye wabo!*" *You belong to them.*

There is a murmur among the assembled people: incomprehension from the whites, smoldering resentment in the confirmation of the four robbers.

Then, with a gesture of derision and disgust, dismissing me, the commander swings away from me. "*Hamba! Hamba suka!*" *Go away!*

The collectors proceed relentlessly on their way. Cell phones, wallets, watches, bracelets, necklaces, brooches, rings of various descriptions are dropped into the black. No one dares to resist anymore. The only sounds are occasional sobs from some of the women, the continued wailing of the first one who had to give up her watch, and sporadic moans from the injured man on the floor. But the attackers no longer move along as evenly as before. Even when no resistance is offered, the loot is wrenched from the victims with excessive force. The women, in particular, are shown no mercy. Each one is slapped in the face, struck with a fist, shoved out of the way or down to the floor, elbowed or jostled viciously in passing. Even when they willingly—some eagerly—surrender their valuables, they are set upon. It is violence purely for the sake of violence. Two or three have their earrings torn from their lobes with such force that they are left bleeding. Slightly built men, too, I cannot help but notice, receive their share of blows in face or stomach, knees in the groin, kicks in the backside. Only the stronger, burlier ones are not interfered with. (Cowards!) I am watching Carla so intently that it catches me unawares when the assailant moving toward me swings a karate chop at my throat that causes me to bend double, retching and gasping, before I know what has hit me. And while I am still standing, bent over, a second attacker kicks me in the stomach. I topple sideways. They pounce immediately, but I manage to roll under a table. A few random kicks still connect with my bent legs, my hunched back, but then it is over. By the time I get to my feet, they have finished with Carla. She stands leaning with both arms on the table, her face covered by a curtain of dark-red hair, gasping for breath, but refusing to cry. A thin line of blood comes trickling from the corner of her mouth.

"My love, what have they done to you?" I ask, trying to cover her with my arms, but she shakes her head violently, fighting to fend me off.

"Don't, don't," she keeps on saying. "Don't touch me."

The black bag filled with loot is carried to where a table has been shoved in front of the main door. Another heated conference takes place. This time the intention is clear: they want to get access to the restaurant's safe. The owner, elderly and apparently asthmatic, is dragged from where he has been huddling, trembling and wheezing, after they hauled him away from the front desk.

"You give us safe keys," demands the gang leader.

"The keys are not kept on the premises," the owner wails. "They're with the security company."

"You lie!"

The leader motions to his henchmen and they start beating up the helpless man. Much sooner than I'd expected, they realize that this will be futile and turn away from their victim; but it is not yet the end.

The aggressors huddle briefly against the front door, some orders are given, and then the four cadres hurry to the back door which leads to the toilets. It also opens to a small enclosed back yard where, it turns out, there is some kind of a storeroom or shed. One of the men moves ahead of the others, fumbles with a bunch of keys—how they got it, I cannot tell; perhaps from behind the counter, or from the belt of the wretched owner—and opens the padlock to the shed door.

We are bundled inside—"You in, you in, you in!"— and then the door is locked behind us. The little space is crowded with bodies. There were a dozen of us when we were held up (I managed to count), and in addition there are the manager and his wife (but he is still with the attackers in the restaurant), four waitrons, two female, two male, and three kitchen staff. Through a high, barred window, dulled by dust and cobwebs, light from a nearby streetlamp filters inside, so it is not totally dark.

"We have to get out of here," somebody says briskly. It is a young, sporty man with wavy golden hair and larger-than-life biceps flexing on his tanned arms. He seemed pretty subdued while the robbers were still in our midst, but right now he is acting with flamboyant macho bravado.

"Why didn't you do something about it earlier?" asks a middle-aged man with a shiny bald head.

"I was at the point of tackling the nearest one," says the muscle man. "But I didn't want to run the risk of one of you chaps getting killed."

Some of the people make disparaging noises, but he seems to be oblivious of the resentment he provokes.

"Anyway," he goes on, clearly assuming that he is in command, "we are in a better position now to break out and have our revenge."

"Feel free," sneers the older man. "Why don't you lead the way, Rambo?"

"You talking to me, old toppy?"

"Can we cut the crap and try to plan something?" asks one of the women. "We may not have much time."

"I think they're just going to let us rot here," wails another, older lady, whose blue-rinsed coiffure has subsided miserably, sitting on her head like a bedraggled hen on a nest.

"We'd be so lucky, Auntie," hisses a young blonde. "If you ask me, they'll come marching back any moment now and kill the men and rape the women."

"I'm sure you can't wait for it to happen!" retorts another woman, as colorless as a field mouse.

"Now, now, ladies," a man with a thin Clark Gable moustache remonstrates. "Let's do something about it. We must try to get a message through to the police or somebody."

"What about sending smoke signals?" jeers Rambo. "Or shall we try to find some empty tins in here and set up a bush telephone?"

"I have my cell phone," I say, suddenly remembering

my earlier precaution which, in all the turmoil, I have completely forgotten about. I bend down and retrieve the nifty little instrument from my shoe.

Everybody starts applauding.

"Good thinking," commends a patronizing middle-aged lady, all dowager but with no teeth of her own.

"What are you waiting for?" demands Rambo impatiently, now that the attention has been deflected from him.

They all huddle around me as I dial 10111, holding the instrument up to the dull yellowish light coming through the high window.

It rings and rings and rings.

All around me mutterings are going up.

"Give me the bloody phone," demands Rambo, as if the delay is my fault.

I keep the telephone out of his reach and try to keep my cool as I wait. (Come on. Come on. Come on!)

Unexpectedly a voice crackles in my ear. "Police."

"For God's sake!" I shout into the instrument. "We're being held up in an armed robbery—!"

"Just hold on," says the voice. "We can't take your call right now."

I hold on and on. There are muffled sounds coming from the outside, but it is impossible to interpret them. They may have killed the poor old manager by now.

I wait and wait and wait. Another few minutes—it

is impossible, of course, to tell the time, as they have confiscated all our watches—and then there is a voice: not the first one, but another.

"You waiting for?" the man says.

"We're in an armed robbery," I say. "This is urgent."

"Hold on, sir."

We go through the whole process again.

This time a voice—once again someone new to the situation, and possibly to the job—cuts through my preliminary explanation to say, "Just a minute, I'm transferring your call to the emergency desk."

But the connection is cut before I can state my case again.

Everything is repeated. Except that, this time, there is a hint of greater efficiency: at least there is a canned voice, saying, "Please hold on. Your call is important to us, and it will be answered."

Then Rambo grabs the telephone from my hand.

With all the bodies, all the breathing, it is getting stuffy in the small room. We are all perspiring heavily. Someone suggests breaking a pane in the high window, but nobody responds. We are all waiting, waiting.

"Godot never comes," says one of the women, laughing nervously.

"Welcome to the New South Africa," says a large pink-faced gentleman oozing bonhomie. He looks as harmless and soft and sweet as a marshmallow.

"What else can you expect?" asks a woman with a sharp, pointed nose. This serves as a password for all the clichés of the past few years to come tumbling out. It is as if everybody has just been waiting to speak their lines—all of them, very obviously, rehearsed a hundred times over. (Some of them, I realize with a feeling of shame, I may have uttered myself.) "When it comes down to it, they just don't have the experience to run a country, do they?"

"It's actually our own fault, you know," the pink gentleman sighs. "We held on for too long. They had no chance to prepare themselves."

"They've had more than ten years now," says a thin girl in what seems to be a beach dress. "And if you ask me, it's going from bad to worse. You know, my boyfriend and I have actually decided to go and join the rest of the family in Perth. This was supposed to be our farewell dinner. Not so, Kevvy?" She spreads tender tentacles all over the limp young man beside her.

He is as white as a calamari, but beams under her attentions.

No one seems to register my presence. Unless they are all, deliberately, pretending to ignore me. Perhaps that is what, just now, rankles most. *Ungomnye wabo*. My head throbs with rage at the mere thought. But I am impotent. I have proved myself to be as impotent as the calamari, or the sea sprite, or the marshmallow, or Rambo for that matter.

"Do you think," a woman asks from the gloom, one of the shapeless mass of helpless humanity under the glare of the dull yellow light that leaks through the window, "do you think the government is in on this?"

"How can you say such a stupid thing?" asks Carla, suddenly flaring up.

"What makes you think it's stupid?"

A bespectacled man with thick glasses through which his eyes peer like fish in an aquarium comes to her rescue. "It's not more stupid or far-fetched than all the stealing and corruption and cashing in that's going on among our so-called rulers."

"Were we any better when we were in power?" asks Carla.

"I should bloody well think so. At least there was law and order."

"And death squads and torturers and crooked police and apartheid ministers fucking their children's black nannies in backyard toilets—"

"But not men who rape three-months old babies or old women of eighty, or who attack defenseless families on farms, or steal money from old-age pensioners, or who live the high life when they do go to prison, or dash to Dubai for Christmas shopping at our expense—"

I cannot take this anymore. What an end to what a day, I think, aware of a blinding headache that is growing worse by the minute. Just stop it, I want to shout. For fuck's sake, stop it! We're all locked up here together and may be killed any minute, and all we can do is argue and talk shit! But what is there I can do about it?

Rambo has passed the cell phone on to somebody else; a woman. I now grab it back from her. As if that will do any good.

The line is still open, crackling. I hope my airtime doesn't run out. That will be just what we need right now.

"Do something, Steve!" Carla whispers almost hysterically in my ear. "Please try to talk to them again. This is a bloody madhouse."

"I'm out of this game, my love," I say stiffly. "You saw what happened when I tried."

"You can try again."

I shake my head, miserable with futile anger.

At this very moment there is a voice on the line once more.

"Who are you waiting for?" a man asks accusingly.

"We are in an armed robbery," I say.

"What is your name and address—?"

"Look," I say, straining not to shout. "Don't ring off, and don't pass me on to somebody else. Just do something to save our lives."

"Where are you phoning from?"

I give him the address of the restaurant. "But for God's sake, hurry up!" I say, no longer trying to control my voice. "They're still here. If you come straight away, you can catch them all red-handed."

The line goes dead.

The other faces are all staring palely at me, like sickly moonflowers in the gloom.

All I can do is shrug.

"Are they at least sending someone?" asks Carla.

"If they come, they come. If they don't come, they don't come."

In the slow, aimless, milling motion of the bodies trapped in the little storeroom, Carla and I are pressed against two of the other hostages. Derek Hugo and Nina Rousseau.

"Having a good time?" asks Derek, grimacing.

"Oh splendid," I say. "Just the kind of night we were looking forward to. A nice change of routine."

"I think we all need a dose of reality," he responds wryly, turning his eyes up to the gray ceiling. "Keeps one from cherishing false hopes for the future."

"Don't be stupid, Chris," says his companion, a harsh tone in her lovely voice. "This is not a time for jokes."

"Perhaps this is precisely a time for jokes."

"If I stay in this stuffy place much longer I won't have a voice left."

"We mustn't be so negative," somebody else says in a strained effort to look at the bright side. "At least we're still alive."

"That is just about the most stupid thing you can say!" the beautiful Nina at Derek's side explodes. "As if something as ordinary and as basic as being alive has suddenly become a special privilege. For God's sake! What kind of a country is this, where one has to be thankful for what the rest of the world takes for granted?"

"There are worse places than this, you know," says the marshmallow man. "You know, I was in the Caribbean recently, and—"

"Then why the fuck don't you go back there and drown yourself in the blue water?" Nina shouts at him. "Or find a nice man to cut you up in small pieces for a stroganoff?"

Derek does his best to move her into a corner where he can try to calm her down—which in this throng is not is not easy. I can hear them whispering urgently in the half-dark.

"Please try to be calm," Derek pleads. "You heard what Steve said. The police are on their way."

"They may just make it worse."

"Can't anybody phone ADT Security or some-body?" asks the toothy dowager. "You know, the police call them in to guard their own stations nowadays."

"Does anybody have a number?"

Somebody does, actually.

Ten minutes later, maybe fifteen, there are siren sounds outside and the police and security arrive simultaneously.

Unfortunately the robbers have left by now. ("They probably couldn't wait any longer," someone comments.)

Something has to be done about the owner of the restaurant, first, and fast. He lies spread-eagled on the floor near the entrance, and he does not look good. But whether they have beaten him up some more or whether, maybe, he has had a heart attack or a stroke, I cannot tell; and there is no doctor among us.

However, the ambulance from Groote Schuur arrives surprisingly quickly. It comes almost as an anticlimax.

Glad to be alive.

After that, we spend three hours sitting around in the restaurant on increasingly uncomfortable chairs, while the police laboriously take statements from everybody present. The scribe turns out to be not very literate and stumbles along innumerable mistakes of formulation and orthography. But in the end it is all done. We stagger out into the cool night air, blinking at a cityscape that suddenly looks completely unfamiliar, even hostile.

Most of the patrons of the place feel the need to shake hands. We must keep in touch, some insist.

Perhaps we can arrange reunions in the future. Should auld acquaintance be forgot and auld lang syne. But Carla and I manage to avoid the others, slipping past them into the dark, through the ornate, surreal doorframe. There is a strange, unsettling feeling about it. As if we are strangers to each other now. As if we suddenly discover ourselves naked in public.

And then we find that our car has been stolen.

10

IT ADDS ANOTHER HOUR TO OUR LATE NIGHT. AT last, just before three, we once again emerge into the outside darkness, heavily redolent of ozone. A young constable—with fingernails chewed down to the quick, but overwhelmingly obsequious—drives us home. The streets are almost deserted. Only in the environs of Long Street are there still signs of life: raucous and extreme, as if each individual hanging round there, driven by obscure desire, feels the need to be as loud as possible in order to affirm that she or he is still alive: Look, look, here I am! Please don't overlook me! After that, as we curve out of the city toward the coast, every-thing dies down again. Night has invaded the place like a tangible presence, a huge dark animal ponderously sleeping, but ready to wake up any moment to pounce on whatever may disturb it.

We drive on in total silence. Only once I dare to break it. It is not even premeditated. At a given moment the words simply break out of me. "What did you mean in the restaurant when you said I was one of them?"

"Did I say that?"

"Yes, you did. And I really want to know exactly what you meant."

"I can't remember. Everything was so—You were there, you should know how it was. I couldn't think straight."

"I've got to know, Carla."

In the flashing light from outside that starkly illu-minates her face from timer to time, I can see her staring straight ahead.

"It was just—" She breaks off, then shrugs. She doesn't look at me again. After some time she tries again. "As far as I can remember, it must have had something to do with living in the New South Africa. They are part of it. You too, in your own way. You don't seem to have any baggage. You can work with whomever wants you to. That's what you have always done. So I thought they might listen to you if you spoke up."

"I don't believe you," I say, very softly.

"I don't suppose it matters anymore." Her voice is toneless, flat.

From Sea Point we turn up the slope, higher and steeper, until we reach our street, the last one claimed—so far—by the urgent push of progress. Further up, there is only the dark flank of the mountain, outlined in black against the stars recklessly strewn across the sky. I see Orion striding on its way. The splash of the Milky Way. The Southern Cross near the black patch of the Coal Sack. All of it so familiar. It should be so comforting, reassuring: unchanging, unchangeable through centuries, millennia, eons. But it isn't. Tonight there is something ominous about it. It is a threatening, alien, unknowable blackness. A dark hole that can suck you in and spew you out somewhere else, in another, alternative dimension, where you cannot ever reach your familiar world again.

"Good night," says the young constable.

"Good night."

He turns in the road, then swings down and roars off into the night. God knows how many other crimes he may still have to deal with tonight. Burglaries, assaults, rapes, murders. And he isn't twenty yet.

We linger at the edge of the road, as if, all of a sudden, we cannot face the prospect of going up along the driveway, following the garden path so skillfully laid out among dark shrubs and flowers, up into the house, one level after the other, past the pool with its stark, clean smell of chloride—the pool from which Silke emerged in the afternoon, naked, trailing her colorful towel after her—and then to the bedroom where we will at last be forced to face each other, alone.

We reach our floor. Our long, wide passage, leading past Silke's door (closed now, sealing its rank darkness inside), and past the children's.

The girls are sleeping peacefully, in innocence and unattainable dreams as light as thistledown. Or are they? One of them—Leonie—is snoring very lightly, like a cat purring in the half-dark (they have a night light on, shaped like a flower with a fairy curled up under it). She moans in her sleep. Something may be hovering, lurking in depths we cannot fathom, ever. The moan turns into a whimper. I tiptoe into the room, lean over her and kiss her on a glowing cheek, straighten the blanket over her narrow shoulders. For a moment she shudders, stretches out her arms, and clings to me. At last lets go again, and now she is fast asleep. (But I know the fitfulness may return.)

We go into our room, where a low welcoming light is still burning. Even before she has stepped across the threshold, Carla has stripped off her dress and dropped it, in her usual, careless way, on the floor. Unclips her bra. I watch the small roundness of her breasts. They are not as firm as they once were, but I find the slight, vulnerable drooping endearing. They are pale in the half-light. The nipples elongated and dark.

Reaching the other side of the wide bed, I start undressing too. We haven't spoken since we drove—were driven—away from the restaurant by the young policeman.

We are naked on either side of the expanse that divides us.

The large window must be open. I can feel a breeze coming from outside, moving through the room, past us, into the rest of the house, where perhaps another window has been left open. Someone must have over-looked it. I may have to go downstairs again later to investigate. Not now. I am too tired. It has been a long day, a near-endless day.

Carla half-reaches out to me. I notice her naked fingers. No sign of her wedding ring. Unprotected, vulnerable, exposed, her fingers seem to be groping for me. But they are unfamiliar, estranged from me, stripped of peculiarity and individuality. They bear no sign any more of who she is, who we are, how we got here. She drops her arm back to her side.

I feel the need to respond. God knows, I want to. Urgently. But I cannot find the gestures or the words.

"Carla." I am not sure whether it is meant as a state-ment or a question.

Her utter silence, like her naked fingers, is a question which I cannot answer.

The night breeze from outside blows more strongly now against my bare body.

Someone should close a window, I think, but absently.

I look at her across the emptiness between us.

"I slept with Silke today," I say.

She doesn't answer.

"I didn't mean to," I say. "Actually, it didn't work out. But I tried. Carla, I'm sorry."

She still says nothing.

It is my turn to stretch out an arm toward her. Even the half-dark I can see how black I am. Except for the thin pale band where my wedding ring used to be.

What made me tell her? I have no idea. My betrayal has nothing to do with sleeping with Silke.

"I must go to the bathroom," I say, inexplicably flustered. "I—"

"Of course," she says.

I go to the bathroom. There is no need to put on a light. I know the place.

The breeze seems to be growing stronger now. I find it inexplicable. This is no ordinary wind, but a blast of clean, cold, cosmic energy.

Then a sound. A sudden crashing sound that scares the daylights out of me. The mirror, I notice, the art nouveau mirror Carla gave me, once, in happier, less complicated times, has been shattered. It hasn't fallen from the wall. It has simply—even in the dark I can see it—shattered, inexplicably, by itself, into a myriad small shards.

Carla comes hurrying from the bedroom on her bare soles, without a sound. (Like Silke yesterday afternoon.)

"Don't come in," I say quickly. "You will cut your feet."

"What has happened?" she asks. "Steve? What has happened?"

"It's the mirror," I say, without looking back at her. "I think we're in for a few years of misfortune."

APPASSIONATA

If music be the food of love, play on
—Shakespeare, *Twelfth Night*

1

Allegro assai

EVEN THOUGH WORDS ARE NOT MY MEDIUM, THEY are the only way to make sure that everybody will know. I am much more at home at the piano. Ever since childhood it has been my dream to become a concert pianist (the vision of posters proclaiming: BERLIN PHILHARMONIC ORCHESTRA, CONDUCTOR CLAUDIO ABBADO, PIANIST DEREK HUGO…), but all it has resulted in is that I am now accompanying more famous and presumably more talented artists. A life like that of the main character in Berberova's *The Accompanist*. How sad. In addition, I am forced to give piano lessons, even if only to gifted pupils. Here, too, there is a sliding scale in operation. One begins with master classes, then you start making allowances, doing favors for friends in the music world, later to their children, finally to friends-of-friends who have little to do with music: a lawyer here, an architect there, preferably someone who has some role to play in the new country and who may at a later stage come to return the favor. It may happen that even in the midst of a busy schedule you may make time for a woman. A beautiful woman, of course. Why not?

But this means crossing an invisible and precarious threshold. I know there are people who find in this the key to what they whisper of as my "failure." Women and music are a suspicious combination, they believe. It has to be either one or the other. Nonsense. I happen to have made something of a study of this. One needn't go any further back than Mozart to prove the contrary. (Old Man Bach may well have been a model of conjugal rectitude, they point out, but with his two wives he did manage to procreate twenty offspring, which must mean something.) Or to Beethoven, who according to one acquaintance "was always entangled in love affairs and sometimes made conquests that might have been difficult, if not impossible, for an Adonis." Or to the wan and sickly Chopin, who was never too weak "to put something in the hole of your D-flat major." Or Schumann, with his elaborate "finger games under dresses." Or the lusty Liszt, who found it impossible to skip anything female that came his way. Or his son-in-law, Richard Wagner, whose inflated ego could be fed only with women. I have always felt convinced that

Casanova would have made a wonderful composer and player of the lute—bearing in mind that famous painting by Balthus of the music teacher playing the pussy of her young pupil like a mandolin. In our own time the register covers anything from the passionate Toscanini, as famous in the role of conductor as he was infamous as a lover, to the Brazilian John Neschling (second cousin to Arnold Schoenberg), who summarized his own lifestyle as that of "a chaser of women and a good-for-nothing." And of course the supremo, Herbert von Karajan. (I realize there are many who do not believe he can be compared to Furtwängler or Böhm or Bahrenboim, but I firmly believe this is pure jealousy. For me Karajan has always been, at least where Beethoven or Brahms was concerned, one of the greatest.) Now obviously I'm not comparing myself to those masters. I am merely trying to illustrate how easily such sweeping statements about musicians and women can end up in a cul de sac. And even if I never became the pianist I had first dreamt of, that doesn't mean that I've ended up a failure. Even in the much humbler category of accompanists there is room for achievement. It need not be an occupation without honor. And this is exactly what I hoped to prove this time, accompanying Nina Rousseau. Because there are not many like her.

I have never been a wunderkind like Wolfgang Amadeus. But I grew up under a piano. In the beginning it was to listen to my mother. Practicing or playing. Then my older sister, Alet. And her friends, when they came for lessons. In due course my little sister as well, and her friends. There's a lot to be learned—and seen—in the course of a lesson like that. Provided you choose your position well. A grand piano is perfect for the purpose. Later, after my parents got divorced and she had some money troubles, she was forced to sell the grand and buy an upright; this drove me to another hiding place, preferably behind the curtains. Much less to see, but by that time I'd mastered different techniques—not just to observe, but in various happy ways to take part.

I suppose I was a precocious child. (But can it ever happen too early?) But I can honestly say that the fringe benefits were never the main dish. I really was, from a very early age, enthralled by music. Even Czerny's five-finger exercises gave me endless pleasure. And the stern metronymic beat of Bach's *Wohltemperierte Clavier*, even Paderewski. But nothing compared to Mozart. From the outset, since long before the divorce, my father had never made a secret of his disgust with my passion for music. That, he repeated in no uncertain terms, was a career for sissies and queers. And although I never gave him any cause for suspecting me of either (I was also a mean hand at tennis, and did well in athletics), he could never suppress his mistrust. If only he'd known!

Instead of turning me into an effeminate boy, music—especially the piano—proved an advantage which even the rugby players and discus throwers gradually came to envy. Music was a brilliant opening to girls. It is amazing how many attractive girls one meets at recitals, operas, and other musical performances. The fact that your mere presence already reveals a shared interest facilitates a next step. Even in the street it can break the ice: pretty women may not make a habit of going about with a harp under the arm or a piano on the shoulder; but any man who knows his music already has an advantage in seeking—and finding—access to an attractive woman who carries a violin or flute or clarinet case on the sidewalk, in a suburban train or a bus. How often during my years of studying abroad did I not strike up an acquaintance with a music student from the Juilliard School in New York or the Royal College of Music in London after an encounter of that kind? Not that it always turned out an infallible recipe. I remember one early morning when a lovely girl with long blonde hair—the spitting image of Jacqueline du Pré—took a place opposite me on the train from Kenilworth, where I lived for a while after returning from London, to Cape Town station. She had a violin case on her lap, and I was promptly seduced by her hands. From the possessive way in which she held the case, it was evident what a role music played in her life.

But on this occasion there was more than music involved. There was something about her, an unmistakable whiff, something that made me suspect she'd just had a night of passion behind her. My knees felt wobbly. For all I knew, this might be a new chapter beginning in the history of music. In my head I was already rehearsing an opening line which would engage her interest well before we reached the main station. But just as I prepared to play the opening gambit, she snapped open the clasp and prepared to raise the lid. I couldn't help leaning forward. What was she going to produce from that case? Perhaps a Lupot, an Urquhart, a Kloz? Or maybe a Guarneri or a Testore? Dared I even think of an Amati, or—who knows?—a Stradivarius? The moment had come. I was already leaning forward at an angle of 45 degrees. One last moment of unbearable expectation. Then she raised the lid.

Inside the violin case was a Cape Salmon.

A great love, carried on the wings of immortal music, was stifled in the bud.

But this was an exception. On the other hand I can recall any number of unforgettable encounters made possible by music. More often than not associated with a specific composer. With the pretty, unruly clergyman's daughter Lulu it was Chopin who provided the access to a Garden of Earthly Delights long before I was supposed to enter in the thrall of such pleasures. There were passages from Beethoven (especially the "Moonlight" sonata and *Les Adieux* and the *Hammerklavier* and number 32) that caused the blonde Margie almost literally to melt. The redhead Karolien found it impossible to resist Dvořak. (Interestingly enough, it was another redhead, the smoldering Carla—mother of my two cutest little pupils, Francesca and Leonie—who recently, many years after Karolien, confirmed the irresistible attraction of Dvořak.)

My first lessons I received from my mother. And she was good, no doubt about that. But we locked horns from the outset. It started with arguments because in her eyes I never practiced enough. I suspect she suffered from a Leopold Mozart or a Johann van Beethoven complex. But I had no desire at all to be in the category of their sons. I wanted to become a good pianist, for sure; perhaps even something of a wizard at the keyboard, but not a freak of nature. And ironically enough, in the years after my father had left us, we started quarrelling because by then she found that I was spending too many hours at the piano.

She wasn't very good with theory either: her forte was playing as such. While in a somewhat unnatural way I was fascinated by theory from an early age: I wasn't content just with playing, I also wanted to figure out why this or that had to be done in a certain way. It was an unexpected little incident that made me decide to leave my mother and find another teacher. I was fifteen at the time. There was a piano recital in the Cape Town city hall. Lamar Crowson, if I remember correctly. Not one of his best evenings. But what I remember was coming into the foyer from the bathroom during the interval and finding in a dark corner an elderly gentleman on a chair, his back turned to the world, with a score on his knees. I couldn't make out exactly what piece it was; all I could make out was Mozart's name on the cover. The man was reading with such ferocious concentration that I couldn't help stopping in my tracks to watch him. And then, as I stood there gazing at him, he pressed an index finger on a phrase in the middle of the page he was studying, and started laughing.

Right there it struck me that there was a dimension missing from my music studies. Until I managed to find out why the man had burst out laughing like that, I simply did not understand enough about music. What I needed to master was not just a new vocabulary, but a new kind of alphabet. The very next day I set to work on my mother. It was not easy: if I am stubborn by nature, it comes straight from her. But after three weeks of nonstop nagging and the threat to quit studying music altogether (something I had never had in mind at all), I won the battle.

My first music teacher after my mother was a young German, Christa. More girl than woman: she had just turned twenty-one. But she had a formidable technique, matched by a theoretical background that amazed everybody she worked with. Her father, Herr Roloff, was almost seventy at the time though he looked closer to ninety: a small, frail, bent little figure that looked more like a mosquito than a man, and with an outrageous white mane—a cross between Toscanini and Einstein— that clearly never came into contact with brush or comb. (Christa's mother, it was rumored, who must have been his third or fourth wife, had started as his student, but then fell pregnant before she turned twenty.) Apparently he had been a conductor in Berlin, but after a few strokes he'd retired from music, although it didn't seem to have influenced his amorous activities. And in the course of time I believe it was more through him than through Christa that I came to discover the inner world of music. In his inimitable mix of German and English he could keep me spellbound for hours with his accounts of concerts he had attended or performed in: the quirks and tics of all the great conductors, the tensions and electrical currents among members of the orchestra (the drummer who had dreamt all his life of an unforgettable moment of his own, and who attained it by rising to his feet in the middle of one of the most serene cantabile passages in the adagio of Beethoven's Ninth, and banging away with all his might on his biggest tympanum for forty-five seconds before he was led offstage and never came back), the idiosyncracies of soloists, all the techniques and strategies one might have recourse to in order to coax from an orchestra, an instrument, or an audience exactly what you desired. After the few years I'd spent in his company even I had learned to laugh—or cry, or fall silent in amazement—with a score in my hands. He drew me so deeply into music that I came to have the weird feeling of no longer being a receiver of a given piece, but a co-composer of it: that I no longer approached the score from the side of the reader or the musician, but from the point of view of the composer himself. That with every new movement or passage or phrase I could sense intuitively what was going through the composer's mind: Let us take a shortcut here—How about turning on the screw right here?—Let's pull out all the stops now—Come, let's rein in the listener and give him precisely what he is not expecting—After that, music was never the same again.

And while he was encouraging me to understand music from the inside, Christa helped me to master the technical tricks and fluencies with which my ten fingers could give, in sound, shape to what her father had made me understand. And so much—so much!—more. Where Herr Roloff's way of talking was delightful and comic—colorful and enchanting precisely because it was so riddled with errors of grammar and pronunciation—Christa's was charming, seductive, musical, irresistible. When she spoke, it sounded more like singing than speech. (Frau Roloff, on the other hand, a tiny mouse of a woman, never really formed part of the setup: it seemed she couldn't ever settle into the South African way of life, and soon returned to Nuremberg, her city of origin. I believe she came out on visits a few times, never for long, and then faded completely from the lives of her husband and daughter.)

In retrospect, I suppose the outcome was predictable—at least for an outsider; but most certainly not for me. And I am convinced that when we made love for the first time behind the piano in my mother's living room (one afternoon when she was giving lessons in the music department at the university and my younger sister and two brothers were doing sport or drama or choir practice or other extramural activities) it must have been as much of a miraculous shock for Christa as for me. Most improper, of course. And if ever the school were to find out about it, we would certainly have been suspended, both of us. But no one ever got wind of it. And until this day I still cherish a feeling of profound gratitude toward this person who had made me understand so much about the world, and not only about music. She taught me all I ever needed to know about finger exercises and staccato and legato and rubato, everything from cantabile to allegro assai. Today I can console myself with the knowledge that with

Christa I was merely following in the footsteps of a Gounod or a Debussy and so many others, who all learned incomparably more from their female teachers than playing the piano.

I never really thought of an end to the relationship with the Roloffs. If something of that kind ever turned up in my thoughts, it would have had to do with the expectation that Herr Roloff's health would finally break down, or that he, or he and Christa together, would eventually return to Germany together. He always seemed to be living on the very edge of death. But then it was Christa who died. In the most senseless manner imaginable. A green truck jumping a red light just as she was crossing with a plastic bag of groceries from Pick 'n' Pay. Instantaneously, apparently. That also contributed something to my spontaneous linking of love and music: from that Thursday afternoon death also formed part of the equation. Christa, Christa. To be complete, not one of the three could ever again exist for me in isolation from the two others. A chord of three notes. In E-flat minor.

Afterward, other teachers took over. First in Cape Town, later in Johannesburg, still later in London, New York, and Paris. Each contributed something to the pianist—and the person—I became. But all of this, however necessary or ingenious or virtuoso it might have been, turned out to be merely embellishments and variations on the original theme. Like Bach's *Goldberg* or Beethoven's *Diabelli*, or Chopin's improvizations on Mozart's "Là ci darem la mano." The basic theme had already been settled, the foundation laid. And from that time, when I was barely fifteen, I have been tuned in to the final movement announced so many, many years later by Nina Rousseau.

It was soon after the catastrophe that I met Nina. The accident that had everybody guessing and speculating—the kind of gossip that could keep some newspapers going for days on end. Promising young pianist Edgar Devine drowned in farm dam: postmortem reveals that he may have been strangled before body landed in water. Rumors about a relationship with world-famous soprano.

And everybody knew about Nina Rousseau, of course. Or thought, or hoped, or guessed, that they knew. The cognoscenti spoke about Cecilia Bartoli and Angela Georghiu or Renée Fleming or Elina Garanča. Apart from Anna Netrebko, no other soprano on the world stage seems to have experienced such a meteoric rise in recent years. Thirty-seven years old! And proudly South African, moreover. There was, first, her breakthrough as Donna Elvira at Covent Garden. Followed by appearances at the Met, La Scala, the Opéra de la Bastille, the Salzburger Festspiele, you name it. Then the unfortunate relationship with the charismatic conductor Werner Schicksal, his tragic suicide in Linz (hanged from a beam in an outbuilding), and her nervous breakdown. After which she rushed back to South Africa to rest, and hide away, and find her feet again. And just as she started thinking about returning to the stage, there was this mysterious accident on the farm in which her accompanist (and presumably her lover) died under such suspicious circumstances.

2

Andante con moto

THERE WAS A BEETHOVEN RECITAL IN THE Baxter on the evening I met Nina. Several of us were involved. In the first half there was the "Spring" sonata (opus 24) by the visiting German violinist, Heinz Stöckli, the "Archduke" trio (opus 97, number 7) in which Stöckli and I played with a local cellist, Maria van Damme, a few arias from *Fidelio* by students of Angelo Gobbato, and then my most important contribution to the evening, the *Appassionata*. The second half, after the interval, was devoted mainly to a couple of the late string quartets, but by that time my attention was no longer fully focused on the music. (At any rate, the stringers were not really evenly matched.)

It was the interval that made the difference. To begin with, I had obligations toward the two friends I had invited to the recital, the painter David le Roux and his stunning wife, Sarah, a photographer: we often went to concerts together, and they have been among my most enthusiastic supporters over the years. From my side, I have a particular appreciation of their work: on my walls are photos by Sarah and several paintings by David. Her work offers a remarkable combination of two qualities which usually tend to be mutually exclusive: compassion and relentless realism. Her camera refuses to lie or to pretend: her black and white contrasts expose all hesitation and uncertainty, relentlessly reveal all compliance or compromise; while her choice of subjects—women, more often than not—reveals an understanding, and in fact a compassion for human vulnerability. And in David's work, particularly in his wonderful blue paintings, there is a way of looking at contrasts and clashes, ambivalences, a kind of bifocality, which makes one realize that the world is never quite as it seems: behind the surface there is always something else hovering to tease and challenge the spectator.

Before the recital, we met in the foyer where I gave them their tickets, and we arranged to meet during the interval. But as it happened, I was drawn into a conversation with Maria van Damme in her dressing room immediately after the trios, during the *Fidelio* arias. We had met before, and of course we'd rehearsed together for the concert, but we'd never really had a chance to talk. Maria is a handsome woman. Strong, imposing, a classical beauty, with an almost frightening passion for music. And I have always had a weakness for female cellists (based on an image no doubt fixed in my id by Jacqueline du Pré). The energy of the interaction with the instrument, the way in which the bow is handled like a weapon—rapier, sword—the defiant posture with legs wide apart. In the back of my mind I always remember Sir Thomas Beecham's devastating attack on the woman who had messed up during a repetition: "Madam! There you sit with one of God's greatest gifts between your legs, and all you can do is scratch it!" There certainly was nothing Sir Thomas could have reproached Maria for. On the contrary. I had been watching her for a long time. But the problem was that she was married. To a piccolo player. Which under ordinary circumstances would not necessarily intimidate any would-be suitor—but he was known for his uncontrollable temper, the kind of man who wouldn't hesitate to shoot. But in the end it was exactly his temper that resolved the matter when Maria decided she was not going to take it any longer. And only a few weeks before the Beethoven evening they were divorced. Which probably explained why that evening in her dressing room revealed so many contradictions in her, one moment she was vulnerable and wounded, the next defiant and aggressive. In the course of our conversation it became clear that we had much more in common than either of us could have imagined—not only music, but an addiction to reading, a love of mountains, a special weak spot for France, even cats. We agreed (not quite definitely, but at least tentatively) to meet during the interval, after my *Appassionata*, in the foyer, followed, perhaps, by a meal somewhere nearby during the second half of the concert.

Then, at the interval, after I'd made sure that Sarah and David had something to drink, Angela Gobbato turned up to introduce me to someone. Nina Rousseau. The soprano. *The* soprano. Recently returned to the country following the suicide of Werner Schicksal in Vienna (and then, of course, the second blow with the death of her accompanist Edgar Devine). The first I noticed was the long, long blonde hair (Jacqueline du Pré once again) streaming from her lovely shoulders down to the small of her back. The slender contours of her body in the long dark-blue gown. The two eyes, blue as a painting by David le Roux—ultramarine, Prussian blue, cobalt, a touch of Touareg blue. Even if I hadn't known anything about her, I could have fallen for her on the spot (even though I'm supposed to be a mature and circumspect man!—fifty-two years old, undoubtedly too old for her; but love has never cared much about age differences). But then Angelo started singing her praises, filling in what the newspapers had missed. Concluding most gallantly, "Derek, if you can persuade this diva to return to the stage, your life will not have been in vain."

I've known Angelo for years. I'm familiar with his enthusiasm and his sense of the dramatic. But with Nina Rousseau he was absolutely spot-on.

As the bells started ringing for the start of the second half, I hurried to apologize to Sarah and David (fortunately this was not the first time I'd let them down like this, and they waved me off, amused and understanding). Afterward I returned briefly to the dressing room to proffer a complicated explanation to Maria, but she had already left: not a promising start to future relations, but right now there were more important matters on my agenda. I would try to think of something plausible later.

Back to the foyer where Nina was still waiting— praise the Lord! We moved outside into the balmy night, found a quiet spot on the slope of a lawn at the back, and started talking in the generous dark.

First, predictably, about my *Appassionata*. Of which she did not approve unconditionally. The *allegro assai* at the beginning and the *allegro ma non troppo* at the end, yes. But she had quite strong reservations about my slow middle movement, the *andante con moto*, which she found too "sweet," too much cantabile, too much dolce, too little *con moto*.

"What about the darkness?" she insisted.

"It is surrounded by darkness," I argued. "The beginning and end are imbued with it. But the middle is meant to be peace and quiet and tranquility, it is inward-looking and serene."

"Serenity doesn't mean sweetness."

"The contrast remains important."

"I agree. But it can only be effective if one doesn't allow oneself to believe that peace and quiet and tranquility—and how did you put it?—serenity can exist on their own. In the very heart of the peace and quiet there must be something lurking. Darkness, danger, dread, a threatening presence, whatever. That was what I missed in your playing."

"Perhaps you're only thinking so—if I may presume to say that?—because of what happened to you. You are conscious of darkness and dangers other people may never be aware of, because you know about invisible things lurking everywhere."

"I think I was born with a cowl," she responded with what sounded like a deliberate attempt at making light of what I'd said. "I've been consorting with ghosts ever since I was a tiny girl."

"What kind of ghosts?"

"There are ghosts everywhere, if only you know where to look. You should come out to our farm one day—it's at the other side of Tulbagh, in the Winterhoek

Mountains. A wonderful old place. Somewhat dilapidated, I'm afraid, because my parents spend most of their time in the city and my brother is always dashing from one wine show to another in Europe or wherever. But it's lovely. That is a place of peace and quiet, I can tell you. At least from the outside. But who knows? There have been people living there for ages. In the beginning, as far as I know, there was a Khoi settlement. And there are Bushman paintings under all the cliffs. Later, of course, the Dutch moved in. But early in the nineteenth century one of mother's ancestors, a crusty old Scot, bought the place. And called it Lammermoor. He had a lot of Scottish baggage, you see. Doted on Sir Walter Scott and Robbie Burns and all of those worthies."

"And where do the ghosts come in?"

"Oh they're everywhere. In the kloofs. In all the old Bushman caves and hollow cliffs. Even right inside the homestead. Under the floors. In the attic. The old people used to tell about a murder that was committed right at the beginning, when the house was first built. A corpse sealed up right inside one of the walls. You should see those walls." She stretched out her arms. "But you really ought to come and see for yourself."

"Is that an invitation?"

"Who knows? I may do just that. But I don't know you well enough yet. Give me a while."

"Sounds like an unusual kind of place."

"Aren't there any ghosts in your own family?" she suddenly asked.

"Not as far as I know. We're an unimaginative lot. City dwellers, all of us."

"Pity. My family thrive on murder and mayhem and adultery and scandals. Can you imagine?—in a place like that, lost in the mountains, all green pastures and waters of peace." A smile. "I suppose that is why I was hoping to find it in your *Appassionata* too."

Our conversation ran on and on. We were like two survivors in the Namib coming upon a pool of water after weeks of wandering in the desert. After a long time we saw the audience emerging from the building and scattering into the night—some downhill toward bus stops and stations and the Main Road, others uphill to the parking lots. And still we went on talking, as if each had recognized something in the other which we dared not let go of again.

The theater lights inside were turned off. The darkness drew closer. The high rump of Devil's Peak appeared more black and louring than it had been.

A nightwatchman came past on his rounds.

"You must not stay here," he warned, lighting up our faces with his torch. "I'm sorry, sir, sorry, madam, but it is not safe to be here. You must go home now."

I stood up and offered her my hand. "Are you coming with me?" I offered. "We still have so much to talk about. What about a nightcap at my place?"

251

"I'd love to." She hesitated. "But only if you promise not to make a pass at me." In that voice. With all the rich darkness of a mezzo—although I was soon to discover that it could reach out to a coloratura.

"I promise," I said quietly, But my thoughts were weighed down by the darkness she had been looking for in my *andante con moto*.

In the car, round the mountain along De Waal Road toward Mill Street, where we could turn up to Oranjezicht, we went on talking nonstop, still glowing with that exuberant feeling of discovery and recognition and affirmation. And even in the house, in the large lounge dominated by my Bösendorfer, it continued.

It must have been at least seven Jamesons later (normally I never have whiskey, keeping it only for guests) before she stretched out her left arm and looked at her watch and said in a voice that sounded shocked, "My God! Do you realize what time it is?"

"What difference does it make?"

"Don't you have appointments and stuff in the morning?"

"Not tomorrow—today. And you?"

"I'm still without a job. I haven't had the guts to face a new start."

"Then it is high time."

"Not yet."

"Nina." I got up to stand before her. "I want to help you to make the effort."

"You have no idea what it may cost you."

"I'm prepared to try. Anything. Everything. I promise." In that intimate, late-night darkness I was prepared to promise whatever she wanted, no matter how outrageous.

"You don't know what you're saying."

"Just give me a chance."

"We can talk about it later. When it's light again. When we've both sobered up." She also stood up, tarrying for a moment. Then, resolutely, she said, "Look, it's too late to go home now. Do you have a place for me to sleep?" Adding immediately, with stern authority in her deep blue eyes, "But only if you promise—I mean promise—not to interfere with me."

"Promise." We sealed it with a very formal handshake.

I took her to the spare room, placed a glass of water on the console beside her bed, fetched a toothbrush and other toiletries from a drawer in the guest bathroom, and then decamped to my own room at the back of the house.

Ten minutes later she knocked on my door, still in the long dark-blue robe she'd worn to the concert, but barefoot.

"Do you by any chance have a T-shirt or something I could sleep in?"

"Let me see."

After I'd made sure that she had everything she might need for the night, I quietly withdrew to my own room again.

Predictably, I hardly slept at all. Still I felt like a daisy in the morning. I made us breakfast—mainly fresh orange juice, fruit, yogurt—and the conversation spontaneously resumed from where we had left off the previous night. Mostly about opera, for obvious reasons. Her favorite roles. From *Gianni Schicchi*, from *Traviata*, Mozart, Donizetti. And the lieder of Richard Strauss, and Schumann, and Schubert, and Wolf. It was a revelation to see how similar our tastes were. And gradually the conversation became more personal as well. The disappointments and loves in my life, and why I had never married. The disappointments and loves in hers. She very obviously believed in living fully. Live now, pay later. Even though every relationship, so far, had ended in loss or failure. But so much more than the facts of her life were involved: what touched me was not so much what she told, but the how of it—the conviction with which she spoke, the passion smoldering in her voice like a barely contained veld fire.

I even dared to ask her about her recent losses. The German conductor, Werner Schicksal. Her accompanist, Edgar Devine. About Schicksal she didn't say much. Only that, in his own terms, he'd loved her very much, but that he'd tried to control her whole life and had been unbearably jealous. She chose not to speak about the suicide and of course I didn't push her. On Devine she spoke with unexpected vehemence, not hesitating to use crass language—which, coming from someone with her heavenly looks, quite startled me. But I soon discovered that she was, at heart, an unvarnished Afrikaner wench, as down to earth as a clod of earth; and that that soon turned out to be part of her charm.

"At heart, Edgar was a fucking bastard, Derek," she said. "A bloody fine pianist, but a low-down shit."

"You were lovers," I dared to point out.

"What has that got to do with it?" Then with unexpected bluntness: "All right, he could fuck like an angel. That is to say, if angels know about fucking. But he treated me as if I was just there for him to use. One thing I can tell you—no matter how shocking it was, I gave a sigh of relief the day he died. That was what made me realize that I had to choose between love and music. It just isn't possible to find room for both. It simply doesn't work out for me."

"But for God's sake, Nina, surely you don't have to go to such extremes." Gazing urgently into her face, I could feel my throat contract at the mere thought. "Any artist manages to make room for both." I hesitated for a moment, then took the plunge: "I have always accommodated both the piano and women."

There was something almost condescending in the way her deep-blue eyes looked at me. "Have you ever thought of where you might have been today if you'd given all your energy to music? I listened very carefully last night, Derek. I think you're bloody good. But you're leaving too many of your creative juices behind in bed. From what I've heard, you fuck too much."

I gasped for breath. "You shouldn't listen to so much gossip," I said caustically.

She shrugged. "That's for you to say. You can make your own choices. It really is none of my business."

If only she could have known how much I wanted it to be her business!

It was at that very moment, I realized afterward— for right then I was too confused to think straight—that I decided: Come what may, Nina Rousseau, you're going to end up in my bed.

Surprisingly calm and self-contained she returned to our conversation: "I'm not you, Derek. I'm not other people. If art and love are two horses you, or they, can harness to the same cart, it has nothing to do with me. But I cannot. I'm what I am, no more, no less. I've tried in the past, and every time it was a fuck-up. I have made my choice, and that's that." With that she stretched out both of her arms on the breakfast table, took one of my hands between hers, looked me in the eyes, and said, "That is why I asked you last night: Please don't—don't ever—try to make a pass at me. It's not because I'm a prude. I may be the very opposite. But if you're considering to work with me, or to be friends, then please put everything except the music out of your mind. Will you promise me that?"

"Do you realize what you're asking, Nina?"

"I realize it better than you may ever think." She was still holding my hand between hers. "This is not a whim, Derek. It isn't madness either. It's—" For a long time she didn't say anything. Then she added very softly, "It's life and death. I know what I'm talking about."

She must have thought that I'd decided against it, or tried lightly to evade it. For she suddenly demanded, "You must tell me now. If you're not prepared to promise, I'll understand and accept it—but then it's the end. Once and for all. And if you do promise, that will also be once and for all."

What else could I do? I took her right hand in mine, as if I was taking an oath, and said, "All right. I promise."

Soon afterward, we cleared the table together, and then she went with me to the music room where the Bösendorfer was waiting.

She sang. Like a fucking angel. In a manner of speaking. *Se vuol ballare. Quanto amore. Che gelida manina. Vissi d'arte, vissi d'amore. Là ci darem la mano.*

When at long last—not just reluctantly, but sadly— we stopped, we sealed with a handshake what had, really, been agreed: Yes, she would return to the stage. And this time I would accompany her.

The news caused an almost immediate sensation. There was even international interest. Given Nina's celebrity, and her recent silence, it was only to be expected that the music world would sit up. What it might mean for my own reputation, was incalculable.

Neither of us was in a hurry. This had to be a recital the Cape would not easily forget. Which was why we owed it to each other to take our time, to ensure that everything, every note, every pause, every gesture, would be perfect.

For three months we prepared. Mainly in the mornings. But often in the evenings as well. The afternoons I had to devote to my customary chores: giving lessons to the gifted and their offspring.

But there was more than music at stake. For me, perhaps more than for Nina, it was an opportunity to get to know each other without any undue pressure. Every day there was something new about her that intrigued or charmed me, making her ever more special. Her dedication and her passion, how she could be playful and light-footed like a little girl, or deeply serious with a frown between her pensive eyes, especially when she was working on a new score, or mischievous and teasing. Or comical, even frivolous or downright silly. Underneath it all there was that brooding sensuality which consumed me with desire. But I kept very strictly to our agreement: while she was slowly rebuilding her confidence and her appetite for life, it was imperative not to make her feel threatened in any way, or to cause her any reason for suspicion or the slightest uncertainty.

Often, when our hectic schedule made it possible, we went out. To concerts or plays in the evenings, or to see a film—she loved the cinema. But we also, unashamedly, pretended to be tourists, drove out into the winelands, or up the West Coast, or went on long hikes—along the contours of the mountain above Camps Bay or from the cable station round Devil's Peak to the Rhodes Memorial, or in Kirstenbosch, or along the Sea Point promenade, or the sandy beaches of Noordhoek between the dunes and the sea, or browsed in the shops and boutiques of Fish Hoek. Or in bookshops. Nina couldn't resist junk of any description. Her whole house—a rambling, half-restored, half-dilapidated old Victorian construction in Woodstock, on the mountainside—overflowed with books and bric-a-brac. Everywhere on windowsills and tables and ottomans and old-fashioned display cabinets and crooked shelves and sofas and chairs the beautiful and funny and precious and worthless souvenirs of her travels and our excursions were accumulated. Dolls, dolls of every conceivable description and provenance, painted chicken eggs, carved ostrich eggs, obscene netsuke from Japan, woodcuts with monstrous phalluses from Africa and India and Indonesia, figures and figurines of alabaster or ebony or ivory, beads of quartz and tiger's eye and ultramarine and agate, tin toys from Taiwan, masks from Mozambique or Mexico or the Congo or Bali, marionettes from Singapore and Thailand, stones collected from the Great Wall of China or the palace of Diocletian in Split or a Mayan temple in Yucatán or the ruins of Machu Picchu, papier mâché from Guatemala or Norway. And mugs from everywhere: Mozart mugs from Salzburg, tankards from Belgium and Bavaria. And glasses from Prague, from Helsinki, from Copenhagen, from Burano. Let alone everything she'd brought back from the concert halls or opera houses where she'd performed: teaspoons from La Scala and the Met, from the Salle Pleyel and the Royal Festival Hall, from the Bayerische Staatsoper in Munich, the Marinskij in St. Petersburg. And matchboxes and soaps collected or stolen from every hotel in every city where she'd sojourned.

She had a story to tell about every item, mostly funny, or endearing, or moving, or scabrous.

"Are you making all this up or is it true?" I often asked her.

"I'm just a good listener," she answered cryptically.

"Who and what do you listen to?"

"To whatever the ghosts want to tell me."

"What ghosts?"

"Each one of these things has a little ghost inside. All you have to do is to tune in to them, then you find out what they have to say. Especially at night, for that's when they come out to play."

"Nina, you're impossible."

"You needn't believe it if you don't want to. But I promise you it's true." As prim as a Sunday school teacher.

Then back to work. Her whole house had been planned around her Steinway in the front room with its barred bow windows—just as mine had been around the Bösendorfer. And every excursion and journey of discovery returned, infallibly, to the piano with its white and black notes. (No sign, so far, of Chopin's D-flat major with its alluring little hole.) Every day a little way further, a little bit closer to where we wanted to be.

Sometimes I got the impression that every day also brought us a little bit closer to where I wanted to arrive. It was no longer the simple sexual desire it had been in the beginning. Every day we spent together, revealing something more of the dark side of her moon, she became, in a much more than readily definable romantic way, more indispensable to me—Nina with her musical voice, her laugh, her sense of fun and her lewdness, Nina with her sensitive hands and graceful feet, often sporting a precious ring on a middle toe, Nina with her dirty stories and her flights of fantasy, her ghosts and fairytales. Indispensable, for sure.

Yet I must admit, probably to my shame, that the way in which she constantly kept me at a distance, evading my attentions even before they could turn into proper advances, the way in which after a copious meal at home or in a restaurant, after a hike or a drive, even after a long bout of practicing or the unexpected bonus of a lied or an aria, would invariably—accompanied, always, by that secret, ironical little smile—offer me her hand, could drive me up the walls. There were many times when I kept tossing and turning in my bed after she'd taken her leave (on many of these occasions she stayed to sleep over in what had soon become, for both of us, "her" room) driving me to the unsatisfying solace of my own hand.

On some occasions this even surfaced openly, especially when a conversation was dunked too liberally in wine or whiskey. Once, after such a handshake, when I dared to bring her hand to my mouth to press an old-fashioned gentlemanly kiss to her knuckles, she responded by doing the same to my hand. And then lightly to hold on to it.

"You can't do this to me, Nina!" I protested.

"What?" As if she had no idea of what I was talking about.

"Do you realize what you're doing to me?"

"No. What?"

I was so carried away that I pressed her hand against my erection. To my surprise she made no attempt to jerk it away. She even, briefly, lightly, folded her fingers around it, gave it a little squeeze, then said, "Poor thing. You'll just have to use your hand."

"Nina, please!"

She leaned over, gave me a sisterly little kiss on the lips. "You know what we agreed." Adding with all the warmth of her heavenly voice, "Sleep well."

It was this persistent, and increasing, frustration that must have been to blame for what happened between me and Carla.

In the beginning she was no more than a voice on the telephone: a melodious voice, but nothing exceptional, nothing like Nina's. The kind of call I receive several times a day: a woman who wants to know whether I would consider giving lessons to her children. Two girls of ten and seven.

"Sorry, Madam," I said promptly, "but I have no vacancies at the moment."

"Perhaps you could just give me a chance, Mr. Hugo."

"I'm really very sorry, but—"

"I can assure you I'm not just another doting mother who believes her children are a gift to mankind. You must have to deal with many spoilt brats. But these two have real talent."

"There are many other music teachers in town, Madam. If you'll please excuse me now—"

"I'm not talking about teachers, Mr. Hugo. You are a pianist of exceptional talent. I heard you play at the recent Beethoven recital in the Baxter, and I—"

"That is most kind of you. But it is quite simply not possible. Good-bye."

One learns to grow a thick hide. But I hadn't reckoned with her perseverance.

The day after the call our departmental secretary came to me in a free period between two lessons, with the news that there was somebody to see me.

I glanced at my timetable, frowned, and said, "I don't have any appointments for this afternoon, Lindie. Did you schedule anything?"

"I don't know of anything either. But—"

At that moment the door to my classroom was pushed open and somebody came inside past Lindie. An exceptionally beautiful woman. Smallish, slim, with the most stunning deep-red hair I'd seen in a long time. And a smile as wide as a blessing.

"Derek Hugo," she said. Not a question, but an irrefutable statement.

"Yes—?" I hesitated.

"I phoned you yesterday."

"I'm sorry, but I don't recall making an appointment."

"We didn't. But—"

"Mr. Hugo is very busy, madam," Lindie interrupted hastily. By this time she knows how to handle such situations. (Apart from that, I should add, she disposes of numerous other talents, none of which has been left unappreciated.)

In ordinary circumstances I would have very promptly brought the conversation to an end. But this was only a few hours after my last practice session with Nina and, if possible, she had been even more irresistible than usual. Her voice had been like liquid fire. The cadences and phrasing and rhythms of her singing were still throbbing through my body. The memory of her long blonde hair was like a river in which I would willingly drown myself. And she had been wearing a light summer dress that had modeled every curve of her long, lovely body in silky caresses. After the last aria, "Oh smania! Oh furie!" from *Idomenio* she bent over and remained standing like that for a while before she slowly stood up again to whisper, "Jesus! What's happened?"

"You were unbelievable," I said.

"I'm exhausted." It took another while before she could compose herself. (Not that I wanted her ever to compose herself again.) Then she looked at her watch and said, "There's still time."

"There is always time," I said quickly. She could not have missed the innuendo.

"Would you mind if I had a quick bath?" she asked. "I'm soaked from head to toe."

I got up. "Let me run you some water."

"I can do it."

"You deserve to be spoiled." I walked ahead of her to her room, ran a bath in the en-suite bathroom, added half a bottle of oil, and took a large white fluffy towel from the cupboard. "All for you."

"Thank you, Derek." She gave me a quick hug, then quickly skipped past me, avoiding me in her usual deft way. "If I'm not out in fifteen minutes, please give me a shout."

She disappeared into the steaming bathroom, leaving me high and dry in the passage.

The door was left open.

That open door has bothered me ever since. Was it an invitation? Any reasonable person could draw such a conclusion. But I knew Nina too well by then. The way I interpreted it—after much harrowing deep thought, I may say—all she'd meant to convey with it was, *I trust you*. And then she'd left it to me to prove that I was worthy of her trust.

Perhaps I'd simply been a bloody fool. But I couldn't run the risk of abusing her trust and forfeit, in the process, everything we had established over the preceding weeks.

A few minutes later I heard her singing from the bathroom. Accompanied by sounds that conveyed that she was getting out, drying herself, getting dressed. The thought of her naked limbs surrounded by clouds of steam was enough to make my knees wobble. But I collected myself, and went to the piano. And started playing the middle movement, the *adagio con moto*, from the *Appassionata*.

"You know," she said on the way to Woodstock in my car, "I think you're slowly getting the hang of the *Appassionata*."

I smirked. I couldn't think of an answer. But the hand she quietly rested on my knee was a much better comment than anything I could have come up with.

From her house I drove to the Baxter, and up to the Music Department just beyond. And here I was now, with that beautiful redheaded woman opposite me.

That was why I didn't send her away. "Look, I can't promise anything. But bring the kids round tomorrow afternoon—Lindie, will you try to find a slot?—then we can have a go."

"Oh thank you very much!" she exulted.

"Madam—"

"Please call me Carla."

"Another of my favorite women's names," I commented soberly, holding on to her lovely hand with the long fingers—a pianist's fingers—just a fraction longer than was strictly required. The next afternoon she was there. With the two girls. Two delightful children, and indeed exceptionally talented. A tad younger than I usually prefer to accept them, but we agreed on a trial period, twice a week; and even before that was up, I told her they could stay on. Sometimes Carla brought them herself; otherwise she sent them with an au pair girl. Blonde and German, most promising. But not in the same category as Carla. What a magnificent creature she was, redolent with mellow fruitfulness.

One afternoon while the au pair was still there with the children, Carla also turned up. She wanted to discuss the girls' progress with me, and after the German girl had gone home with her charges, Carla remained behind. After that, from time to time, it happened again.

It was all very much aboveboard. But there are so many ways of transmitting messages that have nothing at all to do with the subject of discussion at any given moment. And in every respect she confirmed the general perception about redheads: the submerged sexuality, the physical awareness, the passionate tendencies, whatever. Sometimes when I lay awake at night, I felt no doubt or ambiguity at all about my situation: if Nina were to give the slightest hint that she might be available for more than we had agreed to permit between ourselves, I would not have hesitated for a moment. But in the meantime Carla had become a kind of lightning conductor that, who knows, might alleviate the frustration. Not that I was really expecting any fireworks. She was married. She clearly was besotted with her husband, a top-notch architect as far as I could make out, and doting on her children.

And yet—Where there's a marriage, I have discovered so many times, there is always a chance of something going wrong. The old folksy wisdom that marriage is the main reason for divorce. Cynical? But my fifty-two years in this world has not left me blind. And even in Carla I have sensed something of the kind, even if it was kept well below the radar. A casual remark about her husband often being so busy that he has to work well into the night after she has already gone to bed. The hint of a minor irritation here or there: that he didn't share her love of music—that she no longer has enough time to devote to her real passion, ceramics—the way in which, in the first years of a marriage, one keeps dreaming about concerts and adventures (she still hoped to tackle the climb to Machu Picchu one day, to visit Angkor Wat, to follow Gauguin's footsteps to Tahiti) and how you gradually learn to live with compromises, pruning your expectations. Or more specific worries: she loved old things, old houses, old furniture, rambling gardens; for her husband everything had to be new and modern and streamlined and precise. He'd sold their old Victorian house in

Kenilworth and built a new monster of glass and steel without ever consulting her. Actually, he despised her just a little bit—

One afternoon, it must have been about a month after the girls started taking lessons with me, there came a moment when all of a sudden everything landed on a razor's edge. It started in a very relaxed way: she'd arrived just as the children were preparing to go, and we all started chatting. I complimented Carla on the girls' progress. To draw them into the conversation I asked them about their plans for the future.

"What would you like to do when you grow up?" I first asked Francesca. "I hope it will have something to do with music."

"Oh yes," she replied with great confidence. "I want to play the piano in big concert places. And the flute. And I think the violin. And then I'd like to sing, too."

"Don't you think that's a bit much?" I asked cautiously.

"Maybe it is." A small vertical frown appeared on her forehead. "Because, you see, I want to play tennis and hockey, too. And run the hundred meters at the Olympics."

Before she could finish, little Leonie pushed her aside to take over the limelight. "When I grow up," she announced, "I want to be a widow."

Both Carla and I gawked.

"You know my best friend, Danita?" Leonie continued, unperturbed. "Well, she has an aunt who is a widow. And she is terribly rich and she has beautiful clothes and she travels all over the world and she always brings us chocolates."

"But do you realize what it costs to become a widow?" I asked with a straight face. "Your husband will have to die first."

Leonie reflected for a moment. "Oh that's okay," she decided. "You see, men are so useless. I'd much rather travel all around the world than just stay at home all the time."

"But suppose he doesn't want to die?" I asked.

"*Ag*, then I'll just kill him or something."

Thereupon Carla quickly thought of something to conclude the conversation. Just then the au pair also turned up—that sexy little slip of a girl—and took Francesca and Leonie home with her.

"You coming with, Mummy?" asked Leonie.

"I'll be coming a bit later," said Carla. "We still have a few things to discuss."

I gave them a few minutes to get on their way, then went to close the door after them. There was, suddenly, something very definite about the gesture.

"I hope you realize how very special those two are," I told her. "Even though Leonie is clearly headed for the gallows."

She couldn't handle flippancy as smoothly as I had. "Children aren't everything," she just said, almost solemnly.

Perhaps, I thought afterward, Leonie's naïve childishness had moved something like a shadow across the day, as if a very beautiful woman had suddenly veiled herself in black.

I came closer to her. Very close. "Carla, what's the matter?" I asked.

That was when she told me about their previous home and the move to Fresnaye.

"Please don't get me wrong," she said suddenly. "I don't want to criticize or anything. And in many respects Steve is exactly the kind of man I need. We understand each other. We feel the same about so many things." The briefest of pauses. "The sex is wonderful." Followed by a much longer pause. Then her voice grew darker and she spoke more slowly. "But you know, that's not all there is to life. Sometimes I wake up at night and just lie there peering into the dark, and then I start wondering: Is this all? Is this really all? And I can't even explain to myself what it is I'm missing. Perhaps it just comes with growing older."

"How can you talk about growing older?" I asked very sharply. "For God's sake, Carla, you're not even in your prime yet. Everything can still happen. The whole wide world is lying there just waiting for you."

Without knowing how or why it had happened, I realized that our discussion had become deeper, darker. I started telling her about my frustrations. Not about Nina, of course: that would be a kind of betrayal I couldn't even think of. But about all my early dreams. Those posters: Berliner Filharmoniker. CONDUCTOR CLAUDIO ABBADO. SOLOIST DEREK HUGO—what had become of it all? Here I was stuck in giving lessons. Or accompanying really gifted artists. Like, one of these days. Nina Rousseau. But where did it leave me? Was that what I really and truly wanted? Was that what I should like to remember one day when I was as old as Wilhelm Kempf was when I heard him play in Paris (breaking a string on a Liszt)? Or Arthur Rubinstein in Chicago? Or Sviatoslav Richter—?

In some inexplicable way she had landed next to me. She was stroking my hair. And I knew: once a woman gets her fingers into a man's hair—That is the first intimacy.

"Don't talk like that, Derek," she said. "It's people like you who make it possible for others like me to go on dreaming. To go on believing."

Whatever it was, I did not answer. I just moved in behind the piano and started playing. Dvořak. There are times, I know from long experience, that music can convey more, and take one further, than words.

That was a moment, I'm sure, I could have taken her in my arms. But I know that something in me

273

was still holding back: I couldn't do it to Nina. (Even though the thought made no sense: there was nothing at all between us about which I could "do" anything. She had made that so very clear, so many times. Or was it, rather, a fear of betraying something of what I felt for her—and therefore in some strange way a form of betrayal of myself?) But my reserve might also have had something to do with her, with this woman, Carla. To hold back, precisely at a moment when her yielding seemed possible, even likely, not to abandon myself, might in fact render the next abandonment easier, more pleasurable. After the sonata I remained seated without moving for some time. Then stood up and turned to her. She was standing there, waiting. Her lips slightly parted. A whiff from her, the merest hint of a fragrance, that suggested: Here I am. I am ready for you.

And then the telephone rang.

It was Nina. She knew that I had no pupils scheduled for that hour. She wanted to discuss our practice that evening.

After the call, as I replaced the phone, Carla was standing at the door, her small handbag neatly tucked in under her arm.

"I'm sorry," I said. "That was my—It was Nina."

"It doesn't matter. It was time to go anyway. I've already taken up too much of your time."

The next moment she was gone.

The next step caught me unprepared. If during one of my nocturnal waking hours I had to predict what would happen next, I might have guessed that Carla would either come up with a full-scale new onslaught, continuing from where we had been obliged to let off, or not to return at all. What happened was that for the next lesson she brought her husband with her. Was it a way of showing schadenfreude? Or of bolstering shaken bravado? Even a complicated, feminine way of "putting me in my place"? If I was baffled, I don't think I showed much of it. And she pretended that she was simply using the opportunity of introducing me to the rest of the family.

I rather liked her husband, Steve. A bit of a show-off, as if he felt obliged to prove something to himself, compensating perhaps for some deficiency, some early sense of deprivation? But a well-cultivated man, even though—as Carla had duly warned me—not much of a music lover. What did somewhat surprise me was that he knew about Nina, had heard her name, had seen photos of her. (I got the impression that Carla was not very pleased to learn about it.) He even knew about our upcoming concert. For the rest, he clearly doted on his children. And he seemed over-demonstrative about his wife. I had the impression that the moment they arrived home he might drag her to bed to reconfirm his claim on her. As if that was really necessary. (But between them, perhaps, it was.)

They didn't stay long. Everybody assured everybody else that we would meet again, soon, get together for drinks or a meal, at their place or mine; and that they—or Steve, at least—would most certainly be coming to the concert in three weeks' time.

After that they left. I stayed behind to gather from my music room what I meant to take home with me; then locked up and left. Here and there in practice rooms students were still at work. A couple of pianos. A contralto practicing her arpeggios. Farther down the passage a flute. Still more distant, a cello. I often find the most magical moment of a concert this tuning of instruments before the music begins: a fluid world of sound like the void-and-without-form of the world before creation. And our building during practice hours reminds me of it. Everything is still tentative, nothing formed or definitive as yet. Anything may yet happen.

Only a few days later there was a turning point. Both Nina and I were exhausted after a succession of utterly depleting—yet deeply satisfying—sessions; and we decided to take the evening off for a meal out. Moreover, we had reason to celebrate: that afternoon, at last, we had finalized our program. I had bought a small gift to pay homage to her: a delicate golden chain with an ultramarine pendant. By that time I knew that blue was her favorite color. With her shimmering blonde hair the effect was amazing.

It was my turn to choose the restaurant, (how different everything—everything!—would have been if it had been her turn!) I remembered the place after a meal with some of my colleagues: a peaceful interior (it used to be a church hall, but had been renovated and furbished very tastefully), quite close to my home in Oranjezicht, with muted, unobtrusive classical music, fine food, candles. Just what we needed, we agreed. The place was called Chez Alice and there were subtle reminders, particularly in the mirror-like entrance, of entering into a different kind of space.

The summer evening was balmy and gentle to the face, and we decided to walk the two or three blocks from my home. Not a very wise decision in retrospect, but this is such a laid-back quarter that the violence and crime the newspapers constantly rant about seem like rumors from a distant land. Moreover, our regular long walks along the mountain or in Kirstenbosch or the long beaches at Kommetjie or Noordhoek had always been so relaxed that we had more than enough reason to feel completely at ease. It was only a fortnight before the concert and such a little haven of peace and quiet was exactly what we needed.

The elderly owner, a generous little man who loved talking about music without ever making a nuisance of himself, offered us a table close to the entrance, where we could still enjoy something of the evening breeze while we had our meal.

Just after we'd taken our seats I gave her the small velvet box with the necklace. She was as delighted as a child. After she'd hung it round her neck she leaned over the table to give me a thank-you kiss.

"This is just for now," she smiled. "I promise you there will be a proper thank-you as soon as we're alone again."

What could she have meant? Nothing really unpredictable, I suppose. And yet—! As on so many other occasions I couldn't help feeling an almost feverish anticipation.

We were still busy with our hors d'oeuvres—a shrimp cocktail for Nina, avocado and thin slices of smoked chicken for me—when two familiar faces appeared in the doorway: none but Carla and her husband (what was his name again? Yes, Steve, of course, the architect). It was he who first recognized me and approached with outstretched hand: Hail, fellow, well met. Carla seemed slightly hesitant. With reason, I suppose. I introduced them to Nina, trying to make up my mind whether I should invite them to join us; but that might turn out awkward, and we would really prefer to be together on our own. Still, there was something electric in the atmosphere. Even at that moment I was thinking that, in spite of what had happened—or not happened—between us, it might not be impossible for Carla and me to resume, one day, from where we had been interrupted.

Steve and Carla proceeded to their own table, fortunately quite far from ours, so we could continue to eat and talk in the cozy ambience of the candlelight. Even though it was supposed to be an evening of relaxation and escape, we could not get away from the recital: every aria, every movement in each aria, discussed separately and in relation to the others; Nina's view of each turn and repetition, and of what she expected of me as her accompanist.

We were so engrossed in our conversation that we were barely conscious of what was going on around us. It was only when I looked at my watch and discovered how late it was that we realized, surprised, it was time to think of going home. She would be spending the night at my home again. By this time it had almost become routine. And yet, on this occasion, there was the prospect of her promised thank-you. But I did not want to let my excitement get out of hand. Even if it were to end, as every other time, in disappointment, I would try to accept it in advance.

I called for the account and prepared to pay.

At that moment there was a commotion at the front door and a group of masked men came storming in from outside. Brandishing guns in their swinging hands. My first reaction was indignation about the melodrama. For a moment I thought it was some kind of student prank. But I was immediately shocked into a double take. This was no prank. The men were deadly serious.

I still find it difficult to recall the details of what exactly occurred in the chaos that followed. If I remember correctly, we were all ordered to stand. Then to lie down. Then to get up again. They demanded everything we had with us: money, credit cards, cell phones, watches, jewelry, rings.

We both, in the same instant, thought of Nina's pendant. She raised her hand to her throat and pressed it against her collarbone.

"Derek!" she whispered urgently. "Derek, they're not going to get this."

"There's no point in asking for trouble. We've just got to do whatever they want. Otherwise—"

The words were suspended heavily between us, like a hard, dead weight.

What that otherwise might be, we preferred not to know. Perhaps the fact that they were all masked was a good sign: without masks they might afterward be identified by any of us, which might make them decide to kill us. But how could one be sure?

Every thought in my mind remained preoccupied with Nina. The program we had just finalized. Our concert in two weeks. The pendant. Nina's whispered words: *I promise you there will be a proper thank-you as soon as we are alone again.*

It was almost impossible not to lose all control.

From there on the confusion in my mind only gets worse. What I do remember is that at a given moment Steve approached the attackers. Which was a reckless, foolhardy thing to do. And I remember the offensive, arrogant, domineering way in which he tried to intimidate them. As if he'd been delegated to negotiate on behalf of all of us. It made me furious. What right did he have to act like that, to place us all in jeopardy? Throwing his weight around like that while our lives were at stake! Didn't the man realize—?

I think one of them pushed him back. That took the stuffing out of him. All for sweet blow-all. But at least it did not seem to make things more dangerous for the rest of us.

Moments later we were all herded into a store-room in the backyard like a flock of sheep. The door was locked.

There Steve took the lead again, although this time it was really Carla's doing. She stuck her hand into her bra and took out a cell phone. She must have hidden it there while we'd all been cowering on the floor. She quickly pressed it into Steve's hand. He dialed the police. Once again I was infuriated by the way in which he tried to order them around. It surprised nobody when they made him hold on and on. Inside the shed it was getting more and more hot and stuffy. Some of the women were getting hysterical. Most of the men were not acting very impressively either. Steve's bravado evaporated pretty soon when the police failed to react as promptly as he'd hoped. But I couldn't waste too much time on him. I was in quite a state myself. And I had my hands full with Nina.

I suppose it was everything she'd had to cope with over the last few years—the suicide of her conductor, Werner Schicksal, the mysterious death of her lover-accompanist on her family farm—that made her react so immoderately. She was talking non-stop, in a bitter, bitchy, nagging, quite incoherent way. About the coming concert, nothing else. As if we'd already lost everything. She even started blaming me, as if it was all was my fault. It was I who'd brought her there, it was I who'd—

It came almost as a relief when Steve came to me in the throng and struck up a conversation. Hardly a conversation. Some wisecracks, a few stupid, almost offensive attempts to make jokes. Even so, in those circumstances, it was a necessary diversion. Until I was forced to return all my attention to Nina.

And then, unexpectedly, it came to an end. People from a security company arrived, with the police hard on their heels. It still took an eternity to take down statements from everybody. But at last, long past midnight (one had to guess the time, nobody had a watch anymore) we could go out into the cool darkness of the night—as peacefully as if nothing untoward had happened at all. We walked the few blocks home. Nina was carrying her shoes in one hand.

My keys had been taken, of course, but I always keep a spare master key behind a bougainvillea in the garden, so it was easy to get into the house.

Nina immediately went to have a bath. I'd expected her to turn in directly afterward, but—like me—she was clearly too wide awake from shock to think of sleep. She came to sit with me in the music room, wrapped in a blanket from head to toe. Much too warm for such a balmy night, but in spite of this she had bouts of cold fever that made her teeth chatter uncontrollably.

I poured us Jamesons. Except that this time we were mainly silent, it was like that first night we'd returned from the Baxter and went on talking until nearly daybreak; and when at last we'd gone to bed, she had worn my old T-shirt while I'd spent most of the night thrashing and spinning about in futile frustration. Since then, I could not help thinking, every single thing in my world had changed. Completely. And yet it all seemed, on the surface, no different from before.

We kept on drinking in silence, and every now and then I refilled our glasses.

Only when the first light came oozing through the large bay window she turned her beautiful eyes to me and asked, "Well? What now?"

"How do you mean, 'what now?'"

"We cannot just go on as if nothing has happened."

"It's been a terrible night," I said cautiously, my jaws tight because I'd had too much to drink. "But if you look at it properly, nothing has really happened. We managed to get through it all without anybody getting really hurt."

"Nothing can be the same after this, Derek."

"It depends on us." On unsteady legs I went to her and kneeled on the floor in front of her. "We cannot— we dare not allow this thing to disrupt our lives. What has happened was truly terrible. But now it's over. We can only go on."

"How can you say that? It will never be over."

"Only if we allow it to stay with us."

"It will haunt us forever."

"You and your ghosts." I wanted to sound flippant, but my tongue was unwieldy. "I thought you'd learned long ago to cope with your ghosts."

"Not with something like this, Derek." She emptied her glass, like many times before, shivered lightly and pulled a face, then held her glass out to me, empty.

"You sure?" I asked.

She merely nodded. I had my doubts, but dared not turn her down. I went to pick up the nearly empty bottle and poured for her. Not for me this time.

"What about our concert?" she suddenly asked.

"What about it?"

"We'll have to cancel."

"No!" I was beside myself with consternation. "It's got to go on as we'd planned it. We've got to!"

"You mean, even if the country goes to hell, the show must go on?"

"We'll make music because we've got to prove, now more than ever, that we need music. It's more important than thugs and violence."

"It won't be so easy."

"Of course not. It's not easy at all. Perhaps it will be the most difficult thing we can think of doing. But we've got to. Otherwise we've lost. And then everything will be lost forever."

She slowly shook her head from side to side, but said nothing.

When I looked up again after some time, she was fast asleep, snoring lightly through a half-open mouth.

I took my time to get up, considered for a moment to pick her up and carry her to her room and put her to sleep there. But suppose she woke up? She needed this oblivion. At the same time I didn't want to abandon her here. What if she woke up unexpectedly to find herself alone? And so, with a weary sigh, I turned round and settled as well as I could on the sofa opposite her large easy chair. Not for a moment did I expect to drift off. Yet when I came round again, it was high day and the sunlight was stabbing at my eyes like the knife of an attacker. The headache was unbearable.

Nina, as far as I could make out, was still fast asleep.

But when I returned from the kitchen, with fresh orange juice and strong black coffee and a few slices of toast on a large tray, she woke up. For a moment she stared uncomprehendingly at me, clearly unaware of where she was or who I might be. But then she moved on her chair, stretched out her legs, groaned, pressed two fists against her eyes, and asked in a daze, "What the fuck has happened?"

As I tried to explain, she started remembering. But she was in a wretched state. I tried my best to make her eat something, then coaxed her into drinking the juice and the coffee, stuffed a handful of pills into her mouth, helped her to her bed, drew the curtains, and left her. Even before I'd reached the door she was fast asleep again.

I groped for something to mend my own headache, then telephoned the Department, asked Lindie to cancel all my appointments for the day, and went to my own bedroom to dive under myself. Toward evening I woke up. Some time afterward Nina came stumbling from her bedroom, and once more I offered her some juice and something to eat. Slowly life began to move on track again, like my grandfather's old Ford coughing and wheezing in the mornings. But it was only the next day that we could start talking about the future again.

In the beginning Nina remained fiercely and unreasonably set against any idea of even thinking about our concert. Only very slowly, through several days, could we start discussing it again. To cancel, was unthinkable. But it took endless patience before I could persuade her just to think about it again, instead of flying into a senseless rage the moment it was mentioned. For the moment, all she wanted to do was rest. Just rest.

That was how we decided to go to her old family farm on the other side of Tulbagh and spend a few days in the mountains. Out of the world. Out of reach of all demands and expectations and obligations.

If we came back to find that she still couldn't face it, I promised, we would abandon the concert. But at the very least we should keep the options open. Give it a chance. See what happened.

3

Allegro ma non troppo

O F THE ROAD TO TULBAGH, PAST WORCESTER, I remember very little. For most of the time Nina remains sitting with her head against the window, dozing. I am listening to a CD, Beethoven's early sonatas, abandoned to random thoughts. Green and blue the world flows past. Gradually the mountains draw in more closely, enfolding us, contracting our space. It truly feels as if the whole known world, everything familiar, is falling away from, us. What is left, was only us, here, now.

In the late morning we turn off from the dirt road and cross the rattling motor grid into a long lane of gnarled oaks that look as if they have been guarding the entrance to the farmyard for centuries. Through the

trees one catches glimpses of the whitewashed homestead: originally built in the early nineteenth century,
Nina has explained, but rebuilt and added to like a nest
of sociable weaver birds as and when family needs
dictated. Now it is a rambling, congenial mess. Massive
walls, an attic upstairs, with a rickety outside staircase
leading up to it; wide stoop with an old-fashioned curved
veranda and small diamond-shaped windows on either
side, with panes of colored glass. It immediately
reminded me of my grandparents' home in Wellington.
But it also brought back other memories. For a while I
couldn't trace them clearly, but gradually they returned:
it was one of a cluster of old Victorian houses in
Claremont. Where I once spent a pleasurable week.
With a girlfriend, of course. Her parents had gone away
somewhere and we had to look after their cats—a very
musical brood with names like Mozart, Figaro, Susanna,
and Papageno. (But we were so occupied with each other
that we didn't pay much attention to the cats.) An unforgettable week, in which the old canopied four-poster in
the main bedroom, an heirloom from some distant past,
collapsed one memorable afternoon. It was the most
beautiful of the group of old houses left in the area,
tucked away in a quiet, shady quarter which somehow
had been overlooked by developers and had remained
untouched among the encroaching flat buildings and
shopping malls sprawling all over the place with

American brashness. But only a few months after our memorable *Hochzeit* in that delightful old place everything was sold and demolished and replaced by a monstrosity of a building with the depressingly predictable name of Claremont Heights. I once tried to visit friends there, but got so hopelessly lost in the ultramodern labyrinth that at one stage I thought I'd never get out of it alive. Afterward, whenever I wished to see them, we would meet at Cavendish or somewhere else, not just because I was scared of getting lost again but it was so depressing to remember the wonderful old home that had once stood there and where the girl and I—I know she was a cellist, but cannot for the life of me recall her name—had spent such an unforgettable week.

And now I seem to recognize, in Nina's old—and much rebuilt—family homestead of Lammermoor, the spitting image of that long-lost dream place. Originally conceived, she has told me, by a maternal ancestor who had moved in some time after the arrival of the British settlers and wished to commemorate his loved, lost fatherland by bestowing on it this name from Walter Scott.

The most striking addition to the homestead is the solid, old-worldly bars and grilles protecting all the doors and windows.

"One will certainly feel safe here," I observe in flippant mood, remembering our recent visit to Chez

Alice. "I'm sure absolutely nothing and no one can get in here."

"Not out either," Nina says cryptically. She opens the trunk and takes out her suitcase. "Come, I'll show you."

She takes me round to the back door: the front door key, it appears, has been in her brother's keeping and he forgot to hand it over when he left for a wine show in Bordeaux. Behind the heavy grille the back door has been painted a bright sunflower yellow. But it is clearly of recent inspiration, and done rather hurriedly, as there are still small patches of the original color visible through the yellow. It obviously used to be blue.

I follow her with my eyes as she strides on ahead of me: the grace of her movements, her long legs in the faded jeans, the brief loose top, her feet in skimpy sandals, offering glimpses of her soles as she walks. The swaying of her long hair, loosely gathered in a ponytail that swings to and fro in pace with her easy gait. Honey-blonde, wheat-blonde; amber-blonde in the deeper shadows. I can feel my throat constrict at the thought of being here alone with her over the next few days and nights, just she and I. Everything ponderous with possibility, heavy as swollen summer grapes. Even though I remain only too conscious of her grave warning: *You're not allowed to make a pass at me*. I know only too well the fragile tension of her nerves. After the trauma in the restaurant it is imperative that she be allowed to relax completely. And for that she needs to trust me implicitly. Otherwise—oh yes, indeed, I'm only too conscious of all that. But it still cannot prevent me dreaming, perhaps hoping.

From the back stoop we have a clear view of the whole wide Winterhoek valley, all the way to the Witzenberg range opposite. Patches of green vineyard, dark orchards, interrupted here and there by a golden wheat field. The stark white of houses and outbuildings—sheds, cellars—most of them thatched, surrounded by so much generous green. Three bateleur eagles circling lazily high above the valley, their calls almost inaudibly distant in the blue sky. A sense of space opening around us in all directions. Just the two of us in all this infinity, this abundance of green and blue. She and I. Nina and I. Islanded in days—and nights—of music.

She unlocks the door and escorts me on a guided tour of the homestead. Somewhat to my disappointment the interior does not resemble that long-ago house in Claremont. A random assortment of rooms which confirms the first impression of a sociable weaver's nest: a large kitchen with a black Aga stove built into what must have been the original wide hearth; a vast front room with a table that must be able to seat sixteen people—and then, unexpectedly, a gleaming black

Bechstein against the inside wall. From there a long passage with broad floorboards of Oregon pine stretches all the way to the front door.

Directly opposite the dining room is Nina's bedroom. The door is open and in passing I can see an enormous four-poster which immediately brings back memories of that distant week with my nameless cellist—the only aspect of this house that revives that early experience. But I resolutely suppress all the thoughts it stirs up in me. And Nina doesn't hesitate for a moment before leading me further. On either side of the passage are framed photographs, many in antique oval frames, most of them yellowed, or printed in sepia, others more recent—including several of Nina in a variety of opera roles, either on her own or with other singers: Bryn Terfel, Rolando Villazon, Placido Domingo.

Among the older ones there is one that makes a particularly strong impression, and I believe this is significant: a young couple, he seated, she standing, in formal gear. Presumably from the time of the Boer War. In spite of the stern pose something in the young woman immediately touches me: clearly a very beautiful girl, with long black hair wound up in a braid high on her head. One gets the impression of a person who might readily roam about the mountains barefoot without caring a hoot about what people might say. The man appears rather ordinary, almost nerdy, in his high collar with turn-up ends, like a moth that has tried to fly up his neck and then given up, his formal suit, the chain of a pocket watch draped over a stomach not yet visible but clearly ready to start showing itself soon. Her grandparents, Nina explains.

One thing in particular strikes me, even though I have an idea that it used to be quite commonplace in its time: the man is seated, while the young woman stands next to him.

"How come?" I ask her. "It seems most unacceptable to me."

Nina smiles. (The first carefree smile I have seen on her face in the last two weeks.) "That's easy. Family rumor has it that this was taken just after they returned from their honeymoon. At that stage, the story goes, Oupa couldn't stand. And Ouma couldn't sit down." Adding wickedly, "You see, we are a rather hot-blooded family."

"What happened to your grandmother? I suppose she had twenty-one children and then died a good Christian death?"

"Sadly no," Nina says. "She had only one child. My mother. You see, she was never meant to be a farmer's wife. She wanted to see the world. And she wanted to sing. I'm sure I inherited my voice from her. But there was no way, in her time, in her surroundings, to break away and follow her own head. The only chance she ever had to sing was at Communion or suchlike functions. Can you imagine—?" She breaks off abruptly. "But you know, I have an idea that in his own way my oupa did try to understand. A year after the wedding— against all the dire predictions and warnings of the family—he allowed her to go overseas. Even though one of her mother's sisters had to go with her as a chaperone." A pause. "She stayed away for a full year. They never wanted to talk much about it, but as far as I could make out, she left the aunt behind in London or somewhere and went on alone—to Paris and Vienna and Milan. Everywhere she went to concerts. Opera, especially. This is what I managed to piece together from casual remarks over the years. If you ask me, she would never have come back on her own."

"Money ran out?"

"That too, I suppose. But there was another reason. When she came back, she was pregnant."

"But—"

Nina nods. "And hard on her heels an Italian followed. Quite by chance, everybody tried to argue. But it was only too obvious what was going on. The man even came to visit the family here on the farm."

"And then?"

"He died before he could go back. Very unexpectedly."

"An accident?"

"Nobody knows for sure. Something ungodly, the old people said. Perhaps it was her husband, my grandfather, who just couldn't take it anymore. Or her father. Or she herself. But how can we ever be sure? All we know is that from the day of his death my oupa kept her locked up here in the house. Behind these thick bars you can still see all over the place. She had her baby right here on the farm. But she and Grandpa started sleeping in separate rooms. And she lived for another thirty years, can you imagine? Cooped in like a bird in a cage. Or a monkey in the zoo. Oupa bought her the Bechstein. There must have been something that kept him tied to her in spite of everything. And she was beautiful, of course." Nina points at the portrait. "That hair. The family still talks about how besotted he was with it. And it never turned gray. As black as a raven's wing until the day she died. And long, all the way down her back. But what use was it to her? She never even played the piano. From time to time she still sang a bit—sat there in front of the keyboard, but never pressed a key, only sang. Or hummed. Stopping whenever somebody came in. Then withdrew into her room again. Poor thing." A long pause. "All that passion, and all in vain. And it runs through all our generations."

"Surely that cannot be the reason why you refuse to commit yourself?" I dared to say.

"I've told you so many times, Derek. I have no choice. I cannot risk dividing my concentration. You know I've tried. Several times. But it never worked out. Werner. Edgar. I must sing. Otherwise it will all have been useless. Just as it happened to Ouma. It's like a curse on me."

I cannot think of anything else to say. Or rather: there is much I can think of, but nothing I can say out loud.

We proceed down the passage, accompanied by creaking floorboards, a whole symphony of creaking and groaning ranging from deep bass to high C, away from the ancestral wedding portrait and farther and farther away from Nina's room with the generous four-poster.

More portraits, portraits. And a mirror too. A beautiful, striking mirror with an art nouveau frame which seems somewhat out of place among the starkly rectangular photographs. The frame is formed by a naked girl with long flowing hair, her slender arms outstretched around the mirror which has the shape of a harp.

"And this?" I ask.

Nina shrugged. "Just another story, about another lost love or lust."

More family photographs. Then, unexpectedly, a smallish unframed painting by David le Roux, unsettling in its own way, representing a young woman in a narrow street between tall windowless buildings: one half of her is wearing a very smart outfit, the other half is blatantly naked. There is nothing really erotic about it, yet I find the painting inexplicably disturbing. As if in its simple, almost elementary subject matter it touches on something of endless complexity.

And Nina confirms my impression. "It was my brother who bought it," she explains. "I'm not quite sure that I like it. I've often been tempted to take it down, but I've never actually got round to doing it. Every time—I don't know, but it is as if something is holding me back. It has a kind of evil fascination."

"I know the artist," I tell her.

"And?"

"A very ordinary, decent kind of chap on the surface. But you're right. There are hidden depths in him. Some years ago he got married to a colored woman. Very beautiful. A photographer. At the time it was already legal, of course, still it took guts to challenge the old white establishment. And they have the two most exquisite kids. An advertisement for the rainbow nation."

"I've always thought," says Nina, "that if I ever decided to marry—not that I will, but if—I'd prefer a black man."

"And why?"

"Oh well, you know, white men are so—" The sentence remains incomplete between us. After a while she says, "But come, I must still show you to your room."

Once again we are accompanied by the creaking floorboards. Right at the end of the passage, just left of the locked front door which leads to the stoop, we reach the room intended for me.

"This used to be Ouma's," says Nina. "I hope you don't mind."

"Why should I?"

Everything inside looks very prim and proper, with no hint of all the passions and frustrations of the past. A single bed, a wash stand with pitcher and ewer. And an old porcelain chamber pot on the bottom shelf. A bookcase with books shoved in haphazardly, some upright, others horizontal, several back to front. Many popular paperbacks—her brother's taste?—but also a *Collected Shakespeare*, a scuffed Walter Scott in a deep red binding, some Dickens, an incomplete set of Edgar Allan Poe, Murakami's *Sputnik Sweetheart*, three or four novels and short story collection by Sestigers (two Lerouxs, a Brink, De Vries, Adam Small, Ingrid Jonker's *Rook en Oker*, a couple of Rabies). On the walls some more family photographs. Also a print of one of Magritte's enigmatic works in which the seen and the unseen appear to challenge one another. And a large poster of a Lempicka exhibition in Vienna. This one is unashamedly erotic, although the aloof and clinical style lends it a distance that makes it appear almost frigid.

"Let's go and find something to eat," Nina suggests.

We've brought food in a cool box which she rapidly unpacks on the kitchen table. A few tomatoes, an avocado, garlic, prawns, and lettuce are cut up, sprinkled with lemon juice, and within a few minutes we can sit down to lunch. After that we immediately proceed to the large front room where the Bechstein is already waiting, its keyboard open, the sheet music waiting. The rest of the afternoon is spent practicing. In the beginning she is still nervous and unsure, but as she gathers confidence and her throat and jaws relax it begins to flow more smoothly. After the first half-hour her voice has warmed up and we can start working seriously. There is something new, something different in her voice today. A kind of emotion—rich and deep but magnificently contained and controlled—which gathers me in its spell. Every note is thought and felt through, pursued in all its possibilities and promise and ramifications. But it involves so much more than notes, tempo, phrasing, volume—halfway through the afternoon I'm forced to acknowledge that I have never heard her sing like this before.

There is something disconcerting about her selection of scores too. Songs of farewell, one might say. "Addio al passato." "O mio babbino caro." "Un bel di." And then, above all, that stupefying aria from *Lucia*, the mad scene, "Ardon gli incensi"—"The incense is burning, the sacred torches flaming"—I would never have believed that after Callas anyone could sing that aria more perfectly. Except possibly Sutherland. Or, more recently, the incomparable Netrebko. But the way Nina sings it in this early evening—because by this time dusk is already insinuating itself into the front room, as the sunset begins to burn through the open windows as if all the world outside is going up in flames—makes me feel as if the very blood is curdling in my veins.

We only stop when she is too exhausted to go on, as the sky is bleeding its last.

"I have a feeling hell must look like that," I whisper, entranced.

Nina shakes her head quietly. To my surprise there are tears on her cheeks. "The inside of hell is much worse," she says without looking at me.

Afterward, she goes to run a bath while I get busy in the kitchen. I have brought all the ingredients we'll need for a canard à l'orange, my favorite dish. I have always believed in the way food and music complement each other, and ever since my teenage years it has been the principle on which I've based my culinary activities. In the beginning it was prompted largely by my mother's unreliability in that domain as she tended to get so distracted by preparing or practicing for the next day's classes that she would completely forget about food; and that inspired me to take over. During my first few months in London, while I was still hunting for digs before I was to start at the Royal College of Music, I ran into a weird woman in Stepney, a Mrs. Fernandez, who had a flat to let in her ramshackle old house.

She was a rather startling sight herself, with a nose like a gnarled sweet potato, her thick glasses stuck together with safety pins and affixed to the aforesaid nose with Scotch tape; her hair, suitable for a Muppet, was dyed a brilliant red and sprouted thinly from her head in all directions. But the house was even more unsettling. She regarded herself as an artist (one reason why she was particularly interested in taking me in as a lodger); but all her wild, abstract paintings were hung on the outside walls of her home, none inside. It says something about her skill that, as far as I could establish, not one of them had ever been stolen. But what struck me most forcibly was her way of matching music to every dish she prepared on the mammoth gas cooker in her large kitchen. There was a set and unvaried pattern to this: a lamb stew would be cooked exclusively to the accompaniment of Beethoven: the Ninth Symphony for a leg, the *Missa Solemnis* for a rib, a piano concerto for a curry. For poultry there was only Mozart (a symphony for turkey, chamber music for chicken—with a piano as the solo instrument for a casserole, violin for curry, flute or clarinet for roast, horn for à la King, opera for duck).

Berlioz, sometimes Wagner, went with beef. Bach was excellent with entrées. And Shostakovitch or Debussy were prescribed for dessert. All the music was played fortissimo on her somewhat rickety pickup, reverberating to the very foundations of the house. I was tempted by the setup. But in the end I turned the flat down, as I couldn't live with the prospect of always having the music imposed on me, without any room for personal choice.

When I informed her of my decision, she pronounced a formal curse on me with Old Testamentian fire and brimstone. I can no longer recall all the details, but they included that my right arm would wither, that I would never find a woman prepared to marry me, that I would grow as deaf as Beethoven and as blind as Bach, and that I would die a violent death. I remember thinking, this evening in the kitchen on Nina's family farm, that not much seems to have come of those terrible prophecies. I have survived until fifty-two, with no sign of a withered hand, not even from excessive masturbation, with my eyesight and my hearing intact, and not much prospect of a violent death in this barricaded farmhouse as impregnable as a medieval fortress. (The closest I have so far come to such an end was that night in the restaurant Chez Alice, when Steve and Carla—presumably—saved our lives with her cell phone.)

Memories from my encounter with that old witch, Mrs. Fernandez, now return to me as I prepare the duck, registering with some amusement that I am actually playing a selection of Mozart arias from a CD by Anna Netrebko. It becomes an extension of our afternoon session; and I turn it up loudly enough for Nina to hear in her bath across the passage.

I grate the orange peel and press out the juice. One peeled orange I stuff into the duck with a sprig of rosemary. Then sprinkle the breast with a dribble of olive oil, wait for the oven to heat up evenly, and place the duck inside in a stoneware bowl, surrounded by potato halves. I open a bottle of wine—the grossly underrated Devonet from the Clos Malverne, an amazing blend of Merlot and Pinotage—and pour two glasses for the wine to breathe.

How would Nina react if I were to go and knock on the bathroom door and offer her a glass? And sit down on the edge of the bath beside her. Perhaps with a candle, for ambience?

No, no, I must restrain myself. What she needs is to relax completely (that night in the restaurant has scarred her, even more than I thought at the time) and the only way to make this happen is by allowing her to trust me unconditionally.

I take a mouthful of wine, allowing its heavenly bouquet it to fill all the cavities in and around my mouth. Then I get up to cut a few oranges into paper-thin slices which I arrange around the edge of the large oval platter on which the duck is to be served; and I start preparing the sauce which will be poured over the duck when it is ready. The orange juice, rind, a dash of Van der Hum (sometimes I use Cointreau), a small sprig of rosemary, must be allowed time to get acquainted (but not overly familiar) before they are introduced to the duck. I know some people like preparing this even before the baking starts, but in my experience this easily leads to a messy mush; and what I want tonight—what I plan to serve to Nina—is a duck brown and crisp on the outside, but marrow-tender inside. Accompanied by a simple salad with a honey-and-mustard dressing and a touch of balsamic vinegar, a few small vegetables—baby marrows, red peppers, carrots, beetroot—all of it cut into strips or thin slices, briefly sizzled in oil in the pan, it does justice to the whole. Add Mozart to this, and wine, and it may just turn into a memorable night after all. In my mind I recall the stinkwood four-poster I briefly spied in Nina's bedroom through the open door. (Hopefully it will not collapse under us as it happened with the cellist in Claremont. But even if it happens, it need not be the end of the world.)

In a while—forty-five, sixty minutes—I shall open the oven and test the duck, remove the foil, do some basting, and allow the process to go its way (interrupted from time to time by more judicious basting, but always taking care to prevent the duck getting soggy).

I have just topped up my glass when she returns in a full-length Indian dress of muslin or something similar, which loosely follows the contours of her body, fanning out around her legs as she walks. One of those garments that suggest that she is naked underneath. A long line of small, dark-red buttons runs all the way from her throat to the bottom seam. Her blonde hair is loose on her shoulder, still bearing a hint of dampness from the bath. She is not wearing any makeup and her face looks clean, vulnerable, naked. She is barefoot. In my state of turbulent and gradually gathering desire I find her irresistible. She is like music turned flesh. A flute sonata. An aria for soprano. But I control myself, and when I look up once into her deep blue eyes I get the impression that she is conscious of my restraint, and appreciates it.

After the first basting she helps me to carry a table from the kitchen—not the old, heavy one that stands in the middle of the floor on its sturdy legs, ready to face any onslaught, but a smaller, more slender yellow-wood one from the back wall—and place it on the stoop. Nina fetches a white cloth from a drawer in the massive kitchen dresser and brings it outside, with silver cutlery and two tall candles. Together we lay the table. Then I bring two chairs and we take our seats as we wait, each with a glass of the dark-red Devonet from heaven. Light from the kitchen spills through the window, but not too abundantly to disturb the night outside. High above us stars lie scattered across the dark-blue sky as if they've been flung up like water from a basin. Far opposite, the serrated mountains are outlined in black against the high horizon. The long, deep valley below us is a pitch-black emptiness, with here and there dull yellow stains of farmyards. A dog barks in the distance. In an oak tree behind the house a nightjar screeches, and an answer comes from further down. From the farm dam we passed earlier on our way to the oak lane, frog choruses are chanting like a Bach cantata or a great oratorio. Nearby are the sound speckles of crickets. Here we are far removed from the city and its steady drone of traffic and the ever-present threat of violence. Everything seems unbelievably peaceful.

Only occasionally, at long intervals, there is a slight shiver that causes the hairs on my neck to stand up, before it creeps down my spine. As if something is not altogether fine. As if this tranquil night provides a hiding place to ominous things that pose danger precisely because they cannot be named.

We do not talk much. After her singing this afternoon I find it difficult to reach for anything as mundane as words. It is comforting, reassuring, deeply satisfying just to be sitting here with her. To study the candlelight spreading and moving across her cheekbones, when from time to time she makes a movement and her eyes catch the light, and it settles in her hair: blonde as daylight. Yet bearing, in this night, darker shadows than before. To drink my wine, occasionally to fill up our glasses again, fetch a new bottle, then to listen to the night again.

But below the silence and the calm I steadily keep on knowing about her, knowing about the feverish desire still brooding inside me like an afterglow of the sunset.

Then it is time for me to go to the kitchen and fetch the food: the quick searing of the vegetables in the pan, the warming of the sauce before pouring it over the duck, the final arrangement on the large platter, then carrying it outside where I place it between the serenely burning candles. *Introibo ad altare Dei.*

I fill the glasses up again. We clink, and drink. And eat. Nina makes small sounds of delight deep in her throat. (Would this be how she would react when she makes love?)

Remote from the world, we huddle in our small pool of light in the dark. Less than two hours from Cape Town, yet light years removed. My thoughts wander off in all directions. I think of prehistoric times Nina has told me about, when small communities of Khoi and San were living in this valley, always on the move, always coming back. Peaceful, yet with enough internecine violence to keep these valleys and mountains steeped in uneasy tension. Much later, the first nomadic white farmers arriving in this valley of Roodezand, the Land of Waveren, with their memories of Europe and an ever more distant world they so urgently tried to transport with them, and the inevitable clash with the otherness of Africa. The first explosions of violence, unleashing something which after more than three centuries is still pulsating across the land in dark swells and surges. Here we are caught in our eternal, minuscule world of music—Bach, Mozart, Beethoven, Chopin, Mahler, Shostakovitch—surrounded by the darkness and stars and exploding supernovae and dark holes of a still incomprehensible cosmos. A cosmos inhabited by the ghosts of ancestors and forgotten gods and invisible beings that continue to seethe in resentment and—who knows?—may at this very moment be preparing revenge for injustices and evil we do not know about, or even want to know about, anymore. How insignificant this urgent desire burning inside me compared to those incomprehensible powers around us? And yet it is real: terrifyingly real, in the blood coursing through my veins, the heat throbbing in my temples, the dryness in my throat. Nina, oh my God, Nina. You with your heavenly voice, you with your long blonde hair in a cataract over your smooth shoulders, you with your hands cupped around the glass in which the wine is gleaming deep and dangerous against the candlelight. What may yet happen to us tonight? How will the new day find us, if it does?

She remains sitting when, much later, I get up to take the dishes to the kitchen and stack them in the sink. When I come back, she has refilled our glasses with the last wine. Once again I sit down opposite her. The depths of her eyes are as dark as the valley below us, the night sky above. She drops one of her hands in mine, leaving it there like something she has shed or forgotten about.

"Shall we go in?" I venture when our glasses are empty again.

She doesn't answer but gives what I take to be nod.

I get up, conscious of how difficult it has become to control my breathing. Behind her chair I stop and place my hands on her shoulders. Like two demonic talons in the treacherous light they lie on the smoothness of her skin, against the blonde hair which seems to be accumulating and gathering and holding more and more shadows. I can smell its fragrance. It makes my head spin. I am no longer sure about what is happening, what I am imagining, what is not happening.

"Come—?"

She is unsteady on her feet as I accompany her inside.

As we reach the door that stands open at her room, I stop. She leans back against me.

"Nina?"

She does not answer. Just quietly shakes her head against my chest.

"Can't I stay with you tonight?"

Another light motion of her head, the movement of her hair which in this half-light appears even paler than usual, as if she has brought with her something of the daylight from before.

"Do you know how much I desire you?" My voice is rough and unfamiliar in my own ears.

"Don't say that, Derek. Not ever. We dare not. That would make you like all the others."

"I love you, for God's sake!"

"No. Remember our agreement. You promised."

I sigh, and remain silent for a long time. I can feel my hands trembling lightly as I slide them from her shoulders to fold them over her breasts. For a brief moment she seems to yield, then stiffens.

"No, Derek. Please." Looking up at me. "It's time to go to bed."

"Suppose"—I try to say it lightly, but my throat is taut—"suppose I come to you deep in the night?"

A brief laugh. "Don't forget: I'll hear you. These old floorboards creak something terrible. I'll hear every move you make."

I sigh. "All right then. So good night."

And then she turns round and kisses me. Without warning. Her tongue foraging deep in my mouth. I gasp for breath. All manner of unruly things are happening to my body. My left hand steadies her against the edge of the door while my right hand gets busy with undoing the long row of tiny red buttons. Moving down from her taut throat, between her breasts, across her stomach, until I find myself on my knees in front of her. Then I rise up again. My hand remains busy. She moves her legs apart. There are no knickers under the muslin of her dress. She is unbelievably, deliciously wet under my fingers. As if her whole body is dissolving in moisture, as if she herself—and I—are beginning to melt into it. Between my fingers I palpate the small swelling of her clitoris. Until suddenly, like a switch being turned, she stands back from my grasp, breathing deeply. Her mouth is still open, there is spittle on her lips.

"No, Derek! You must go to bed now."

With a parched throat, breathless, stiff-legged, I retreat down the long passage to my own room, accompanied all the way by the creaking and groaning of the floorboards.

Somehow I seem to manage to reach my room. Reluctantly, numbly, I close the door behind me: a final creak, a sad double sound. My head is throbbing with an unbearable headache. I tear off my clothes and slide into bed. On my fingers her smell still lingers. Every woman, I know ever since my first encounter with a girl, has a taste that belongs exclusively to her. Christa, behind the piano. The pastor's daughter Lulu, the boisterous Maggie, the inexhaustible Jenny, Linda, all the way down the alphabet and back. Each one, every single one, utterly unique. There may be a generic common denominator, but ultimately each remains incomparable. And from this night on I know I will recognize Nina's anywhere on earth.

It must be hours that I remain awake, trying to calm down. Staring through the dull light of the dusty bulb with fixed and burning eyes. The pitcher and ewer, the rickety bookcase. The red Walter Scott. The shadows of the heavy bars in front of the window. The stains of splattered mosquitoes on the walls. The knots in the dark pine boards of the ceiling glaring down at me like accusing eyes.

At some stage I must have fallen asleep. When I wake up, lost in the night, it is from the sound of creaking floorboards. Approaching from far away, nearer and nearer. All the way from Nina's room to mine. It is pitch dark. I must have switched off the light, although I cannot remember doing so. My head is bursting with a migraine. But the creaking of the boards is unmistakable. I cannot believe it. Imbloodypossible.

At the same time, there is no way I can mistake it. But every separate creak, every whispering footstep, is clearly defined.

How well I remember taking leave of her on her doorstep. The small musical moans and whimpers with which she reacted as we stood so close together. The unbuttoning of her dress, from top to bottom. The taste of her tongue. The taste of her cunt. The wetness on my fingers.

And now she is back. On her way to me.

In the utter darkness—here in the Winterhoek, far from neighbors and houses, the nights are medieval and absolute. Except for an occasional, very rare car coming past soundlessly on the distant main road.

Right at my door the footsteps stop. My body is strung as taut as a wire. I am aware of perspiration on my forehead. I push the sheet away from me.

Then I hear the door open, the sad double sound.

I push myself up on an elbow. It is almost impossible to distinguish anything. But I can imagine discerning her, pitch black on black, in the rectangle of the door. She approaches on bare feet. The light motion she causes in the musty room moves across my naked body like a barely stirring breeze.

The floorboards groan as she approaches.

Right next to my bed she stops.

My breathing is very shallow. I move aside.

"Come to me," I whisper with difficulty. It doesn't sound like my voice at all.

For a moment she hesitates. I put out my hand. She is naked too. I touch a wrist and pull her closer. And then, without hesitation or transition, we are together. My god! I have expected her to be passionate, but not like this, not this utter and total surrender and abandon.

I no longer know for how long we are entangled, only that it is incomparably wonderful. Her taste, her smell, which I have already experienced so fleetingly in the passage, is all over my face, my hands, my whole body. Everything happening in utter darkness, which somehow makes it even more intense.

Except right near the end, as we briefly roll apart and become aware of a late-night car passing silently on the distant road. A fleeting cavalcade of light patterns along the inside wall. Sweeping across all the objects in the room—bed and table and pitcher and bookcase; and us. For one moment she is caressed by the passing light. The smooth bare limbs, the small shadow of her pubic hair, the dark stains of her nipples. The long pitch-black rippling hair.

Then darkness once more.

I close my eyes very tightly as if it were possible to exclude that image, and once again press my face tightly into the fragrant and fatal darkness between her legs.

Only after a long time do I become aware of her thighs gripping me more and more tightly. And of something like a coil, like a thick braid, being woven more and more suffocatingly around my neck. Until everything in that black night begins to turn and whirl around me and I realize that I am not going to get out of that black noose again.